TOO LITTLE TIME

TOO LITTLE TIME

Geoffrey French

MARCHMAN PUBLICATIONS

Welshpool

Copyright (c) Eric Geoffrey French 1993
The moral right of Eric Geoffrey French to be identified as the author of this work has been asserted

Published by Marchman Publications, Welshpool, 1993
Illustrations: Monica Pratt
Design: Jennifer M Braithwaite

Conditions of sale. This book is sold subject to the condition that it shall not, by way of trade or otherwise, be lent, re-sold, hired out or otherwise circulated without the publisher's prior consent in any form of binding or cover other than that in which it is published and without a similar condition including this condition being imposed on the subsequent purchaser.

MARCHMAN PUBLICATIONS
Canal Yard, Severn Street, Welshpool

ISBN 0 9521710 0 7 Too Little Time (pbk)

Reproduced, printed and bound in Great Britain by
Welshpool Printing Co , Welshpool

British Library Cataloguing-in-Publication Data
A catalogue record for this book is available from the British Library

CONTENTS

Acknowledgements	7
Preface	9
1: I'll Be Seeing You	11
2: It Seems To Me I've Heard That Song Before	20
3: Sonny Boy	29
4: I'll Walk Alone	41
5: You Started Something	53
6: Just One Of Those Things	64
7: Is You Is Or Is You Ain't My Baby?	75
8: Silver Wings In The Moonlight	83
9: I Don't Want To Set The World On Fire	92
10: This Is The Story Of A Starry Night	99
11: I Don't Want To Walk Without You, Baby	105
12: Taking A Chance On Love	112
13: Our Love Affair	121
14: Wish Me Luck As You Wave Me Goodbye	128
15: A Little On The Lonely Side	135
16: There's A Boy Coming Home On Leave	146
17: The Lambeth Walk	154
18: Run, Rabbit, Run!	162
19: It Had To Be You	174
Prologue as Epilogue	187

To Kerstin
For her patience

Acknowledgements

A short novel rarely carries lengthy acknowledgements. However, I wish to return courtesies received from many people, including: Trevor Hearnshaw; Doug Le Vicki, Executive of the Glenn Miller Society and the Friends of the Herb Miller Orchestra; Tom McGee, Editor of "Betty Grable's Hollywood"; John Miller, Director of the Herb Miller Orchestra; Ray Pallett, Editor of "Memory Lane"; Charles Wilson, Editor of "Nostalgia". My recollections of wartime Blackpool were supplemented by Pip Beck, Bill Dainty, Jack Greenwood, my cousin Edith Hartland, Miss Patricia of Blackpool's Music Hall Tavern, Mike Simkin of the Headlands Hotel, and Major Chick Yuill of the Salvation Army, Blackpool Citadel Corps. Geoffrey Butcher's "Next To A Letter From Home", a masterly history of Major Glenn Miller's American Band of the AEF, provided valuable background. Finally I must acknowledge the kindness and wisdom of Billy Amstell, Vice-President of the Ambrose Circle, Freeman of the City of London, whose musical career so far spans seven decades not out including many years with the Ambrose Orchestra, Roy Fox, Jack Harris, Geraldo, Stanley Black, Geoff Love and others.

My chapter titles may recall songs once familiar to some readers. Other musical compositions of the Golden Age are mentioned in the narrative.

Where lyrics are cited in whole, in part, or in parody, this is by kind permission as follows:

"A Nightingale Sang in Berkeley Square" (Manning Sherwin/Eric Maschwitz), 1940, reproduced by permission of Peter Maurice Music Co Ltd, London WC2H 0EA.

"Roll Me Over" (Desmond O'Connor), 1944, reproduced by permission of Peter Maurice Music Co Ltd, London WC2H 0EA.

Copyright EMI Catalogue Partnership and reprinted by permission of CPP/Belwin Europe:

"The Whiffenpoof Song" (Meade Minnigerode/Tod Galloway/George Pomeroy)

"Coming In On A Wing And A Prayer" (Jimmy McHugh/Harold Adamson)

"At Last" (Harry Warren/Mack Gordon).

PREFACE

John Miller, Director of the Herb Miller Orchestra and nephew of the late Major Alton Glenn Miller, having read this novel more or less straight off the wordprocessor, was kind enough to tell me he liked it and that it had brought the war era in Blackpool alive for him. I treasure this compliment and thank Mr Miller for permitting me to quote him.

The story is fiction of course. Its main characters are figments of my imagination, and no similiarity whatever is intended, nor should any be inferred, to any actual person or persons alive or dead - most emphatically not to any of the distinguished musicians and entertainers who over the years have nurtured the Glenn Miller tradition and the memory of the Golden Age of popular music generally.

Nevertheless almost all the settings are historically authentic, although I have changed the names of some locations and tampered a little with other details. Moreover, various real personages are introduced, notably the late Ted Heath and` Major Glenn Miller himself, my account of their participation in the Jazz Jamboree at the Stoll Theatre in October 1944 being based on fact, apart from some fictitious conversational exchanges. The amazing ten year-old Victor Feldman did indeed perform under Major Miller's sponsorship - though "Terry Cullerton", of course, did not.

1
I'LL BE SEEING YOU

She was tall, erect, smartly turned out, more attractive than a woman of her age has any business to be. Confident of herself, independent, she stood at the bar counter, one foot on the brass rail, sipping easily if somewhat incongruously at a pint of mild and bitter.

Well preserved she undoubtedly was, if that description implies expert makeup and grooming to offset the ravages of age. Just the same, there was something more to it than blue-rinsed brittleness: there had to be, to bewitch a barman almost young enough to be her grandson, especially at Saturday lunchtime with a coach-party of thirsty Yanks vying for his attention.

The something more consisted of a musical voice, a twinkling eye, a ready smile, and most of all an outgoing cheerfulness that belied her seventy or so years.

"He died early this year, you see," she explained.

She was simply stating the fact, but the barman said, "Oh, I'm sorry," as convention required.

"That's OK, don't worry about it. We all gotta go sometime. He'd had a good life."

"Yes."

"A Kraut fighter shot him up over Aachen. You ever hear of the place? Neither did he till then: November '44 it was. His ship kind of crawled back to England on two engines. They should never have made it, but they did. Those old Forts could really take it, you better believe me. Crash-landed on a beach. He and the skipper and two others were still alive. Out of ten, can you imagine? He was in hospital the rest of the war but they patched him up good. All the time we were married Hank never worried about a damn thing. His whole life after that mission was bonus, he always said. A pity he didn't get to come on the trip, though. He was really looking forward to it. We'd had our names down six months." She took a pull at her beer and remembered solemnly while the barman wiped the counter. "But when he knew he wasn't going to make it himself he told me I had to come anyway." Her eyes sparkled again. "That was one of the last things he said to me. 'You gotta go to England. And when you get to Blacksley Parva, have a pint of English mild and bitter at the Bull's Head and see if Albert remembers.'"

"I bet he would have," said the barman. "He remembered all the Americans."

"He was your Dad, I guess."

"Albert? No, my grandad."

"Oh my God!" She drew it out in American fashion "Gaaahd" and mixed a laugh into it. "You sure know how to talk your way into a girl's heart."

"Sorry, love," he grinned.

"That's OK, kid. I'll be honest, I got grandchildren too, only they're not as old as you yet."

Another customer signalled. The barman excused himself and turned away while she glanced around reflectively. Low ceiling and smoke-blackened oak beams, snug wooden settles in corners and under bow windows. How old? Two hundred years? Three hundred? Four even? You never knew in England: everything went back such a long time.

Scattered among the sporting prints and horse brasses were other decorations. Harshly intrusive once, they had faded, mellowed, blended into their surroundings. These were the trophies and souvenirs of forty years ago: cannonshell casings, a pair of officer's epaulettes, a huge broken propeller blade. A framed motto on the wall proclaimed:

You can always tell a gunner
By his hands and nervous stare.
You can always tell a bombardier
By his manner debonair.
You can always tell a navigator
By his pencils, books and such.
You can always tell a pilot
But you cannot tell him much.

At the end of the bar counter a glass case covered an American officer's cap and on the wall above it was a large framed photograph of a handsome, uniformed youngster posed stiffly at attention outside the main door of the pub. This was evidently the owner of the cap, for in place of headgear his mop of curly hair was topped by a brimming, carefully balanced pint glass of ale. The ink-scrawled legend read "Look, Ma, no hands!", with the signature "Louie".

An impromptu quartet of elderly American tourists was singing to the photograph, glasses outstretched in salute:

... We shall serenade our Louie
While life and voice shall last,
Then we'll pass and be forgotten with the rest!

The fact is, she thought, they *have* passed and been forgotten. Did anyone today care what these paunchy old farts had once been, what they had done, what they had come through all those years ago when they were young and smiling and gallant - and also homesick, bewildered and terrified to breaking point? Was it even possible for anyone not alive then to comprehend, let alone care?

Yet someone had cared, someone had remembered. Someone had preserved the souvenirs and dusted them week by week - and as the years slipped by, new generations too young to remember had had the grace not to throw out the increasingly meaningless relics of a time long gone.

Or had they in fact lain discarded in some attic and been hastily resurrected to honour today's visit, to loosen tongues and purse-strings, to keep the drinks flowing and the tills ringing? Now if the wall-varnish behind the photograph didn't show any mark, that would prove ... What a nasty idea! She dismissed it hurriedly. So what, just as long as everyone had a good time?

The barman returned. She drank up and handed him her glass.

"He said to have a pint, but he wouldn't have minded me having two."

The barman began refilling the glass. "You really like it?"

"Sure do." She winked and smacked her lips. "I could get hooked if I stayed long enough. Really English, isn't it?"

He shook his head. "Used to be. Not so much now."

"Come on, what are you saying?"

"It's a fact. Things have changed. It's all lager these days, you know, especially with young people. There's plenty of pubs wouldn't be able to serve you a mild and bitter at all: they don't keep it."

She shook her head. "Say, that's kind of disappointing."

He smiled and pushed the refilled glass across the counter. "I suppose it would be if the beer was all you came to England for."

"Well, I did have other reasons as well."

"Of course. I was just kidding."

"I know." She fumbled in her purse, paid him and raised her glass. "Cheers: that's what you say, isn't it?" She took a sip and went on. "It wasn't just because of my husband either, I guess. I got other reasons - my own reasons, but I couldn't possibly tell you what they are. Truth is, I couldn't even have told my husband." She touched his arm in a faintly suggestive gesture, but then shook her head. "Aw heck, my big mouth. No, dammit, I'm not going to tell you. We'll talk about something else instead."

They did, while the others in the coach party quaffed their beer and recognised old acquaintances among the locals and played darts and swapped reminiscences of Sam and Warren and Tom, and the day the Krauts hit us over Holland before there was a single P38 in sight, and that other time when a diving 190 sliced through a Fort clean as a whistle and the two halves went down with little bundles falling out and someone swore he saw every goddam 'chute open, but jeez, they couldn't all have got out, it stands to reason, don't it? An' say, wasn't there some guy in your outfit was balling the kitchen maid in one of them fancy manor houses and her ladyship caught them so he knocked her off as well before he came back to base?

The drinks flowed, the reminiscences went on and on, and the indefatigable quartet of serenaders brought the Whiffenpoof Song to its comfortless, haunting climax:

We are poor little lambs who have lost our way
Baa, baa, baa!
We are little lost sheep who have gone astray
Baa, baa, baa!
Gentlemen songsters off on a spree,
Doomed from here to eternity!
Lord, have mercy on such as we -
Baa, baa, baa!

And the proud crest of the United States Eighth Air Force mounted above the bar looked down once more over some of the men who had bought its glory with their courage and their blood.

The crest above the bar of another East Anglian pub not far away was that of RAF Bomber Command. There were other differences too. The elderly coach-party went in more for sports jackets and blazers, less for tourist gear. And in place of the lush apocalyptic sentiment of the Whiffenpoof Song was the amiable vulgarity of one of those ribald ditties traditionally regarded by the British as a suitable accompaniment to war. A lone voice warbled the first verse -

I'll sing you number one, then we'll start to have some fun
Roll me over, lay me down and do it again!

- and back came the chorus with a will -

Roll me over in the clover
Roll me over, lay me down and do it again!

Beneath the superficialities, though, much was the same - the jovial high spirits of old fogeys reunited with other old fogeys, the thoughtful silences amidst the hubbub, the wistful peering at the wartime souvenirs around the walls.

The next verse of the song seemed to add a poignancy to the yellowing framed photograph showing a group of aircrew in flying gear, posing with their WAAF driver alongside her van, their Lancaster bomber in the background -

I'll sing you number two when she shows me what to do

Roll me over, lay me down and do it again!

Roll me over in the clover

Roll me over, lay me down and do it again!

- and the rough innuendo of the third verse was washed away by the adjacent photograph of a self-consciously grinning, fresh-faced sergeant pilot seated in the pub bar next to a civilian girl, his service forage cap perched on her head and her hand resting innocently on his knee while she leaned across to plant a curiously chaste kiss on his cheek-

I'll sing you number three when her hand has reached my knee

Roll me over, lay me down and do it again!

Roll me over in the clover

Roll me over, lay me down and do it again!

- while the next photograph, showing as it did a pale and undersized pilot officer with one arm in a sling giving the thumbs-up sign as a salvage crew prepared to apply a bulldozer to the mangled remains of a Wellington bomber, invested the fourth verse with intimations of courage, skill and high tragedy -

I'll sing you number four when she's down upon the floor

Roll me over, lay me down and do it again!

Roll me over in the clover

Roll me over, lay me down and do it again!

Here too the walls of the pub had their other trophies - polished brass cannonshell casings, rank insignia, propeller blades, squadron crests - recalling scenes of disaster and heroism now unbelievable: the navigator who nursed a crippled Wimpey safely down under the directions of the dying pilot; the crash-landing Lanc that went up like a Roman candle, frying all the crew except the rear gunner, who jumped out of his smashed turret with seconds to spare and got away without a scratch; the WAAF MT driver who drove her van under the whirling propellers of a Stirling that had just taxied in, which you could do because there was plenty of clearance underneath them, only it wasn't a Stirling, it was a diverted Lanc, so she and the van got chopped to pieces.

Still, it was all a long time ago and these lucky ones who'd survived against the odds remembered and reminisced without tears or false sentiment, knowing it could just as easily have been themselves and unashamedly thankful it hadn't been. So they grinned, slapped one another's backs, exchanged addresses, fraternised with villagers, compared pot bellies and called for more rounds.

Not everyone in the bar-parlour was taking part in the reunion. In one corner a rather butch, sharp-featured woman in her late thirties, wearing black library-framed spectacles and a severe suit, sipped an iced tonic-water and addressed her whisky-drinking male companion with weary patience.

"I have to try to talk to him at least. Give him a chance to tell his side of it."

"He doesn't have a side."

"Come on. There's always another side."

"No there isn't. He just didn't care. It was all number one with him."

"Well, I'm going to talk to him anyway, if I can."

"Why?"

"My idea of ethics, dear boy, professional ethics."

"Tripe," he pronounced and took a mouthful of whisky. Indignation, disbelief and contempt chased one another across pasty features already disfigured by what seemed to be a permanent anger. A few drops of his drink spilt down his chin when an elderly man carrying a couple of tankards lurched against him. "Dammit all, watch what you're doing!" he flared.

"Sorry, squire," said the other equably. "Bit of a crush in here."

The angry man's scowl and grunt as he turned away were designed to make clear that he was unappeased. The offender shrugged and moved on. Returning to his table he spoke in a low tone to his companions. They shot covert glances towards the angry one. Their burst of laughter was not lost on him. His expression darkened further.

The butch woman consulted her watch. "Better drink up. Time we got going."

"I don't know that I really want to."

She sighed. "Now he tells me! You didn't have to come at all, you know. Why did you?"

"Just curiosity. Now I'm not sure I should have."

"Suit yourself. We've got tickets. We may as well not waste them. But it's up to you. I'm going anyway."

She got up. The impromptu choir had reached the hackneyed improprieties of the last verse of "Roll Me Over" as they pushed through the throng and made their way out of the pub. The aggressive-looking BMW which the butch woman extracted expertly from the car park seemed to suit the two of them equally well, in their different ways. As they drove off he was still grumbling.

The aircraft floated easily at a thousand or so feet under a blue sky decorated with puffballs of bright cloud. It was one of those small single-engined jobs that practically fly themselves in such conditions. The pilot sat relaxed, enjoying the brilliant late-summer landscape of green fields and hedgerows, clumps of trees and neat villages. Flying was fun on a day like this. Even on other days it was better than sitting in a tailback on the stinking M1.

He was alone as usual. He preferred it that way. Alone, you didn't have to answer to anybody, you kept your secrets, and if you had problems you could jump in the plane and flip over to Paris and think them out quietly or just decide to ignore them. He'd felt differently once briefly - briefly was the word all right! - a long time ago when there'd been a woman in his life, but that had ended in storms.

Yes, on your own was best. Best for him anyway. Always had been. Not likely to change at his age. Pushing for sixty already? Could it be true? Still, that's not so old these days, sort of middle-aged. Anyway he looked a lot younger. Always had done. Lucky that. Helped in his business. He glanced down musingly at the khaki-coloured holdall and long flat black case on the passenger seat beside him.

He ran his fingers over his smooth dark hair, reassuring himself. No bald patches yet. And a fortnightly visit to Trumper's ensured that the immaculate forties-style short-back-and-sides - a source of permanent despair to them but he insisted on it - was never marred by tell-tale grey. The slacks and pullover had no beer gut to cope with either: a daily jog, a weekly workout and a continuous calculated abstemiousness ensured that.

He glanced at his watch and peered down again, looking for landmarks. His destination ought to be in sight any moment. Yes, there it was, shimmering faintly in the far-off heat-haze. A mite of diminuendo on the throttle and the slightest adjustment of trim would dip the nose of the aircraft sufficiently for a long, lazy descent. Then with the slight breeze on this heading he'd drop her straight on the runway. He hoped the tarmac hadn't developed any potholes. His might well be the first aircraft to land at the field since it closed ten years ago. But they'd assured him it was OK.

Officially closed the airfield might be, but on this day it was far from deserted. The hardstanding outside the hangars had been taped out as a bus and car park where harassed marshals were trying to range the flood of arriving vehicles in some sort of order. As the arrivals were slotted in one by one, drivers and passengers swelled the crowds streaming on foot towards one of the hangars. The fifties-and-over age group was the most heavily represented, but there were plenty of younger people too. English was the preponderant tongue but not the only one. Several camera-toting contingents emerged from tourist buses with continental European plates, including at least one that was German.

As the well-fed representatives of Bonn democracy climbed ponderously down, the butch woman was alighting from her BMW. She glanced idly in their direction. Her companion did more than glance: he halted in his tracks and glared his hostility.

"What the hell are they doing here?" he asked ill-humouredly of no one in particular.

"Same as you and I are, I should imagine," the butch woman replied. "Paid their money, I expect, so they're entitled."

"You'd think even they could show a bit of sensitivity - "

"About what, for heaven's sake? It's all a long time since, you know. Shouldn't be surprised if they've been invited. In my experience these old codgers who were in it don't harbour grievances." She took his arm and began propelling him towards the hangar, but he shook her off.

"And I do, is that it?"

"Yes, since you ask."

"And you disapprove?"

"Yes again."

"Then why are you here?"

She regarded him with distaste and spoke carefully. "Because it's my job, and because there are some people I disapprove of more than I disapprove of you. All right?"

He grunted, and they walked on.

A few yards in front of them an erect seventy year-old American woman with a lively walk and a twinkle in her eye had lost no time in making acquaintance with one of the German contingent.

"Did you say a fighter pilot?"

The German nodded diffidently.

"Not FW 190s?"

He nodded again, not sure what to expect.

"Oh my Ga-a-ahd, would Hank have liked to meet you!" she exclaimed. "It was one of you guys chewed up my husband's ship on the way back from Aachen. Could even have been you, I guess ... " And as the German hesitated she patted his arm, grinned broadly and went on: "Well, times sure do change, don't they ... ?"

The crowds gradually thinned out. The marshals relaxed and began chatting among themselves, interrupted less and less frequently as arriving vehicles dwindled to a trickle. From a couple of miles away, noticed by only a few, a light aircraft made its landing approach. The pilot judged his gradual loss of height to perfection, swooped in to a textbook landing and taxied to the far side of the hangar away from the latecomers still straggling through the ticketholders' entrances.

The propeller stopped and a few moments later the pilot climbed out carrying his holdall and black instrument case. He held a belted raincoat over his arm as well. The weathermen had forecast a change of temperature later towards evening, maybe some rain, maybe some mist. He hoped not the latter: it would delay him getting home. Might even have to stay the night in some draughty village pub.

Meanwhile the sun was still up and he did not remove his dark glasses. The two or three people who saw him walk to the hangar did not recognise him.

Once inside, however, he replaced the shades with a pair of rimless spectacles, and at once his identity was unmistakable.

2
IT SEEMS TO ME I'VE HEARD THAT SONG BEFORE

It was gloomy inside the hangar. With his khaki holdall, instrument case and raincoat to carry, the pilot had to take a modicum of care as he picked his way, purposefully but without haste, through a litter of cables, electronic equipment, packing cases, discarded plastic and lengths of rope.

Along a dusty corridor running down the side of the hangar were doors leading off to what had once been offices. He entered one of these, grimaced at the peeling paintwork, cracked windows and general air of dilapidation inside, but without hesitation flung his raincoat over one of the two battered stand chairs which, with an ancient table, constituted the sole furnishings of the room.

He unzipped the holdall and took from it the Second World War uniform tunic, cap and tie of a major of the United States Air Force. He was already wearing the trousers and shirt. As he began knotting the tie there was a perfunctory knock and the door opened.

"Thank God you're here." There was relief in the voice of the dinner-jacketed oldish man who entered the room.

The pilot continued working on the tie. "Relax, Adam. We set it all up yesterday. What's the panic?"

The other pointed to his watch. "This is cutting it a bit fine, even for you."

He grinned. "Have I ever failed?"

"There could always be a first time."

He threw Adam the uniform tunic to hold while he shrugged himself into it.

"Not with me, chum, you know that."

Adam smiled. He did know it. The pilot fumbled in the holdall and passed a hand mirror to Adam.

"Hold, would you?"

Adam obliged. The pilot buttoned up his tunic, peered into the hand mirror and adjusted the set of his tie. "Everyone on places?" he asked.

"Sure. Ready to roll."

"Good boy." He donned the cap with a flourish and threw up a mock salute. "Do I look OK?"

"Spot on." Adam consulted his watch again. "Shall we go?"

"Yep," said the other, extracting a conductor's baton from the holdall and a trombone from the instrument case.

A few moments later they climbed a short flight of steps leading up to the rear of a wooden platform occupying most of one end of the hangar. Plywood side screens concealed the empty spaces on either side of the stage and were high enough to act as supports for the rails on which a set of stage curtains had been rigged.

The stage itself was occupied by a full "big band" of musicians arrayed in conventional fashion, brasses on one side and reeds on the other, with piano, bass and guitar behind, flanking the drums at stage centre. A male and female vocalist, he dinner-jacketed, she in long forties-style evening dress, sat demurely on hard chairs to one side.

The now-uniformed figure advanced to front centre stage. His eyes behind the rimless glasses flicked from side to side checking the readiness of the musicians. The muffled tuning-up sounds they had been making died away with a subdued roll-and-rimshot from the drummer as the orchestra leader placed his trombone on a convenient stand and held his baton ready. At front of stage Adam peeped briefly at the audience through the break of the curtain, then turned to the orchestra.

"Quiet now, everybody. Ready to go. Lights!"

The stage lights came on and Adam looked questioningly at the orchestra leader, who responded with a thumbs-up and raised his baton.

On the other side of the curtains the footlights came up and stilled the low murmuring of the audience. But the curtains remained closed as the orchestra blasted into the unhurried strains of "I Sustain the Wings", the short and somewhat solemn signature tune used by Glenn Miller while serving as a captain with Training Command.

Only on the final flourish of the music did Adam step out into the pool of light provided by a single spot. He adjusted the stand-mike and acknowledged the polite applause that greeted him. "It's nice to see so many of you," he remarked conversationally. "This is going to be a memorable occasion."

More polite applause, mingled with some whistling and stamping, showed that the audience shared this opinion. He went on. "I'd better do the formal part now, so I'll say it properly - Good afternoon, ladies and gentlemen. My name is Adam Gates, and it is my pleasant task to act as your host on this notable and indeed historic occasion. Let me begin by calling upon the Ambassador of the United States of America to address us. Ladies and gentlemen: it is my privilege to present His Excellency Chester J. Harmon Junior, formerly Colonel, United States Air Force, and now his country's ambassador to the Court of St. James."

A follow-spot picked out a silver-haired figure of distinguished appearance making its way from front row centre up the proscenium steps and on to the stage. After a quick handshake Adam Gates retired behind the curtain, and the ambassador, alone at the front, launched into his speech.

"Mr Gates, distinguished guests, members of the Royal Air Force Bomber Command and the United States Eighth Air Force, ladies and gentlemen. We have assembled here today to be reunited with friends and comrades from long ago, to pay tribute to the memory of those who lost their lives in the great cause for which we fought, and to listen to some wonderful music - music that is of our time yet timeless because it will never die. All that is more important than speeches. But a speech there has to be - or so I was told - and that being so I am honoured beyond words that it has fallen to me to make it ... "

As the ambassador's sonorities rolled on, Adam Gates waited behind the curtain, glancing occasionally at his watch. He frowned at the approach of a stagehand from the back of the stage. The bandleader exchanged two or three brief sentences with the stagehand, gesticulated impatiently and signalled to Adam, who went over.

"What's the trouble?"

The stagehand began to speak but the bandleader cut in.

"Some crazy woman journalist seems to have got in backstage and won't go away."

Adam grimaced. "Okay, leave her to me."

"Thanks. And if you're not back quick enough for the intro?"

"You do it over the mike from back of curtain and let the ambassador find his own way off stage."

Adam hurried down the steps to the backstage area. He took in the severe suit, the cropped hair and thick-framed spectacles. Dyke, he decided with distaste, and went straight into the attack.

"Look, I'm sorry: we had a press conference yesterday morning. Why didn't you come then?"

"Partly I didn't have time, and partly what I have to ask him about he wouldn't want to discuss in a press conference." I'm as tough as you, said the dyke's eyes, if dyke she was.

"I'm sorry, but I don't know what you mean."

"I want an exclusive, and that's what he'll want too when he knows - "

Adam shook his head impatiently. "You're talking in riddles. There isn't anything I can do for you. He's on stage now and the orchestra starts blowing as soon as the ambassador finishes talking" - he tapped his wristwatch - "in about three or four minutes at most."

He tried to look dismissive, but she stood her ground and brought up her secondary armament.

"Sure. I'm not stupid. But what about the interval?"

"What about it?" Come on, come on, there isn't time for all this. He repeated the watch-tapping ploy.

"He could see me then. At the interval." So you don't like dykes, said her eyes. Well, this dyke doesn't like straights who don't like dykes. So what?

"He'll be busy, and - "

"I only need ten minutes," she said; and you can drop dead where you stand, added her eyes, but I'm not going until you give me something.

" - and to be honest, even if he isn't, he won't want to bother with the press." He made to take her arm, but she wasn't having any and backed off.

"Tell him I want to talk to him about Terry Cullerton."

"Who?"

She took a step towards him, shaped her mouth and spoke slowly, with soft emphasis.

"Listen carefully. Watch my lips move. Terry Cullerton. Cull-er-ton. C-U-L-L-E-R-T-O-N. Terry Cullerton. Got it?"

She turned on her heel with the confident air of one who knows she has fired the winning broadside. "I'll be back at the interval. He'll see me."

Damn all journalists, Adam thought irritably as he hurried back on stage. They think they only have to wave a press card and everybody will jump. Trouble is, we do jump: in this business we've got to, and they know it. He whispered a fast "Tell-you-about-it-later" to the orchestra leader and paused behind the break of the curtain as the ambassador went into his peroration:

" ... and the best part of that day was the last part, when worry, exhaustion and fear were soothed away by the music of that fine officer and gentleman, Major Glenn Miller, with the American Band of the Allied Expeditionary Force. For our generation, and I think for many younger people too, that music has pretty much the same effect today. So I'll just say one last thing and then let the music take over. It is simply this. There is nothing in my life that I am so proud of as the memory of having served with you in the great battles we fought for freedom all those years ago."

Adam listened to the applause, judged his moment, nodded to the orchestra leader and stepped through the curtain. An exchange of courtesies, then the ambassador returned to his seat while Adam announced through the microphone, "Ladies and gentlemen, the Gary Milner Orchestra!"

The curtains drew slowly apart and the honey-smooth sweetness of the most haunting of all signature tunes flowed out, penetrated deep into the memories of the audience, imprinted yet another groove in the pattern of indelible nostalgia. Lips tightened, hands clenched, eyes moistened. Even before the curtains were fully open, the spine-tingling magic of "Moonlight Serenade" had done its work.

The emotional tension was notched yet higher by the expertly-arranged spectacle on stage. "GM" monograms were everywhere - on the music stands, on the immaculate mid-brown blazers of the musicians, on the bass drum, on the flats that hid the backstage area from the audience's view. Above the stage a huge glittering silver-spangled sign read "The Gary Milner Orchestra" in lettering so richly elaborated that "Gary Milner" could almost be mistaken for "Glenn Miller". The parallelism was further reinforced by a huge black-and-white blowup photograph of Major Glenn Miller hanging at one side of the stage and matched by another of Gary Milner, similarly uniformed, on the opposite side.

Most remarkable of all was the figure of Gary Milner himself, at front centre, facing the musicians and conducting in exact simulation of the understated, curiously stiff Glenn Miller style. The applause that welled forth from the massed humanity packed into the rows of makeshift seating down on the hangar floor held something bigger and more powerful than ordinary audience politeness. It expressed emotions generated by months of anticipation and suddenly supercharged by recollection of youthful dreams blasted by war; of youthful innocence dissolved in a cauldron of hideous perils; of youthful comrades who got screaming drunk yesterday and today screamed as they died; of youthful girls who betrayed their last lover with you today and tomorrow betrayed you with their next but in an odd way kept faith with you all; of youthful yearnings for it to be over so you could just go home. And the essence of those half-forgotten, suddenly-sharpened pains and joys seemed distilled and concentrated in the sounds drawn from the musicians by the gently-moving hands of a long-dead orchestra leader now miraculously resurrected.

The butch journalist, separated from these emotional tides by both a generation gap and her stock-in-trade of professional detachment, was nonetheless aware of them as she made her way back to her seat alongside her male companion. But she was not surprised to discover that they meant nothing whatever to him. His words dropped like lead weights into the last few bars of "Moonlight Serenade" as it drew to its exquisite close.

"Well," he grunted irritably. "Did you see him?"

"No. He was on stage by then. I'm seeing him at the interval."

"Humph." He paused, then flung his next words loudly into the applause rising from the rest of the audience. "Bloody swine."

"All right, all right. Keep it down."

"He is a bloody swine."

She noted the faces turning their way, frowning in annoyance. She had had enough of his relentless carping.

"Yes," she hissed, "but just shut up about it for once."

Up on the stage, Gary Milner remained motionless through the applause, his back still turned to the audience as Adam Gates returned smiling to the microphone.

"No need to ask if you enjoyed that. No need to tell you, either, that that's the kind of music you'll be hearing for the rest of this concert." Adam turned slightly and gestured towards the still-motionless bandleader. "Or that the man who has done more, perhaps, than anyone else to keep the Glenn Miller tradition alive is with us here today. The melodies are the same, the arrangements are the same, the brilliant musicianship is the same, even the appearance and the name are nearly the same. His voice rose. "Ladies and gentlemen, meet the leader of the orchestra, Gary Milner!"

There was a drumroll and clash of cymbals as the bandleader turned to face the audience. The resemblance was uncanny. The rakish angle of the cap, the rimless glasses over alert, schoolmasterly eyes, the sensitive mouth and determined jaw - this was Glenn Miller reincarnated, it must be, or so one could easily be persuaded to believe for as long as the performance lasted, and perhaps even for longer than that as far as some of the more fanatical members of the

Gary Milner Appreciation Society were concerned.

There was a murmuring among the audience. Then someone began to clap, others followed suit and the sound crescendoed and roared into an explosion of applause.

Among a party of American veterans and their wives somewhere near the centre of the hangar a nice-looking old lady who'd drunk mild-and-bitter to her husband's memory an hour or two before was one of the first to rise to her feet, her eyes shining like a young girl's. She clapped furiously, calling excitedly to all around her, "Gee, isn't he just da-arrling? Oh my Ga-a-ahd, isn't he beautiful?"

Some of those who heard smiled at her naive enthusiasm, but even as they did so the infection reached them. One by one they too stood up and cheered. Within seconds the entire audience was doing the same.

Even without her it would have happened. It was what always happened. It was intended; it was planned and expected; the glitz never failed. On it, and on the music, Gary Milner had built his fame, his wealth, his life.

Even in such a career as his, though, today was something special. It was bound to be with this audience, at this time and in this place where many of those present had been enthralled forty years earlier by the music of Miller himself only days before his disappearance and death.

Adam shot Gary a sidelong grin. "How about this then?" he exclaimed into Gary Milner's ear through the storming applause. "Be great today, Gary. Be great more than you've ever been before: they deserve it."

Gary's nod of acknowledgement was almost imperceptible: the cool image was vital to the legend. But he risked a brief murmur. "It'll be the best ever."

Adam strode offstage. Gary made a stiffly correct military salute, then removed his uniform cap, laid it aside and took the microphone. He did not speak until the last of the applause had died.

"Mister Ambassador, distinguished guests, ladies and gentlemen: good evening, and thank you for your generous reception" - he smiled self-deprecatingly - "especially bearing in mind that we haven't actually done anything yet. But we're going to, I promise you we are, because that kind of warmth means a lot to us, particularly when it comes from an audience as special as this one."

His delivery was friendly, relaxed, resonant with sincerity. Much tuition and practice had made it so. There were no Americanisms of idiom or accent: he had long since made a careful judgment of the limits beyond which his resemblance to a long-dead hero should not be pushed. It was in obedience to this judgment that he continued in a modest, confidential tone.

"Now one thing I have to make clear, if you'll bear with me for another moment." He made a downwards gesture. "To members of the United States Eighth Air Force who earned this uniform the hard way, let me acknowledge that I'm only entitled to wear it as a stage costume lending atmosphere to a stage performance. And to members of Royal Air Force Bomber Command let me say as an ex-RAF pilot myself that I'd gladly use my own old uniform on stage" - he smiled again - "only it wouldn't suit the role I play." He waved a hand at the orchestra behind him. "While I'm on the subject, I might as well mention that some of the more decrepit boys in the band" - a rustle of mock-protest among the musicians - "are old enough to have done their bit as well." He indicated one of the saxophonists. "There's Jimmy Cradock here, he was in Burma with the Fourteenth Army, and Frank Thorogood behind him was in the Western Desert with the Eighth ... "

As Gary Milner proceeded with the introductions the temper of the butch journalist's male companion did not improve. He glanced around the intent faces of the people around him, then burst out again in bitter tones.

"God, what a nerve! Listen to that! What a bloody nerve!"

The journalist shrugged impatiently. "Are you surprised? It's a stage performance: he said it himself. He's just winding up the audience."

"Yes, but all that pilot stuff!"

She shrugged. "He *is* a pilot." She raised a hand, forestalling his protest, and returned her attention to the close of Gary Milner's speech.

" ... and Harry Boothroyd was in the Navy: we call him the Pride of Pompey. So you see, this is a special occasion for us just as it is for you. In fact, we're pretty much in the same mood as you are. Which is a good cue for trotting out that good old warhorse which never fails to set feet tapping and put us all, yes, 'In the Mood'!"

He turned, raised his baton and propelled the orchestra into a performance of the piece that had more than just the machine-like precision that any random collection of sessions men can be relied upon to give it. It had that something extra, that sparkle and freshness which a gifted orchestra leader coaxes from expert musicians playing for the umpteenth time a number which they can all perform in their sleep and sometimes have done. The Gary Milner Orchestra never failed to deliver that something extra, and it was Gary Milner who inspired them to do it. This was the talent that made him the undisputed custodian of the Glenn Miller flame.

Down in the auditorium, the nice old lady with the American party snapped her fingers in time to the music and fairly bounced in her seat. "Dear Ga-a-ahd!" she exclaimed. "Isn't he a honey? Love ya, baby, just love ya!"

A few yards away an angry man writhed in disgust. "The creep. The rotten swine. The nerve he has, saying those things, standing up there like that! How can he? How did he get there? How did he? Just tell me that!"

And his companion replied, "You know how he did it. We both know."

3
SONNY BOY

Terry Cullerton's gramophone was old-fashioned even for 1942. A heavy box-shaped tabletop model crafted in stained oak, it was far too big and clumsy for the stand chair on which perforce it perched precariously in his tiny bedroom. The doors of the contraption were closed, and Terry had stuffed dusters and handkerchieves into a couple of the slats of the soundbox so as to reduce the volume emerging from the innards. "Song of India" came through as if played on toy instruments behind a blanket, but no shortcomings of reproduction could disguise the brilliance with which the Tommy Dorsey Orchestra had transformed the Rimsky-Korsakov melody into a swing classic.

Terry sat on the bed, trying to analyse how it was done. He concluded that the key lay in the restraint with which Tommy Dorsey's soft, sweet trombone preserved the delicate texture of the original melody, built slowly to the sudden brash exuberance of Bunny Berigan's trumpet chorus, then glided in again to gather up the pieces and reassemble them in their former smooth pattern.

The pickup arm scratched its way to the finale. Terry rewound the machine, replaced the needle and lowered the pickup arm to the outer groove again without turning the record over. Once more he listened intently, a mittened hand resting on the cornet lying on the bed beside him.

He wore the mittens to try to maintain flexibility in his fingers. His poky, shabbily-furnished bedroom, with its scrap of threadbare matting and cheap flowered wallpaper showing an ominous patch of damp in one corner, was horrifically cold. Terry accepted this without resentment. Cold bedrooms were normal in wartime: everyone knew that extravagance with fuel was paid for with sailors' lives out on the Atlantic, where despite all Winston Churchill's rhetoric it looked as though the U-boats would win the war for the Nazis even if Rommel didn't do it in the Western Desert.

Quite aside from this, any idea of lighting the ancient black cast-iron gasfire that the room boasted would have been vetoed by Terry's father on the ground of expense. In a world where memories of dole queues and soup kitchens were still fresh and your father was making sacrifices to keep you at school when you could have been out earning for nearly three years, you did not argue about pennies for the gas meter.

There was a good coal fire in the kitchen range - Terry had lit it himself in preparation for his father coming home from work - but of course playing gramophone records downstairs was banned, and Terry preferred to be alone anyway.

In a strict Salvationist household, to have gained permission to play and listen to profane music at all was a sufficient achievement, for the time being at least. Of recent months, as Terry's delight in the dance music programmes purveyed over the wireless by the BBC Forces programme had quietly grown, so also had his resentment of the need to keep it secret - and his suspicion that the austere religious faith whose thou-shalt-nots ruled his life was not so much a conviction rooted within himself as a straitjacket thrust on him by his father.

Withdrawing all his meagre savings from the Post Office in order to buy the second-hand gramophone without consulting his father had been Terry's first serious act of teenage rebellion. The ensuing row had tested all his new-born resolve, but in the end, with many a dire threat and prediction of the perdition awaiting those who strayed from the narrow paths of rectitude staked out by General Booth, Harold Cullerton had allowed Terry to keep his new acquisition provided it remained in his room and was used only under strictly-controlled conditions.

It was a foot in the door to future independence. Terry's realisation of this brought a new and assertive set of the jaw to a face hitherto notable mainly for making its owner look even younger than he actually was - an attribute in which Terry took little pleasure, not yet having discovered the advantages that could be wrung from it if skilfully exploited.

Just now, though, all that Terry's countenance revealed was fierce concentration as he waited for the Bunny Berigan trumpet chorus. He fixed a mute into his cornet, picked up the instrument and put it to his lips. Then he gathered air into his lungs, flexed his fingers and came in exactly on cue.

At first he played cautiously, no more than matching the muffled sound from the gramophone. Of course it wasn't the same using the mute, but he hoped that would keep the sound from reaching his father. After two or three bars, though, the exhilaration of the solo carried him away: he rose from the bed, stood straight and blew uninhibitedly, eyes closed and one foot tapping.

Not for long. A banging through the floor from the ceiling below set the house shaking.

"Terry! Terry!"

He stopped playing, sighed and removed the pickup arm from the record.

"Yes, Dad?" He knew what would come next, and it did: the slow tread on the stair, the door flung open, the rebuke.

"I've told you before, Terry: you're not to play your cornet in t'house. Why do you persist in defying me?"

The tone of gruff peremptoriness did not brook argument, or was intended not to. But all too often the lad did argue nowadays. Now he did it again.

"I was being quiet, Dad." Terry would never have offered the riposte a year ago. It was all this jazz that was at the back of it, filling his head with wrong ideas.

"You were not: be told. It's bad enough wi' them records, but when you start playing your cornet as well - "

"You wouldn't mind if it was a hymn."

The impudence! Yet Harold tried to be patient. "That's where you're wrong, lad. You have to think about t'neighbours. It's a cross a musical family has to bear. Consideration for others comes before music, even sacred music."

Terry sighed inwardly. There was always an answer, and his father always knew it, and it always fitted in neatly with the stern expression, with the long-unfashionable walrus moustache, with disapproval of the present day and anything of his own that Terry wanted to do. Terry dared not say what he wanted to say next - yet suddenly it came out anyway.

"Sometimes I just don't care about other people, only about music."

His father's voice rose. "Never let me hear you talk like that, Terry! Selfishness is a sin and you must abhor it. Doing right comes before music. Music is the servant of religion, never the master. Just think on."

"Some music's got nothing to do with religion, Dad."

"Oh aye!" His father gestured contemptuously at the gramophone. "Yon monkey music of yours. It's all you seem to think about nowadays."

Why did he have to keep calling it monkey music? Aloud Terry said, "That's not true, Dad. I like other music as well. Salvation Army music for one: I do like it, you know I do."

"Aye, 'appen you do," replied his father sourly. "An' if that's so, you'd best be putting your uniform on. You haven't forgotten about band practice at t'Citadel, have you?"

A pretty pass they'd come to, reflected Harold glumly ten minutes or so later as, in uniform and carrying their cornet cases, they crossed the bridge at South Station and turned right at the Royal Oak. That Terry could talk about liking Salvation Army music as well as other music when it ought to be the other way round! In fact, a Salvationist's mind was supposed to be open only to sacred music, and he, Harold, ought to have been more strict about it. He should never have given in over that gramophone.

A green-painted Blackpool Corporation tram from Squires Gate swayed and clanged to a standstill, but they ignored it. Feet were made before trams, in Harold Cullerton's view, and in any case tuppence not spent on a tramride was tuppence saved for something else.

So they walked, following the tram's route along Lytham Road, past the fish-and-chip cafés, the milk bars and the garish souvenir shops, on to the junction with the Promenade at the Manchester Hotel. This was by no means the shortest route to the Citadel on Coronation Street but it was the one they always took. "Blows t'cobwebs off you," Harold would say.

He was right about that today. The autumn gale, very different from the "balmy Blackpool breezes" of the town's pre-war publicity brochures, had cleared the Prom not only of cobwebs, if any, but of almost everything and everyone else except the fast streamlined trams introduced for the comfort of holidaymakers during the last year or two of peace.

There were few trippers in the town just now though. Before the war, the Illuminations had extended the holiday season until well into the autumn. The blackout regulations had put paid to that. Now, even in high summer fewer people came on holiday than in peacetime, partly in response to government appeals to "take your holidays at home", partly because of the discomforts and delays of wartime travel, but most of all because would-be holidaymakers knew very well that they would be hard put to find anywhere to stay, might indeed end up having to sleep on the beach.

For Blackpool, like other seaside resorts, was now in effect a vast training camp devoted to the purposes of war. Not that much military hardware was in evidence. There did not need to be. Basic marching and parade drill required only rifles and a pacing-stick - and not necessarily even those - while gym shorts, plimsolls and a singlet sufficed for physical jerks. By this time, the autumn of 1942, some tens of thousands of rookies had spent their first few weeks - to many it seemed years - in the Royal Air Force being processed by the Blackpool recruit-training sausage machine, with tens of thousands more to come. Hardly a street or stretch of sand between the North and South Piers during the daytime lacked its quota of sufferers at the hands of the hard-driving drill and PT instructors, while Burton's ballroom, the Olympia indoor amusements palace and even such other unlikely venues as the tramsheds served for indoor lectures and training.

At this time of day, though, with square-bashing over until tomorrow, most of the trainees were back at their billets in the hundreds of requisitioned private hotels and boarding houses, slumping exhaustedly on their beds in overcrowded rooms, queuing up to wash their feet, writing letters home, wolfing their evening meals and sharing the household chores. In all these activities they were tirelessly supervised, bullied and mothered by the formidable Blackpool landladies, whose qualification for the task was simple. Occupationally inured to a backbreaking seven-days-a-week slog through the six-month "season" of every year, their contribution to the war effort was to prolong it to cover the rest of the fiftytwo weeks as well.

Nor had the evening invasion yet begun, when off-duty revellers from military units based nearby would flood into Blackpool's myriad picture palaces, pubs and dance-halls. In the competition for the favours of WAAF, ATS and local civilian girls, the miserably-paid RAF trainees were faced not only with British rivals but also with hordes of romantically-uniformed foreigners: sad-faced Poles and Czechs, handsome blond Norwegians, hot-eyed gesticulating Free French, New Zealanders, Canadians, Australians and recently - worst of all - the rapidly-swelling invading phalanxes of jaunty, big-talking, big-spending Americans, whose invincible friendliness and well-intentioned generosity could never offset the fact that they were "overpaid, oversexed and over here".

Not that Terry or his father, after three years of war, gave any of this a second thought. They battled on against the wind along the beach side of the near-deserted Promenade, past Louis Tussaud's waxworks, the shuttered Central Beach arcades and stalls, the tawdry onion-domed façade of Luna Park, on towards the Tower looming next to the huge cream-coloured art deco block-and-clock housing the biggest Woolworth's in Britain.

Harold was still laying down the law. "I don't care what you say, Terry, it's the music of savages. It comes from Africa. Civilised countries send missionaries there to teach them something better."

Terry muttered under his breath. "Not music."

"What's that you say, lad? Not music? They do teach them music, but no, that isn't the important thing - it's religion. A proper, civilised religion instead of all that witch-doctor taradiddle - "

Terry tried again.

"Dad, I can't help it. I like jazz music. I like swing. I don't care where it comes from. I like all music, every kind there is. I like Salvation Army music but it isn't enough."

His father halted in his stride and took Terry's arm. They stood and faced each other.

"What you're saying is the Army isn't enough." The tone was hectoring, challenging. An imp of rebelliousness shaped Terry's reply.

"Perhaps it isn't."

Harold stared at his son as at a stranger. "How can you say that? It's been my whole life."

In for a penny, in for a pound. "Not my whole life," said Terry defiantly. "Not mine."

"Come here, lad." Harold Cullerton took his son's arm again, led him to a tram-shelter that would afford some protection from the wind. "Now listen, Terry. You're a fine musician, brilliant even, the best we've got, you know that. And you're not seventeen yet. You've got your life in front of you. When Joe Braithwaite packs up in five or six years they'll make you bandmaster, no doubt about it. That's something to look forward to, isn't it?"

"Yes, of course it is, Dad." Terry shifted uncomfortably. Could he? Dare he? He plunged. "But it's not just the music. There's something else worries me as well. You said yourself, religion's more important than music."

"Aye, so I did."

"That means the question I want to ask is important too, because it's about religion. So I think it's more important than music too." Now he'd done it. There was no backing out.

"Oh aye? Go on then."

34

"Well, what I wonder is - I'd like to know ... " Terry hesitated, did not know where to begin, plunged at random. "I mean, how do we know the Bible is true?"

Harold would have been appalled even if the question had not been so unexpected. "Who the hangment have you been talking to, lad? Who's been putting ideas into your head?"

"Nobody. Just thinking." You didn't have to get all your ideas from other people, did you? Weren't you allowed to think things out for yourself? Terry stumbled on. "Look, Dad, we believed in God, our family. We trusted in Him, and then Mum - well, she just got TB and died, didn't she? No reason for it: it just happened. Being in the Salvation Army didn't make any difference: God didn't have to let it happen but He did. Why?" Unexpectedly, the tears pricked his eyes, but he fought them back. He wouldn't show weakness. The time for that had been four years ago, when he'd refused for months to accept his mother's death, dreamed night after night that she'd come back to dry his tears, cuddle him, tell him everything was all right. But his father hadn't helped. Would he help now?

Terry made a further effort. "What I mean is, the Bible says the Lord is merciful. But He wasn't merciful letting Mum die of tuberculosis. So that makes the Bible look wrong."

Harold boiled with indignation. How could this be? Had sixteen years in a devout Christian household taught the lad nothing? His lips formed to deliver a sharp rebuff, but he controlled himself. Terry was only a youngster still, even if he did have talent and brains beyond the ordinary. There was a balance to be struck. Harold tried to strike it.

"God's ways are not our ways, you know that. And we must always remember: the burdens He lays upon us are never greater than we have the strength to bear ... "

He was off. Terry gazed out through the salt-stained glass of the tram-shelter to the harsh waters and boiling grey skies beyond the promenade railings. No help there, nor from his Dad's raspings either. He knew these comfortless platitudes already, and plenty of others: his Dad had mouthed them all four years ago, never letting go, never mingling his own grief with his son's, never giving his son strength from his own weakness. Since then he'd retired behind his barricade of Victorian rectitude, firing off edicts from time to time to prevent Terry escaping his due portion of the domestic chores left vacant without a woman in the household. Was that all his father could offer? Was that all Christianity could offer?

The gruff voice was still drearily laying down the law: " ... and there's no merit in faith without effort: we have to hold on hard to God, otherwise we lose Him." Impossible to resist adding, as Harold's thoughts diverted to another tack: "Abhorrence of worldly temptation strengthens faith too, remember that. If you gave a bit less attention to yon monkey music and more to - "

Terry protested angrily. "It's not like that, Dad." Why couldn't his father stick to the point instead of making digs? "It's not just music I'm talking about, I told you."

"No? It's not just music I'm talking about either. You can't have the profane as well as the sacred, you know that, and it doesn't apply only to music, it applies to the whole of life. That's why - "

"Dad, you don't understand. I don't think you want to understand."

Harold was angry as well now. "No? Well, I've lived longer than you have and I understand better than you think."

Terry sighed. What was the use? It was deadlock. He'd tried, he'd asked for help but his Dad wouldn't give it. He just wouldn't listen.

Harold sighed. What was the use? It was deadlock. He'd tried, he'd shown the lad the right way but he wouldn't take it. He just wouldn't listen.

By unspoken consent, they resumed their walk in silence. The wind continued howling, and now it began to rain.

Joe Braithwaite raised his baton and surveyed his band and choir with quiet satisfaction. Everybody here, everybody uniformed and in position, everybody silent, confident and ready, bringing colour and spectacle to hide the tired wartime drabness that the Citadel shared with every other public building in Britain.

In a moment they'd make the rafters ring again. This would be the big one next Sunday. He knew and they knew it would be a cracker and this last run-through wasn't really needed: they were doing it again for the sheer joy of it before going home. He brought his baton down and the first quiet phrases of "The Holy City" flowed out.

Gradually the magic took over, the magic that a Christian prefers to call Divine inspiration and which, whatever its rightful name, unfailingly appears when the varied gifts of people united in conviction of the goodness of what they do are so harnessed, ordered and attuned that technique is automatic and the consciousness is cleared of everything but the pure stream of creativity.

Joe Braithwaite's arms and whole body performed with the rigid precision of a metronome, but inside his spirit was ecstatic, soaring to meet his God. Watching the faces of his musicians and singers he knew that they felt it too. Verse after verse they flew with him, upward and ever upward, closer and closer to the heaven whose existence he never doubted.

Now it was time for Harold and Terry Cullerton, and there they came, the two cornets taking turns to ring out challenge and response, building the edifice of worship higher and higher until it seemed that praise could do no more. Then every voice and every instrument reached down into itself for the last reserves of strength and will and fervency, and a great gale of harmony soared to where the gates of the Holy City swung back, revealing the glory within.

Or so it seemed to Joe Braithwaite as the last notes died away. Breathless, transported, he surveyed the eager faces again, then gave them what they wanted, expected, knew they deserved. He was not an eloquent man, but he did his best.

"Raight-oh, lads and lasses," he said. "That were luv'ly, grand. Just make sure we do it t'same way on Sunday, for the glory of God." He turned, and in a different voice asked, matter-of-factly, "Is t'tea ready, Vera? Yes? Good. That'll do for tonight then."

Terry and Harold were both accomplished musicians. Their sharp exchanges on the Promenade had detracted nothing from their performance during the rehearsal, nor indeed from the exaltation which both had shared with the rest of the choir and instrumentalists.

Now they put away their cornets in the silence that for a musician often has to precede the wind-down. Then they made their way towards the trestle table on which the tea and biscuits were set out. As they joined the queue, Terry spoke.

"Was that all right, Dad?"

"Was what all right? The music?"

"Yes. The solos. Did I do mine all right?"

"Aye." It came out reluctantly.

"What more do you want?" Terry wanted to scream into the silence, but he held his tongue until, mercifully, they were interrupted.

"Ooh, Mr Cullerton, wasn't that nice? You and Terry do play lovely together."

Norah Yardley, fresh-faced, puppyfat-plump, uncomplicated and still innocent, considered herself Terry's girlfriend and in that capacity enjoyed a grudging acceptance on Harold's part. Not that he approved of the way hanky-panky seemed to start nowadays at a far younger age than it had in his time. Still, she was Salvation Army like her whole family, a decent home-loving girl, not one of those fast little trollops. She'd perhaps help to keep Terry on the straight and narrow. Anyhow there was no stopping them seeing one another, what with her being in the choir and both of them going to the same school. Just now she looked a picture with her brown eyes sparkling and soft cheeks flushed from the pleasure of the music. Still, it cut no ice with Harold in his present frame of mind.

"Aye," he replied shortly. "'Appen we do." He picked up a cup of tea, stirred sugar into it with the communal spoon, helped himself to a couple of biscuits and stumped off to join Joe Braithwaite and a group of cronies. Crestfallen, Norah watched him go.

"Oh," she exclaimed. "What's up? What did I do?"

"It's not you, it's me," replied Terry. "Come on, let's get some tea." They helped themselves, made for a corner and sat down.

"What's it about then?" asked Norah. "Is something wrong?"

"Same old thing." Was it really? Wasn't it something more this time? No use trying to tell Norah anyway. He resumed. "Keeps on about my monkey music. You know what he's like. Makes me right fed up at times, he does."

"Oh Terry, what a shame." She reached out, touched him on the arm, made to take his hand in sympathy. "You do seem to rub him up the wrong way."

Terry snatched his hand away. "I suppose you think he's right then?"

"No Terry, no." She searched for a way out. "How can I tell who's right and who's wrong? I don't know what's been going on, but I do know I don't like you and your Dad arguing. I'm sure he doesn't really mean it."

Something snapped inside Terry.

"Oh yes he bloody well does," he blurted. The profanity gave him a perverse pleasure which Norah's shocked expression only deepened.

It was Norah's turn to shock Terry, or at least surprise him, as they said goodnight at the front door of her home, a terraced house not far from Terry's own. For a few minutes they were alone, Terry's father having walked on ahead and Norah's parents gone indoors.

"See you on Sunday, then, Terry," said Norah.

"Um," was all the reply Terry made, and perhaps all that was necessary, considering how unchanging was their Sunday routine of attendance at the Citadel. Yet Norah always seemed to want reassurance that their partings were only temporary.

"And going to school tomorrow of course," Norah went on. Terry made no reply, and there was a silence while Norah wondered if she dared say what she was thinking. At last she managed to get it out.

"Don't you wish we could do something on our own sometime, Terry?"

"Eh?" Terry was startled. "On our own? How do you mean?"

Now the subject was broached Norah gathered courage.

"Oh, I don't know. Do something. Anything. I'd just like us to do something on our own. Go somewhere perhaps. What I mean is, we're always with our parents when we see each other, aren't we? Either that or going to school, and that doesn't count."

It was true enough.

Terry pondered the question. "Sort of go out together?"

"Yes. Just the two of us."

"They'd never let us."

"They might if we asked."

"They won't," replied Terry with conviction.

"Oh go on, Terry, can't we ask them?"

"No," Terry replied quickly.

Norah began to protest, but he cut her off.

"Look, Norah, I won't ask them, and that's flat. But we can do it anyway. If you want to come out with me, you can."

"Where to?"

"The Tower."

The Tower? You mean dancing?" Norah was flabbergasted. Yet the idea held a strange attraction.

"Yes. The ballroom."

"But we couldn't without asking them. And they'd never - "

"Yes, we can. I've done it. I've been there."

"You've been dancing? Can you dance? Who were you with?" Norah was incredulous, and a little jealous.

"I went on my own. I've done it a couple of times. I wanted to listen to the music."

"You mean dance music?" It was one shock after another.

"That's what they play there," said Terry, and added defiantly, "I like it, and so would you."

Norah digested this. New horizons suddenly opened before her, offering temptations previously undreamed-of. And with Terry sharing them! Mysterious forces stirred somewhere deep within her.

It was disquieting. She played for time.

"And your Dad doesn't know?"

"No."

"But how, Terry? How did you do it without him knowing?"

"Promise you won't tell?"

"All right."

"Promise?"

"Yes. I promise."

"Firewatching."

In a flash it all became clear to Norah, and she had worked out a simple stratagem for sharing Terry's forbidden pleasure even before she fully realised she intended to do so. Of her own volition she would never have deceived her parents. But Terry's insistence that there was no other way had pushed her over the edge.

Firewatching was Terry's opportunity. Norah's would be First Aid classes.

4
I'LL WALK ALONE

On his sixteenth birthday Terry had become eligible for the fire guard roster at his school, which meant spending an occasional night on the school premises with another boy and a master. Their duties in the event of an air raid were to look out for incendiary bombs and tackle them with stirrup pumps and buckets while awaiting arrival of the fire brigade and rescue services. Such teams of fire guards, stationed in factories, office blocks, hospitals, department stores and other large buildings of every kind, were a vital feature of Britain's defence against the German air blitz.

Since a subsistence allowance was paid and air raids were considered unlikely in Blackpool, firewatching was popular with the senior boys of Terry's school. A further attraction to those from strict homes was that if a master was compliant and a friend could be persuaded or bribed to cover for a few hours, you were free for that period of time to do as you liked without your parents knowing. In this way Terry had been able to begin secretly exploring the countless Blackpool ballrooms - Tower, Palace, Winter Gardens and the rest - in search of the kind of music previously known to him only through dance-band programmes on the wireless.

The motive that drove Terry to this clandestine defiance of parental and religious authority did not actuate Norah. She was a placid girl, content in the security provided by her family and Salvationist faith. Yet she succumbed to Terry's blandishments after only a brief resistance. It seemed the only thing to do. Full of fear and guilt, she cut her First Aid class one evening and joined Terry at the Tower.

Almost against her will Norah found it breathlessly exciting, even though all she and Terry did was to tour the building from roof garden to basement aquarium and then sit in the ballroom listening to the music. When another opportunity occurred, the temptation to repeat the adventure was irresistible. Besides, by then Norah had secretly learnt the quickstep from a school friend, discovering at once that she was an instinctive and natural dancer. Despite all her trepidations she was eager to try out her new-found skill.

Deception becomes easier with repetition and deceivers more daring and ingenious. For their third evening out Terry arranged for a substitute fire guard until a late hour and Norah concocted a wildly improbable story about time-consuming practical First Aid exercises and tests.

High-spirited with anticipation of the long evening before them, Terry and Norah began it at Hesketh's, near the bottom end of Hound's Hill. The pleasure available there was unsophisticated but popular, so the queue they had to stand in was long, as usual. Also as usual, however, it moved fast. The sweating assistants pounced like tigers on the baskets of piping hot fish and chips dumped before them by the fryers. Measuring the portions, spraying them with salt and vinegar, wrapping them in newspaper, ringing up cash and giving change - all took place in a series of lightning-swift movements, tirelessly repeated again and again. The complications introduced by requests for mushy peas, steamed steak puddings or pickled onions were merely routine, and even the occasional orders for ten or twenty or thirty portions barely disturbed the rhythm, for it was a well-established boarding-house custom to ease pressure on kitchen staff now and then by serving guests with bought-in fish-and-chip meals.

"We can go round the block while we eat these," pronounced Terry, as he and Norah emerged, unwrapping their packages.

Turning right at the corner, they strolled along Bank Hey Street. Norah glanced over at the red-brick bulk of the Tower building on the opposite side, then at the massive 500-foot skeleton of the Tower itself, silhouetted black and stark against the greying sky.

"Such a shame, isn't it?" she remarked.

"What is?" asked Terry indistinctly as he sucked in air to take the heat off the excessive quantity of chips he had unwarily stuffed into his mouth.

"The Lights. Not having them," said Norah. Blackpool residents always referred to the annual Illuminations as "the Lights". "If it was before the war they'd be on by now."

"Mm." replied Terry non-committally.

"The Tower would be all lit up."

"So would everything else."

"Yes. That's what I mean. Oh, I know the traffic was a nuisance but the Lights were so pretty, weren't they? I always thought the Tower looked lovely. Remember those lights all the way up, wriggling like a snake? And now there's nothing, just the mouldy old blackout."

Terry did remember vividly enough the excitement of being allowed up late once a year to walk the Illuminations from end to end with his parents, but recalled that the last time, in 1938, it had palled. Had it been because his mother, by then in the sanatorium, had not been with them? Or had there been something else as well? He gave voice to his thoughts. "We were only kids," he said practically. "We probably wouldn't think anything of it by now."

Norah considered this, wondering from the advanced age of sixteen whether the things she'd been thrilled about at twelve now seemed like kids' stuff. Not all of them, she decided, but before she could say so Terry went on.

"There isn't just nothing up the Tower now anyway," he said confusingly. They had crossed to the other side of Bank Hey Street and were turning left towards the Promenade, between the Tower and the Palace buildings. "There's something there all right. On the platforms at the top. That's why they don't let the public go up any more. Peter Hedley in my class, he says the Air Force have a big wireless gadget they can see German aeroplanes with in the dark. His father's an electrician and he works at Vickers Armstrong."

Referred to in the local press only by such security-conscious euphemisms as "a large war factory in the North-West", the Vickers Armstrong works at Squires Gate by now employed so many local people that few of Blackpool's inhabitants remained unaware that it mass-produced Wellington bombers. As a sideline - though without the knowledge or consent of the management - some of the workers also achieved in their odd moments an impressive output of simple, reliable cigarette lighters for which there was a flourishing clandestine market at half a crown a time. Clearly, anyone's father who was employed in such an establishment must be knowledgeable about all things to do with wireless.

Just the same Norah remained sceptical on grounds of common sense. "Go on, nobody can see in the dark," she said.

"This gadget can. It works by radio waves," Terry insisted. "They used it in the Liverpool air raids, his Dad says." They were turning left again now, on to the Promenade, where they walked along the front of the Tower building while finishing up their chips.

"Didn't help them much then," said Norah, glancing into the deepening dusk over the sea beyond the Promenade. "We never saw any German aeroplanes shot down apart from that one time, did we?" There had been eight successive nights a year and a half ago when watchers in Blackpool had seen the dark sky to the south turn to an angry red glow, criss-crossed by searchlights and punctuated by orange flashes as the Luftwaffe made its bid to destroy the port of Liverpool forty miles away. On one of those evenings there had been a moment when a pinpoint of light had appeared in the sky not far away, fanned to a fierce flame, glided lower and lower, then faltered, fluttered and finally plunged to earth somewhere out of sight.

"That was the most horrible thing I've seen in my whole life," declared Norah. "I mean, those men in the aeroplane, they were dying while we watched."

"They were Germans - " began Terry.

"I know they were Germans," said Norah, "and they were dropping bombs on Liverpool and killing people and they oughtn't to have been doing it and I felt sorry for the people in Liverpool too, but just the same it was them we were watching while they were dying and it was horrible and it was wrong: we oughtn't to have watched."

"Well, we couldn't do anything about it anyway," said Terry dismissively. This was not the first time they had had this conversation, and he was not nearly as certain of his feelings on the topic as Norah seemed to be.

"I know, but - " began Norah, but Terry interrupted her.

"Finished yet?" He crumpled up his chip papers. "Hurry up, we want to go in."

"Not yet," replied Norah, and fell silent as she disposed of the last soggy scraps swimming about in vinegar and printer's ink at the bottom of her package. They paused at the steps leading up to the Tower main entrance, where the crowds streaming from buses and trams at the nearby stops were queuing to pay admission.

"Round the back," said Terry, and they completed their circuit of the Tower building by turning left again to buy their tickets at the smaller and less frequented Bank Hey Street entrance. Taking the back staircase by the ticket office they avoided the trek through the aquarium. At the top of the stairs they shouldered their way through the "long bar", a corridor-like cavern of institutional grimness with dingy brown oilcoth, brass spittoons here and there, and gloomy painted walls unrelieved by pictures or ornaments. It contrived nevertheless to be a lively place, in which half a dozen perspiring staff behind a long varnished counter waged battle against the thirsts of early evening revellers.

Passing through the swing doors at the far end of the long bar,

Terry and Norah emerged into a different world. This was the vast and opulent Tower Ballroom, a palatial arena of Edwardian gilt-and-red-plush splendour, its deep sofas, thick-pile carpets and sprung parquet dance-floor illuminated by enormous glittering chandeliers suspended from the high elaborately-decorated ceiling. Here, before the war, millhands and shopgirls had dreamed of being princes and princesses: here their uniformed counterparts now dreamed of becoming millhands and shopgirls again.

A later age would scoff at the polished shoes and Brylcreemed hair, the collars and ties and dance-frocks, the wooden courtesies of "May I have this dance please?", "Do you come here often?" and - the crucial one - "Would you like me to see you home?" Above all it would sneer at the amazing orderliness of the whole ritual - and most especially at the rigidly-defined evolutions of the dances themselves, among which the stiff and formal tango was considered to express the ultimate in steamy eroticism and the stylised gymnastics of the jitterbug to menace decency and morals.

To the wartime generation, however, whether happy or homesick, excited or bored, eager for the future or fearful of it, the dance hall along with the picture palace represented escape into a fantasy-world of luxury, of glamour, of romance. And while the first two of these phenomena generally evaporated with the strains of the last waltz, if fate was kind the third might not.

When Terry and Norah entered the ballroom there were already several hundred young men and women out on the french-chalked dance floor devoutly hoping for this consummation. Most were in uniform; many had already patronised the vast bar adjacent to the ballroom; all were performing the intricate gyrations of the quickstep under the stern eye of the master of ceremonies, a tall, formidable, grey-haired figure of massive dignity in white tie, white gloves and tails with no obvious duties other than to patrol an imaginary centre line for the couples to dance around and order "Clear the floor please!" at the end of each set.

"Should we go straight on?" asked Norah, not wanting to waste a moment before showing off her new-found dancing skill. Terry nodded, somewhat unenthusiastically. It was the music he cared about. His interest in dancing was strictly limited - and so, he had quickly discovered under Norah's tuition, was his aptitude for it.

Norah placed her handbag under one of the red plush settees, covered it with her rolled-up coat, then joined Terry on the dance-floor. Her confidence in the propriety of ballroom behaviour was evidently shared by others who had done the same. Theft of such articles seldom occurred. Moreover, drugs were neither peddled nor consumed; drinking was common but drunkenness was not; and if sexual traffic between the dancers was by no means rare, boys did generally understand when no meant no, while girls willing to behave "no better than they ought to" usually imposed a modicum of delay and insisted on relative privacy.

That was the crux, when all was said and done. The most important motive for going dancing was to meet members of the opposite sex free from the constraints imposed by social convention elsewhere.

For Terry and Norah, of course, these constraints were not merely conventional but religious. The jolly popular image of the bonneted Sally Army lass selling the "War Cry" around the pubs masked a sterner reality in the personal lives of Salvationists. The spectrum of virtuous behaviour permitted to them was narrow and sharply demarcated, much of it consisting of negatives. Thou shalt not drink or smoke was only the beginning: there was also thou shalt not perform or listen to any but sacred music, thou shalt not frequent cinemas or theatres, thou shalt not dance - thou shalt not, in fact, seek any amusement or recreation outside the Salvationist framework itself lest the beast of sexual licence thought to lurk behind all worldly entertainments be unloosed.

This was why Terry had considered it pointless to ask parental permission to go out with Norah. That it would be refused was certain, since young people out of range of adult authority would inevitably, it was held, infringe one or another of the prohibitions that otherwise hedged them in. After refusal would come closer supervision.

Truly the way of the Salvationist was steep, hard and strewn with mines, especially in a town dedicated to providing the merrymaker with all that most spectacularly and vulgarly offended against the Army's rules.

Little wonder that to Norah, launching out on to the dance floor felt like sailing off on an ocean of adventure. Guilt and duty were left on shore and diminished with distance. Merging with the mass of dancers lent anonymity and therefore freedom to her delight in exercising her new skill. Covertly she watched other more expert couples and took note of new steps she was resolved to learn. And although dutifully shocked by the heavy red-gash-in-a-pancake makeup almost universally favoured by the other girls, she could not help wondering whether she might venture to use just a trace of powder and lipstick on their next evening at the Tower.

The trouble with Norah, thought Terry, was the way she kept on chattering while they danced. Ooh look at this and ooh look at that, and what was it your father said about so-and-so and do you know what our history teacher told us today and I saw a nice blouse yesterday at R H O Hill's but my mother says I've got to save my clothing coupons so I don't suppose I'll be able to buy it even though I've got the money ... What a bore it was when what you really wanted was to watch and listen to the orchestra - a full dinner-jacketed lineup of sixteen or eighteen musicians, plus a glamorous female vocalist in long evening-dress and the leader in white tie and tails. It was only to please Norah that Terry danced at all: he knew he did it badly, and trying not to step on her toes was distraction enough when he was trying to listen to the music. But the way she rattled on it was as though she wasn't even aware of the complexity and deftness of the arrangements, the close interweaving of the harmonic patterns, the contrast of brass against reeds, the thrusting coordination and the subtle commentaries of drama, comedy, grace and power supplied by the rhythm section.

Now the orchestra leader was signalling the start of the third number of the set, and what a number it was too! As the bass-driven, insistent eight-to-the-bar beat of "At the Woodchopper's Ball" spurred the dancers into action, Terry alone remained stationary, forgetting Norah, forgetting himself or where he was and everything else except the flickering fingers of drummer and bass-player, the tripping melody of the opening clarinet solo and the muted brass riffs hinting at the outbursts of energy to come. A couple dancing by bumped into Terry and muttered an apology, then Norah dragged him into movement.

"Come on, Terry." Her patience was wearing thin at last. What's the matter with you?"

"I'm listening to the music," he returned shortly.

"Oh, you," she said. "Sometimes I don't know what I'll do with you, Terry Cullerton." She softened her words with a half-smile. "Still, it is good, I have to admit that."

Terry said nothing, concentrating for the moment on chasséing in the right places. Norah tried again.

"I certainly don't agree with your Dad in everything he says. I mean, this is what he calls monkey music, isn't it?"

"Yes," said Terry.

"Has he every really listened to it?"

"Don't think so. He switches it off when it comes on the wireless and when I play it on my gramophone he tells me to keep the noise down."

"Well, I like monkey music too, just as much as you do," said Norah ingratiatingly.

Then why can't you shut up for a minute and just listen, Terry's inner self screamed, and for a while Norah did just that, as though sensing his thought. Terry was hardly aware of the improvement in his dancing as Norah concentrated on transmitting the subtle bodily signals and pressures that her instinct devised to forestall many of Terry's mistakes while adapting her own steps to those that she could not prevent.

A few yards away from them, in the corner of the dance-floor to the left of the stage, a darkly handsome, gum-chewing American corporal suddenly released his WAAF partner with one arm and flung her to the fullest extent of his other. Her feet twinkled, her rump flashed impudently from side to side, and then they were off, jitterbugging like furies. Within seconds they had been joined by three or four other couples while yet others formed a circle to watch.

Norah's eyes shone. "Ooh look, Terry," she exclaimed. "D'you think we could learn to do that?"

Terry glanced at the jivers. "Perhaps," he muttered grudgingly. He had little confidence that he could. "If I wanted to," he added to save face.

Norah's eyes shone as she gazed at the capering pairs. The men would crouch almost motionless at the centre of individual imaginary circles, manoeuvring their partners around them with careless arrogance, thrusting them out over and over again to the circumference of their territories where the girls would spin like tops this way and that, arms waving in blatant sexual display, skirts flying up to offer repeated glimpses of stockingtops, suspenders and bare thighs that were breathlessly titillating in an age when such sights were rarely exposed to male eyes anywhere outside brothels or "Parisian art" magazines passed furtively from hand to hand.

"I suppose it's wrong though," sighed Norah, fighting and losing a battle not to envy these hussies their boldness in thus exhibiting themselves so shamelessly. She went on. "But it looks such fun." She paused. "Wouldn't you like to learn it, Terry?"

"I'd rather do that," replied Terry, and jerked a thumb towards the stage, where the various sections of the orchestra - reeds, trumpets, trombones - were now taking it in turns to rise to their feet, pointing their instruments up, down and around in unison, working up for the final flagwaving chorus.

"Oh," said Norah. "I think - "

But she did not say what she thought, for at that moment their attention was diverted by the majestic, purposeful advance of two "attendants", as they were delicately known, resplendent in goldbraided Balkan-general uniforms. There could be no doubting their target, and the circle of spectating couples parted to let them through. A few quiet words and it was all over: after an initial show of halfhearted defiance the jitterbugging pairs gave up sheepishly and resumed dancing in conventional style for the few bars of music that were left.

"Oh what a shame," said Norah, shaking her head in disappointment. "Fancy stopping them like that."

"They've got to stop them," replied Terry practically. "If they don't, everyone will do it and there isn't enough room. Besides, the springing of the floor might give way."

"Fancy that," cooed Norah. "The things you do know, Terry Cullerton."

Uncertain whether she was teasing or not, and whether he liked it or not if she was, Terry made no reply as they moved off the floor, retrieved Norah's handbag and seated themselves on the sofa beneath which it had been hidden.

"Well anyhow, I suppose we've both got it bad really, haven't we?" Norah resumed.

"How? What do you mean?"

Her manner became arch. "Oh the monkey music, what else? You wanting to play it and me wanting to jitterbug to it. So it's good we're together, isn't it?"

Terry was watching the musicians changing sheets for the next set. "Uh-huh, I suppose so. Yes."

"Anyway, even if I didn't like it, I'd still come with you."

But Terry's mind was elsewhere. "Didn't like what?" he queried abstractedly.

"The music. Even if I didn't like the music, I'd still come with you." Greatly daring, she allowed her head to fall tentatively against his shoulder, telling herself it didn't matter what people thought, and anyway what was there for anyone to notice, they weren't actually doing anything were they? And true enough they were not, or at least Terry wasn't. "I mean because I like being with you." Still Terry remained passive. "Well?"

"Well what?"

"Do you like being with me, Terry?"

"Yes of course," replied Terry perfunctorily.

"You're not very enthusiastic." Goodness, wasn't he slow! "Perhaps you don't really."

"Don't what?"

At last her frustration came to the surface. "Like being with me," she groaned. "Oh Terry!"

He stared at her in astonishment. What on earth was the matter with her? Girls! Aloud he said, "Well of course I do. I said so. I wouldn't go out with you if I didn't, would I?"

"No, I suppose not." Norah sighed. "Never mind."

The rest of the evening passed off well enough, or as well as Norah had learnt to expect from Terry. As they got off the tram at Waterloo Road and began walking in the direction of Norah's home, she was conscious of a sense of anti-climax. She had expected so much from this evening, though she knew not exactly what beyond some vague sense of togetherness. But Terry's self-sufficient manner and air of abstraction were ever-present. At times he had hardly seemed to notice her at all. Why do I bother? she asked herself despairingly. Yet she knew why. It was because she liked him; and the further question of why she liked him she did not ask, for what sixteen year-old girl, exceptionally innocent even by the standards of the nineteen-forties, could answer that?

Of course Terry's preoccupation with the music rather than the dancing was no novelty. Anyway music was one of the things that made him different from such other boys as she knew, whose main interests seemed to be football, warplanes and sniggering over dirty stories. Their approach to girls consisted of raucous teasing quickly followed by crude attempts to explore their persons. Some girls responded by fending off the boys firmly yet with sufficient ambiguity to ensure that they would try again. Norah was revolted by such games. Whatever his other faults, Terry was no hair-puller; and since the Salvation Army threw them into each other's company in any case, it was natural that they clung together.

Or rather, Norah clung to Terry. She knew her need for him was greater than his for her. Even mutual interest in music gave them little common ground, for the fierce torch of Terry's obsession far outshone the candle-flame of Norah's simple pleasure in choir-singing. It was this obsession that set him apart, lent him an air almost of mystery that fascinated even while it infuriated, challenging Norah to find a way through the barriers to the sensitive, loving soul which, she convinced herself, lay somewhere within.

Yet this evening she was not wrong in suspecting that something more than usual lay behind the desultoriness of Terry's conversation.

As their footsteps slowed and then stopped a block or so from Norah's front door - for Terry was supposed to be at his school, had to return there for the night, and therefore must not be seen in his home neighbourhood - she found out why.

"Well, I suppose I'd better be getting back," said Terry.

"Yes, I suppose so."

They stood in awkward silence for a few moments. Norah wondered tremulously if he was going to try to kiss her and how she would react if he did. But the question never arose.

"Listen, Norah," Terry blurted suddenly. "I'm going to ask my Dad if I can go out with you next Saturday. Will you ask your Mum and Dad?"

Norah's jaw dropped. "But you said they'd never - "

"I know. But it's the only thing I can think of. Look: there's something I've just got to do next Saturday. I'm not on fire guard again for two weeks and I can't think of any other excuse for going out. I'll just have to tell him I want to go out with you and hope he says yes. Will you do it?"

Norah temporised, trying to come to terms with this *volte face*. "Where is it you want to go?"

"Well, I - I'd rather not tell you if you don't mind."

"What? Oh come on, Terry. You've got to tell me. You can't really expect me - "

"All right then. Listen, I'm going in for a competition. Playing my cornet. So I'll tell Dad I'm going out with you."

"Oh I see. Oh good." Failing to grasp the implication, Norah suddenly felt an enormous relief. "It'll be so much better that way. I - I don't like telling lies, and we're sure to be found out sooner or later if we carry on - "

"You don't understand, Norah. I told you I don't want my Dad to know about the competition - "

"Why not? Oh please, Terry, let's just tell him where we're going, it'll make everything so much easier - "

"Not we. Just me. I'm going on my own."

Norah gaped. "What?" she gasped in a small voice. "And what am

I supposed to do?"

"Well, I thought you could go to a school friend or something like that - "

Something snapped inside Norah at last.

"Oh thanks," she retorted, her voice low and angry. "Ta very much. What do you think I am, Terry? Do you think I enjoy being a liar? You've made me tell my Mum and Dad a heap of fibs so we could go out together, and it worries me sick, but I did it for you. I thought you meant we should start telling the truth so as not to feel guilty any more. But what you really want is more lies just so you can go off somewhere without me ... "

"It's not like that - " Terry began stubbornly.

"Isn't it? What is it like then?" she persisted.

"It's just that I have to do it on my own."

"But Terry, why? Let me come with you."

"No."

"Please, Terry, it would be the best way. We could - "

"No," he flared. "I don't want you."

She gasped as if he had struck her. Sensing the hurt, he touched her arm and added hastily, "I don't want anybody, I mean. I told you: I have to do it on my own."

But Norah had had enough for one evening. She shook his hand away and flung at him, "Yes, I see. I'm good enough when you want someone to tell lies for you but not good enough to be allowed to come with you. You must be very ashamed of me, I can't think why." She drew herself to her full height and dignity. "Thank you for a lovely evening, but do your own dirty work, Terry Cullerton. Goodnight." She turned on her heel and her footsteps clicked rapidly away in the darkness.

Momentarily nonplussed, Terry waited a moment before walking slowly in the opposite direction. He put his hands in his pockets, hunched his shoulders and muttered stubbornly to no one in particular.

"I just have to do it on my own, that's all."

5
YOU STARTED SOMETHING

The first half-dozen notes of "Bless This House" told the audience that Terry Cullerton was no run-of-the-mill "discovery". Purity and power of this order bespoke by rights the experienced top-flight professional musician, not a schoolboy in blazer and flannels who looked hardly more than fourteen. In the wings the other "discoveries" stood spellbound alongside a couple of stagehands who nodded and exchanged glances with insiders' appreciation. The pianist, himself in civilian life a professional who knew talent when he saw it, poured all his own considerable expertise into supplying a backing worthy of it.

Terry himself, alone at centre stage, ignorant of devices of stance and gesture, stood stiffly to attention as he was accustomed to do at the Salvation Army Citadel, his only movement a slight lift and fall of his cornet at the beginning and end of phrases. His slight initial nervousness quickly gave way to a well-founded self-confidence, for he had planned and rehearsed with skill, intuition and hairline precision.

Nearly all the audience were in uniform, though a few civic dignitaries were seated in the front row alongside the senior officers. Most of the "turns" were Forces personnel too, though there was flexibility about this, especially in the "Discoveries Corner" item of the programme, where available talent could sometimes be thin. This was how Terry came to be taking part in the competition even though not himself in the Forces.

The Coronation Theatre was above a department store on the corner of Coronation Street and Albert Road, and also, by coincidence, in close proximity to the Salvation Army Citadel. Surprisingly large and fairly well equipped, its main disadvantage was that it doubled as a ballroom. This meant that the seating was not stepped. To make matters worse, some of it consisted of bentwood chairs which squeaked and scraped every time their occupants shifted position.

Just the same the silence was total as the bell-like tones of Terry's playing rang through the auditorium. Long before the end of the first verse he had them, rapt and tense, gripped by the crystal flawlessness of his rarefied, stripped-down technique. He paused, small and vulnerable, his cornet held to his side, and they waited breathlessly as the pianist built up for a second attack which by its switch of style yet caught them unawares. The controlled power was still there, but all else had changed. Sharp, cold austerity was replaced by a lyricism that squeezed from the piece every drop of warmth and fervour of which it was capable. Clean-cut phrasing was now replaced by soaring and sliding glissandos that drove emotion to a peak. If the first version had been Louis Armstrong, the second was Harry James. Then came the moment when in-born stage instinct took over and Terry did something he had not planned: removing a hand from his cornet he made a beckoning gesture that the audience could neither mistake nor resist. The voices rang out, while Terry, abandoning his former rigid posture, allowed his body to dip and rise and sway, leading the audience to the finale with a series of brilliant improvisations that set them roaring.

Perspiring, exalted, Terry removed the cornet from his mouth as the applause broke over him in waves. Now for the first time in his life he knew it for certain, really knew it, that his was a talent beyond the ordinary. How far beyond, only time would tell: for the moment it was enough to feed on the applause, to know without waiting for the formal verdict that he had won, that he always would win, that somewhere inside him, for better or worse, he held the indefinable magic that would make it impossible for him to live out his life as anything but an entertainer. Not his father, not the Salvation Army, not the war, not anything on earth would stop him.

The clapping at last passed its peak and the producer and MC of the show, Richard Royle, tall, suavely good-looking and impeccably groomed despite the handicap of being clad in regulation RAF sergeant's "hairy" uniform, his keen and unresting vigilance well concealed by a practised air of waggish affability, appeared from the wings leading the other two contestants. As though in a trance Terry half-heard the words: "Well done, Terry Cullerton! ... indicate each contestant in turn ... decide by your applause ... prize of a crisp pound note and the chance to be on our next show two weeks from tonight ... young airman who told funny stories, and in my experience anyone who can get a laugh out of life in the Raf must be a real comedian, ha ha - AC2 Len Briggs! ... fine conjuror and the only soldier I've ever met whose girl friend never knows what he's doing with his hands, ha ha - Corporal James Grimshaw! ... finally, too young for the Forces yet but old enough to blow his horn like Nat Gonella - Terry Cullerton! ... no doubt about your decision ... round of applause for the other contestants as our resident queen of song, Kitty Norton, comes on stage to present the prize to the winner!"

The two unsuccessful contestants disappeared and a drum rolled as a vision in white floated from the wings towards Terry at centre stage. Viewed from the audience Kitty Norton radiated all the remote, ladylike glamour of the dance-band singer, tall, ethereally beautiful, utterly desirable, impossibly unattainable.

The arts by which this effect was contrived were somewhat more evident at close quarters. The corn-gold tresses undeniably owed much to the bleach bottle, while the peaches-and-cream glow of the Betty Grable complexion was largely the product of heavy stage makeup. Wartime austerity meant that the low-cut evening gown and long gloves were by no means new, but they were well pressed - and an observer who wanted to be unkind might have remarked the same of the wearer, who at rather nearer thirty than twenty had doubtless, in the euphemism of the time, "been around".

Just the same, neither clothes nor cosmetics had anything to do with Kitty Norton's three most important real assets - a clear and well-trained singing voice fully capable of coping with the popular music of the day, a shapely natural dancer's figure, and an uncomplicated extrovert cheerfulness that instantly lit up anyone within range of it, on stage or off.

In any case Terry, still dazed by the completeness of his victory and the sophistication, as he thought it, of his surroundings, was in no condition to be critical. When Kitty flashed him a dazzling smile, delivered a few half-audible words of congratulation, handed him the pound note and leaned forward to be kissed, he was enslaved. She offered her mouth, in fact, but he was too shy and gauche. He put his cheek to hers and pecked the air, fumbled with the note, dropped it and picked it up again, then stood awkwardly, money in one hand and cornet in the other, unsure what to do next. Kitty linked arms with him and faced him towards the audience while Richard Royle took position at the microphone again.

"Thank you, ladies and gentlemen, thank you." He raised his hand and the applause abated. "Thanks also to Terry and the other contestants for entertaining us tonight. And now, as is our custom, the delectable Kitty takes the winner backstage to meet the cast and see the rest of the show from the wings. And don't forget, folks, you can see him and hear him again on our next show in two weeks' time." He extended his arms and raised his voice. "Terry Cullerton!"

The audience applauded again as Kitty squeezed Terry's hand and led him off into the backstage shambles of ropes, flats, cables and props. There being no separate dressing-rooms, cast members were making up and changing clothes in whatever odd corners they could find.

"Now this is Terry the Trumpet," Kitty called out, squeezing his hand again. "You all heard how he can play, so you'd better be specially nice to him until I get back." Several of them waved, smiled or called a greeting.

Terry corrected Kitty shyly. "It's a cornet, actually."

"Mm? Oh, yes. Sorry. Nearly the same thing, though, aren't they?"

"Yes. It's just that the shape's a bit different, so the tone comes out different too. In the Salvation Army it's only the cornet we use."

"In dance bands it's the other way round. They haven't used cornets since King Oliver."

"I know. I'm going to get a trumpet as soon as I can."

"Oh. You're keen, aren't you?"

"Yes," he replied simply.

She regarded him reflectively. "Hm. Yes, I think so. We'll have to have a chat about it." She started suddenly and removed her hand from his. "Goodness me, you're making me forget myself. Doing a spot just now. See you when I come off, love."

As they stood in the wings waiting for Kitty's cue, Terry was deliriously aware, though she was not, that she was holding his hand again. Then Richard Royle announced her, piano and drums went into the pickup, and Kitty advanced unhurriedly to the microphone and sang sweetly, softly, intimately:

That certain night, the night we met,
There was magic abroad in the air ...

Never having been to London, Terry had little idea what or where Berkeley Square might be, and it is doubtful whether, as a child of the small streets, he would have recognised a nightingale if one had landed on the end of his nose. Still, neither he nor anyone else in Britain during the war could have failed to identify the song, imbued as it was with the nostalgic yearnings of an entire uprooted generation lurching through the wilderness of uncharted wartime perils.

Terry's enchantment was broken by a heavy hand that clapped his shoulder, making him start.

"Hello, laddie, taking it all in, are we?" The voice was ripe, the makeup exaggerated to the point of clownishness, the suit loud-checked and baggy.

Unwilling to be dragged back to reality, Terry hesitated.

"Yes," he conceded.

"Plenty to learn, yes, always plenty to learn in this business. Stanley Moffat, laddie, *you* know, comic, heard of me I expect, haven't you?" Without waiting for an answer he ploughed on. "On the *wireless* a lot, regional programme, or used to be until the fire service started absolutely *monopolising* my time and talents. But we all have to do our bit, don't we? Yes, hardest job in the business, making people laugh, you ask anybody."

"Yes, I'm sure - " Terry began politely but again was cut off.

"Serious job, being funny, you see, deadly serious. I liked your playing, laddie, liked it very much." A playful finger poked Terry in the ribs. "Gave me a real *thrill* on the high notes. Nice when you can thrill people like that, eh? What'll you do in the next show?"

Terry shifted uneasily. This was distracting his attention from Kitty. "Well, I don't know, Mr Royle hasn't said yet - "

"Yes, you certainly do play nicely," Moffat continued. "*Mind* you, if you want to be a pro - you'd like to be, wouldn't you? yes, I'll bet you would, 'course you would, everybody would, wouldn't they? and you've got the talent, oh yes, I can see you've got *that* - well, as I said, if that's what you want you'll have to put an act together - bit of patter, bit of business, p'raps even some song and dance. Build it around your trumpet of course, but it's *presentation* you'll need. Know what I mean?"

Terry almost reminded him that it was a cornet, not a trumpet, but then decided not to. "Well, I haven't really thought - "

Moffat laughed and patted Terry's arm.

"'Course you haven't, 'course you haven't. Takes time. Time and hard work. But you will." He leaned forward and looked searchingly into Terry's eyes, a little too close for comfort. "*Talent* there. Oh yes, I said that and I was right: lots of talent there. Just needs bringing *out.*" He paused dramatically and squeezed Terry's arm. "Perhaps I'll help you. Well, TTFN lovie. I'm on just now."

He bounced away in search of his props while Terry, relieved, resumed his concentration on Kitty as she went into her final eight bars.

The streets of Town were paved with stars
It was such a romantic affair
And as we kissed and said goodnight -

Momentarily half-turned towards the wing, she caught sight of Terry, smiled and slipped him a secret wink.

- *A nightingale sang in Berkeley Square.*

Then she curtsied deeply and made her exit as the clapping came up. She squeezed Terry's hand and grinned with pleasure.

"Mm, just listen to that! Nice, isn't it?" she said and swept back onstage, curtsied again, holding it with careful calculation to milk the last drop of applause. Then she exited again while Stanley Moffat bounded in from the opposite wing bellowing his catch-phrase of "All right then, stop that noise!" and went into his act.

"Listen to them," smiled Kitty. "Aren't they just lovely? Bit slow before the interval, but they're really fine now, ready for anything. You fired them up for me, sweetie, you know that?" She squeezed Terry's hand again. "It's lovely when they give it all back to you, better than a double gin: you'll find out. Here, Terry, come and talk to me."

She led him to a corner where her clothes and makeup gear were scattered untidily about. "Sit yourself down, love." She parked him awkwardly on a battered stand chair. "Tell me about yourself, Terry. How did you get on the show? You're a civvy, aren't you?" She did not wait for answers but went on prattling as she rummaged vaguely among her belongings. Suddenly she turned round and indicated the back of her evening gown. "Look, unzip me, would you? There's a dear."

Terry stood up again, uncertain how to set about it, while Kitty burbled on unconcernedly. "Grand patriotic finale coming up, you know. Got to get into uniform."

The idea of anyone so glamorous wearing uniform was difficult to come to terms with. Even more difficult was summoning up the courage to do as she had just bid him. He began fumbling tentatively under Kitty's directions.

"Higher up, sweetie. There's a little catch: unfix that first, then it'll zip down. That's the way. Haven't had much practice in that department, have you? Never mind, you'll learn soon enough. Fine: I'll do the rest."

Kitty took over, and Terry gaped in awe and disbelief as she yanked the zip to the bottom and stepped unhesitatingly out of the gown. "Chuck me the uniform skirt, there's a duck," she instructed Terry as she flung the gown over the chairback without ceremony. He found the skirt, picked it up as though it might bite, and handed it gingerly to Kitty. "Ta, love," she said matter-of-factly, then climbed into it while removing her slip in what seemed like a simultaneous swift movement. The blithe comment that followed in a muffled voice as she started pulling a light blue RAF shirt over her head did nothing to diminish Terry's embarrassment and fascination. "Gosh, whoever makes these shirts knows nothing about female anatomy, that's for sure. Talk about tight in the wrong places!" Terry knew of no reply he could make to this. Kitty's face emerged. "Here, hold the mirror for me, love." Cocking her head on one side she sighed "Crikey, what a mess!", then flashed a grin and ran a hand through her disordered hair. Terry tried not to stare at her still unbuttoned shirt front. Combing out her blonde tresses and rolling them up with quick fingers, Kitty bubbled on. "Hair above the collar in uniform, you know. Bit of a bore, but they can't have us looking like Betty Grable, can they?" Terry made the comparison in his mind's eye and knew not how to tell her it was no contest. At last she buttoned her shirt and put on her tie. "Thanks, love. You can put the mirror down." She patted his cheek. "You still haven't told me how you came to be on the show. The advert in the paper, was it?"

"Yes," he replied as Kitty, pulling her skirt up, lifted a shapely leg and rested it on the chair. His eyes were on stalks as she unclipped her suspenders, rolled down the silk stocking and replaced it with a regulation WAAF-issue stocking in light blue lisle.

"Live local, do you, Terry?" she asked.

"Near South Station. Off Waterloo Road," he managed to reply. It was an effort to hold his voice steady.

"Oh do you? I'm billeted out that way. So's Dicky. Permanent staff - best billets: you know." She paused, put up her other leg and began a second and equally devastating performance. "How will you get home?"

"I dunno. Walk, I suppose." He did not tell her that he was dreading going home, or why.

"Dicky and I have a taxi booked. Comes out of the funds. We can drop you off, I expect."

"Oh. Gosh, thanks. If it's not too much trouble."

"No trouble, my angel." Completing her stocking-change, Kitty pulled down her skirt, donned her uniform tunic with its corporal's chevrons, then smoothed and adjusted everything with quick movements. "One good turn deserves another. You warmed up the audience for me, remember?" She smiled and patted his cheek again, then turned her back to him and hitched up her skirt. "Seams straight, are they?"

"Pardon?" Terry gulped as his eyes popped again.

"My seams, sweetie. Are they straight? The seams of my stockings."

"Oh - er - yes. They're fine."

Kitty dropped her skirt, turned round to face him again, then regarded him critically.

"Right," she said. "That's me done. Now you. You know you're on stage for the finale?"

"No, I didn't - "

"As soon as Stan finishes his sketch. Thank goodness I'm not in it this time: I was in his last one and he doesn't half knock you about. Just listen to that." Muffled thudding and shouting, accompanied by roars of audience laughter, indicated some kind of mayhem on stage. Kitty clicked her teeth and frowned. "Oh dear, I forgot, you're supposed to be watching the show, aren't you? and here am I stopping you. Oh, aren't I awful?"

"Oh no, no," he responded, his emotions loosening his tongue at last. "I think you're wonderful ... " He paused, covered in confusion. "I mean ... "

"Why, bless you, yes, I think you do mean it," she said. Her smile liquefied his insides. "Well now, let's fix your tie for a start."

She came close and straightened his collar and tie. She ran a comb - her comb - through his hair. Her dancing fingers sent vibrations through him as they adjusted the set of his jacket. She pinched him on both cheeks, then stood back.

"You'll do," she said, smiling. "You see? Stick with Auntie Kitty and you'll be all right. Now, when we go on, keep by me, stand straight, look proud and happy, sing up loud and that's it."

"Please ... " said Terry, his heart bursting, and stopped.

"Yes?" She waited a moment. "Go on, love. What do you want to say?"

"I hope you don't mind if - I - well, I did mean what I said before," he mumbled. "I want to - to thank you for ... "

His voice trailed off.

"Oh Terry, aren't you nice? That was so well said. I'm quite touched."

Flushed with embarrassment, he could say no more; he was too besotted. Kitty's awareness of this was tinged with guilt. This was not the first time her high-spirited good nature had provoked an excessive response from its target. Had she been more self-analytical she might have perceived and reined in the frustrated maternal

60

instinct that inspired the sudden warmth she felt for this undersized, tongue-tied youth with ten times the musical gifts of everyone else in the theatre put together. Terry for his part was in no state for detecting such subtleties as the slight uneasiness in Kitty's smile.

A burst of music and the swelling of audience applause indicated the end of the sketch on stage, rescuing Kitty from having to decide what to do about the moment of tension she had so thoughtlessly precipitated.

"Well, that's us," she announced briskly as the rest of the cast began gathering in readiness at the wings. "Come on then, Terry, remember what I said."

But still she took his hand again as she led him to join the others.

The taxi crept cautiously along a blacked-out Central Drive which at half past ten in the evening was almost devoid of traffic. Blackpool went to bed early during the war, as indeed did most of the country. Petrol rationing had forced most private cars off the roads, taxis were scarce, and last buses and trams ran not long after ten o'clock, compelling restaurants and places of entertainment to adapt their closing times accordingly. It was just as well that "street crime" had hardly been invented, for staying out late generally meant walking home through a blackout that would have been paradise for the muggers and rapists of a more sophisticated later era.

Certainly Terry had walked home from central Blackpool often enough to appreciate the present luxury of riding in a motor car, and at the front too, relaxing in leather-upholstered comfort alongside the driver. From the back seat Richard Royle spoke.

"So you do most of your playing in the Salvation Army band, eh?"

"Yes, Mr Royle."

"Takes a lot of your time up?"

"We have rehearsals one or two evenings a week. Then there are the services on Sunday - "

"You see," interrupted Royle, "it's band call for the next show at seven o'clock Monday. Can you be there?"

Terry hesitated. The thought of the bombshell that would explode when he got home made him gulp. As to the subsequent consequences, they were not to be imagined but would certainly include a ban on future escapades like this evening's. He tried to temporise. "Well, there's a band practice at the Citadel, but I can try-"

"No, no, young Terry. Trying's not enough. Sorry, but you have to tell me now. Yes or no, in or out."

Terry made his mind up. Nothing would stop him, nothing.

"Yes. I'll be there," he said.

"Good," said Royle. "Oh, and this is supposed to be a Forces show as far as we can make it. Of course, anyone can see you're not of age ... but if you were in a cadet corps, ATC or something ... It's for the finale really: everyone in uniform if we can."

"No, I'm not in anything like that." Terry felt deflated. Then Kitty, seated in the back alongside Royle, rescued him.

"Don't be daft, of course you're in something, Terry. You're in the Salvation Army. That's a uniform."

"Oh. But it wouldn't look right, would it? I - "

"Why not? It's a uniform," said Royle. "Well done, Kit. OK, Terry, bring your Sally Ann gear. Doesn't matter what sort of uniform it is, you see." He paused and chuckled. "I mean, Stan Moffat looks a right berk in his fireman outfit, but who cares? He's no worse than the stagehands in their Air Raid Warden rigouts - "

The taxi had drawn to a halt. They were at Terry's house.

"There y'are," said the driver. "Burtenshaw Terrace."

"Right-oh," said Royle. "See you at band call then. Make sure you're there, won't you? Be on time, seven o'clock, no messing."

Terry opened the taxi door.

"I won't be late," he said, then added shyly. "I've had a smashing time. Thank you, Mr Royle. Thank you, Miss - "

"All right, sport," said Royle. "And by the way, the names. I'm Dicky, and the flower of British womanhood on my right is Kitty. Dicky and Kitty." Terry did not notice the proprietorial coupling. "Careful with your winnings, mind."

"Goodnight, Terry," smiled Kitty warmly. "Don't spend it all in one shop, will you?"

"Oh I shall, though," replied Terry seriously. "I'll put it towards my trumpet."

Terry alighted. The door slammed and the taxi revved up. Terry watched it disappear into the darkness, then walked slowly up the path to the house. He had seriously considered staying out until next morning as the only means of backing up the desperate fiction he had concocted for his father when Norah had refused to help his deception. But could he really wander the streets all night in midwinter? What if a policeman on the beat challenged him? And even if he got away with it, what was he going to do about the band call on Monday? Norah had been right about one thing: the firewatching story was wearing thin. He stiffened his resolve as best he could.

He'd have to tell the truth at last and face it out.

Terry had no front door key. The key-of-the-door at twentyone was a reality in that era. He took a deep breath, lifted the door knocker and let it fall. He waited, quaking, for what seemed a hundred years. Then came the muffled sound of steps slowly descending the stairs. His father's voice rasped from behind the door.

"This is a fine time of night to be knocking people up. Who is it?"

"It's me, Terry."

"Terry? What the - ?"

There was a sound of bolts being drawn. Then the door opened.

"And what the hangment are you doing here?" demanded Harold Cullerton. "I thought you said you were firewatching again tonight... ?"

Kitty Norton and Richard Royle undressed quickly and efficiently in the cold half-darkness of her tiny bedroom.

"Isn't he a little lamb, really?" remarked Kitty. "More like thirteen than sixteen, he's that bashful. And so polite! But oh my goodness, I reckon he must be on a tight leash at home."

"If he is, it won't last for ever," returned Royle, climbing into the bed. "Hurry up, Kit, these sheets are cold."

"I'm not a hot-water bottle, you know."

"You bloody are, mate. Best one I've ever had."

"Disrespectful sod," she exclaimed routinely, and pushed the flat of her hand into his face without malice. "Yes, everyone has to shake a loose limb in the end."

"You can start doing it now if you like."

"Filthy beast." She climbed into bed.

"Seriously, Kit, he can certainly blow his horn. Do the show a bit of good if we can keep the Sally Ann at bay. He thinks you're smashing, you know. Work on him."

Kitty giggled. "Dicky, don't be awful. I've got my hands full working on you."

"Not yet you haven't. But you will have in a minute, I promise you that ... "

63

6
JUST ONE OF THOSE THINGS

"It's the irregular verbs I hate most," said Norah. "They're no easier in German than they are in French, if you ask me." She waited. "I sometimes wonder if I did right to give up Stinks." She waited again.

Still Terry did not answer. They had made up after their quarrel, or so Norah made herself believe after contriving to encounter Terry "accidentally" on the way to school on Monday morning.

Terry's habit of thinking about other things while she was talking had not changed, however. Neither, as she would have discovered had she asked him, had his determination to exclude her from the new world of which the Forces show had given him a glimpse.

Norah chattered on. "Well, the worst you could do in the lab is cause an explosion and blow up the whole school, and who'd care about that except the teachers?" She giggled encouragingly, waited in vain once more, then took Terry's arm, brought him and herself to a halt and lifted her attaché case of school books with both hands. "Terry, if I hit you on the head with this would you take any notice?"

"Eh?" He stared in puzzlement. "What is it, Norah? What's the matter?"

She sighed exasperatedly. "Oh Terry, sometimes it's like talking to a brick wall."

"I'm sorry. I was thinking." The realisation struck him that he had to tell Norah at least something of what had happened when he arrived home after the Forces show.

"Thinking!" She was hardly mollified, rather the reverse. "You're always thinking. Why can't - "

"This is serious, Norah. Let me tell you. I did go to that competition on Saturday, you know. I told my Dad I was on fire guard but I wasn't. So when I got home afterwards I had to tell him where I'd been. He gave me a terrible row."

"Oh Terry!" She was horrified. "What did he say?"

"I don't want to talk about it. But it was awful." The less said about it the better. The way his father had raved at him you'd have thought he'd pinched the crown jewels or murdered somebody. What had made it worse was Terry's refusal to promise never to repeat his misdeed. On and on the altercation had gone, but he'd stuck to his guns while Harold threatened all kinds of future reprisals.

Norah stopped in mid-stride and took his arm. "Did you tell him about - about us?"

"Yes. Well, I mean no, not about you. He got it out of me about going to the Tower and that." He gestured exasperatedly. "He just went on and on at me and in the end it came out. You know what he's like. But I said I'd been on my own. So as long as you keep your trap shut you'll be all right."

"Oh." Norah fell silent, digesting the implications.

Terry was irritated by her coolness. It was not the reaction he had expected. "Well, you might thank me."

"What for?"

The unaccustomed acerbity of her tone caught him off balance. "Well, for keeping you out of it of course."

"Thank you then. But I'm not sure it wouldn't have been better for me to clear the air too. As it is, I'm still a liar, aren't I?"

"You can always tell your Mum and Dad yourself if you want to," Terry snapped.

"Yes, I can," retorted Norah. "Only you've made it difficult for me to do that without getting you into more trouble, haven't you?"

Terry grunted. He hadn't thought of that. Nettled, he quickened his pace so that Norah had to half-run in order to keep up. After a minute or so she gave up and came to a halt completely.

"Terry!" she called after him.

He feigned surprise. "What's the matter?"

"What d'you have to go so fast for? It isn't a race."

He knew he was being sulky. Casting around at random for some excuse, he said, "I - er - well, I just want to see what they're doing." He pointed towards a squad of RAF recruits under instruction some way further along the street of boarding houses and private hotels.

"Why?"

"I don't know. I just wonder what it's like. Being in the Raf, I mean."

"Oh," said Norah without interest. She scarcely bothered to look. At 8.30 in the morning the streets of central Blackpool teemed with squads of RAF recruits, the future aircrew distinguished by white flashes in their headgear but their new uniforms no better-fitting than those worn by the others. In groups of thirty or forty, each under an NCO, some would march to the beach for PT or to Burton's ballroom, Olympia or the tramsheds for elementary wireless training, while others underwent foot drill in the street itself. They scarcely impeded the sparse traffic, much of which in any case consisted only of slow-moving horse-drawn vehicles and delivery boys riding bicycles or pushing handcarts. Pedestrians, whether service or civilian, simply ignored them. After nearly three years any novelty the scene might once have offered had worn off. Norah's verdict was uncompromising.

"Awful, I should think." She enlarged on the theme. "Being bossed about and shouted at all day like that! Some of those sergeants and corporals are right bullies."

"Yes, but it's only recruit training in Blackpool: square-bashing they call it. They come here straight from Padgate, where they take them in. First six weeks, that's all. Then they're sent down south - somewhere called Compton Bassett, and there's another place called Yatesbury. That's where they start real training - you know, navigation and gunnery and that, and then they do the flying. And once they've qualified they're all sergeants or officers, so they won't get bossed about then."

Norah sniffed sceptically and resumed walking.

"What I've heard," she said, "is that after they've finished training and they go on operations - you know, bombing Germany - most of them get shot down in about six weeks. That's the average."

"Go on," scoffed Terry. "If that was true, no one'd do it. Who told you that?"

"My cousin from Preston, the girl she works with, her boy friend's aircrew, a WOP/AG she says - they're the ones that do the wireless and the guns, aren't they? - well, last time he was on leave he told her. Six weeks."

"And what did he think about it?" Terry was still incredulous.

"She says he just laughed. Said he wouldn't let it happen to him."

"There you are then," said Terry triumphantly. "He didn't believe it himself."

"Well, he was reported missing a month later, and they haven't heard anything more since."

While Terry assimilated this they approached the drill squad, now drawn up at ease facing the pavement, whence their NCO instructor was addressing them. That these were very new recruits was attested by their odd shapes and sizes and a pallor of cheek that a few weeks of hearty food and strenuous exercise would soon dispel. They had not yet fully grasped that the bark of an old-sweat drill instructor is generally designed to entertain as much as terrorise, thus reducing the need to make use of his bite.

To such a man, the appearance on the scene of a teenage pair on their way to school was meat and drink.

"Now then, my lads," he admonished his victims, "keep those eyes to the front! Do you think that the work of the Royal Air Force comes to a stop every time you catch sight of a bit of gymslip crumpet? Do you think the Blackpool girls have never seen one of your white flashes before? Don't look down, it's the ones in your caps I'm talking about!"

One or two recruits had difficulty in controlling their features. The sergeant swelled up like a turkey cock, his face turning puce.

"Stop grinning there! It isn't funny!" he screamed in simulated high outrage, then paused, gathered himself and flung at them the well-practised, unstoppable, almost totally unpunctuated torrent of his indignation. "No cradlesnatching for you my lads so you can stop fancying your chances, naughty boys who do things of that sort get sent to prison and we can't have that happening because your country needs you though God knows why because a sloppier set of twerps and nancy-boys I've never seen in my entire Royal Air Force career which dates back to before Pontius was a pilot, stop laughing! Well you may have broken your mother's hearts but you won't break mine and do you know why? Is it because I am cleverer than she is? no it is not. Is it because I understand you better than she does? no it is not. Is it even because I can cook better than she does? no it is not. It is because I don't love you like she does and I'll break your hearts before you break mine that's why! SQUA-A-AD! Come on, straighten up there, stop daydreaming. Squad! Ah-tayn ... stand still, wait for it - shun-as-you-were! As you were I said you shower! WAKE UP THERE! Squad-ah-tayn ... SHUN!"

Long before the end of this tirade Norah, blushing, had hurried past the sergeant and fled round the next corner. But Terry hung back, watching the drill squad pensively.

Cast and stage crew, most of them in uniform with tunics and ties loosened or discarded, sat or stood haphazardly around the stage of the Coronation Theatre, smoking and drinking tea from cracked mugs. Richard Royle, clutching a sheaf of papers on a clipboard, was addressing the company from a gangway seat three or four rows from the front of the auditorium.

" ... OK, well that's the running order. Any more questions? No? Right. I'll have it typed and run off, and with a bit of black-market cooperation on the part of an obliging orderly room clerk who just happens to be Kitty here it'll reach you through what the Air Force laughingly calls its usual channels, which has nothing to do with swilling out the latrines. And when you get your copy, for heaven's sake read it in case I've had to make any changes. 'Ello 'ello, what's all this then?"

He turned his head in response to a commotion at the back of the theatre. Living as he did on a shorter fuse than he ever allowed his onstage persona to reveal, what he saw did not improve his humour. He glared at Terry and Harold Cullerton as they advanced down the aisle and stopped a couple of yards from him. Terry was carrying his instrument case. Royle spoke again, ostentatiously addressing no one in particular.

"Ho ho ho hum, and this looks like the first change already." He switched his gaze to Terry, pointedly ignoring Harold. "And just where have you sprung from, Sunny Jim? I thought I said band call was at seven o'clock."

Terry blushed with embarrassment. "I'm sorry, Mr Royle. I couldn't - "

"Only very big stars," Royle proclaimed, "keep people waiting, and not many of them, because it's a habit that's apt to prevent them from becoming big stars in the first place. I've made up the running order without you." He turned away and addressed the company on stage. "Now, unless anybody's got any other problems, I'd just like to go over - "

Harold Cullerton pushed Terry aside and spoke.

"I'm t'lad's father. It's my fault he's late. I told him he wasn't to come at all, but he wouldn't be said no."

Richard Royle swung round again and faced the newcomers with something which, if less than outright aggression, was more than indifference.

"Really? Well, I don't know that there's really anything for us to discuss because you see, Mr - er - ?"

"Cullerton."

"Ah yes. Mr Cullerton. Right. Well, Mr Cullerton, what I'm trying to explain is it's cast and crew only at band call - no outsiders, I'm afraid. We've got work to do. I don't want to be rude, but - "

"I want to see what's going on. I'll be blunt, Mr-er- Sergeant-er ?"

"Royle. Richard Royle."

Harold Cullerton's brow furrowed. "Richard Royle? I've heard that name. On the wireless?"

Royle permitted himself a thin smile. "The very same. 'Monday Night's the Night' and all that. Until the war elevated me to my present exalted status."

"Hmph. Well, Mr Royle," grunted Terry's father, "I don't know that I hold with what you're doing - "

Terry spoke for the first time.

"Dad, please - " he began desperately, but was cut off by Richard Royle's rejoinder.

"With respect, Mr Cullerton, what we're doing is putting on a bit of entertainment if we don't get interrupted too much. And if you don't mind my saying so, it actually doesn't matter a fig whether you hold with it or not because it's nothing to do with you."

Harold Cullerton's expression darkened. He did not flinch.

"I beg to differ, Mr Royle. This is my son we're talking about, and he's only sixteen - "

"You're talking about him: I'm not, Mr Cullerton," Royle retorted with elaborate lack of interest. He rose to his feet. "Young Terry's got talent and I'd have liked him in the show, but I can manage without him. So now if you'll excuse me ... "

Royle began moving towards the stage. Terry, overcome with shame and embarrassment, turned on his heel and fled towards the rear of the theatre.

Then Kitty Norton intervened from her vantage point near the edge of the stage. "Dicky, don't!" she exclaimed, and clattered down the proscenium steps to dash up the side-gangway, intercepting Terry before he could reach the exit.

"Come on, Terry love, don't run off," she pleaded, gripping his arm and propelling him to the top end of the centre aisle. "Now don't move," she ordered. Then she addressed Richard Royle and Terry's father. "Come up here, both of you. Come on and don't let's get in a tizzy."

When they had obeyed, Kitty lowered her voice. "Dicky, stop being awkward: you know you always wish you hadn't. What's it matter if Terry's father stays a few minutes? Go on, Dicky, be nice. For me." Then she switched on her smile at full voltage and played it on Terry's father. "Mr Cullerton, I can understand you want to know what sort of company Terry's getting into, and Sergeant Royle" - she gave a discreet warning nudge - "understands as well, don't you, Dicky? Well, we're not monsters, I promise you." Harold's expression softened a little and Royle said nothing. Pressing her advantage she went on in matter-of-fact tones, "Look, why don't we all quieten down and ask Terry what he was thinking of playing in the show? Come on, Terry love."

Terry glanced about uncertainly, then slowly began opening his instrument case. "Well, I don't know - if you really - "

"Yes we do," she encouraged.

He produced a sheet of music.

"I could play this," he said diffidently.

"Let's see," said Royle, his professionalism taking over, and shot a hand out for the music. "Hm, yes. 'You'll Never Know.' Good one. But can you do it?"

"Oh yes," said Terry confidently.

"I mean do it like the Harry James arrangement?"

"Yes. I've got the record at home, you see." Terry said it as though anyone could play anything if they had the record at home - which may have been how it seemed to him in fact.

"You'll need to do a lot of covering," Royle warned. "You've only got piano and drums here: it's not an orchestra."

"Oh but I can do it all right," said Terry. "Only I - I wonder whether ... " He glanced shyly at Kitty. "I thought that perhaps ... "

Kitty smiled. "You want me to do the vocal, don't you, ducks? 'Course I will. Come on, let's try it."

She bustled them all on-stage, handed the music-sheet to the pianist, who lifted an eyebrow, looked questioningly at Royle and received a nod.

Justifying his self-confidence, Terry did not merely bring off a superb simulation of the Harry James performance: he elaborated on it to cover for the absence of a full backing orchestra. The pianist and drummer followed his lead with professional aplomb, and when Kitty's voice came in, honey-sweet and clinging, the three instrumentalists wove a smooth, intricate supporting pattern of rhythm and harmony to emphasise the helpless longing expressed in the lyric. Then as cornet and vocal built the closing passage to a beautifully blended finale, the company on stage broke into spontaneous applause in which even Richard Royle joined.

"Well well," he commented. "Well well well well well. That was good, young Terry, very good. Thanks, Kitty."

Kitty pecked Terry's cheek. Her eyes shone. Terry held his cornet awkwardly to his side and looked down at his feet, his face flushed with pleasure.

"There you are," said Kitty, addressing Royle. "Smashing, wasn't it? You can just drop one of my other numbers and shove this in instead. Simple. Won't make any difference to the running order and it'll lift the roof off." She turned to Terry's father. "You have to admit that was lovely, Mr Cullerton, now, haven't you?"

"Well, there were some clever ideas in it, I'll grant you that," he conceded. "You sing very nicely, Miss - ?"

"Norton. Kitty Norton. Please call me Kitty."

He hesitated, then managed it with only a slight gulp. "Yes. Kitty."

"He's very talented is Terry," Kitty continued. "He could easily be a professional right now, and once he's got some experience - "

Harold shook his head.

"We're a religious family. Salvationists. Terry's been brought up on sacred music. I don't know if you know it, but the Army doesn't hold wi' nowt but sacred music. Now all of a quick Terry's wanting to play all this jazz. I don't know as I can allow it."

Kitty took his arm and Richard Royle's, leading them aside from the others.

"Mr Cullerton," she said, "can I ask you something personal?"

"What's that then?"

"Do you mind telling me what your job is, Mr Cullerton? I've got a reason."

"I'm a joiner. I work for t'Council. Why?"

"And you go to church on Sundays?"

"The Citadel. I told you: we're Salvation Army."

"Yes, of course: sorry." She flashed a winning smile. "Well, you see, I'm like you. I've got a job during the week. I'm a corporal clerk in the orderly room. Mountains of paper work in the Air Force, you just wouldn't believe. But I was a singer before the war and that's my proper career so I daren't let it go rusty, and that's why I do these shows in my spare time. Same with Dicky here and everybody else in the show for that matter: daytime job, spare-time job. But it doesn't stop us going to church on Sundays, does it, Dicky?"

"Eh?" Royle's eyebrows lifted in startlement, then he recovered himself. He spoke without conviction. "Oh yes. Regular as clockwork, that's us."

"There you are, you see, there's no reason why Terry shouldn't do the same, whatever job he has - even if he goes on the stage," concluded Kitty with another smile. "Anyway we won't stop him. But give him a chance to do something he wants. Dicky and I will look after him when he's here, won't we?"

Royle chipped in. "Kitty's right, Mr Cullerton. Terry does have a lot of talent. We can help him to learn how to use it. And it's true what she said before as well: we're not ogres just because we're on the stage."

Harold fought with himself and lost. What could he do after all? Imprison the lad? Thrash him? He had never done either of those things even when he had the power: harsh he might be, but cruel he was not. Now that moral authority no longer sufficed to intimidate Terry - his inability to prevent the lad coming here this evening had shown that - what weapons were left? And for all the paint and powder this young woman seemed a good sort: if she and this Richard Royle kept an eye on him ...

Harold played his last card. "But it's all Forces, isn't it? I'm against the war, if you want to know. It's not a popular view, but I'm not ashamed of it. I'm a pacifist."

Royle hooted with laughter, taking Harold aback. "So am I, Mr Cullerton, so am I! So's everyone I know! Not popular? Ye gods, it's the most popular view in the Air Force! If they gave me the chance don't you think I'd burn this uniform and run back to Auntie Beeb right now?" Royle patted Harold's arm and employed his most persuasive tone. "Don't you see, Mr Cullerton? That's why we need the shows: to cheer everybody up and forget about the war for a bit."

"Look," said Kitty, "why don't you come and see the next show? Dicky can shell out a complimentary." She smiled archly. "I can make him."

"That's kind of you, Miss - er - Kitty, but I don't think so really, thanks just the same. It's against - well, no thank you." He frowned and shook his head doubtfully. "I don't know as I'm doing the right thing, but - well, we can see how Terry gets on for a week or two. I have to say it's on sufferance, mind you: I still don't hold with it all. And it mustn't interfere with his Salvation Army responsibilities ... "

Yet in his heart he knew that it would. He should have prevented it somehow and he hadn't. He had failed in his duty to the Lord, and to his son. The guilt lay heavy on him.

Kitty's bedroom was enlivened by a few personal items - her makeup things and one or two ornaments on the dressing table, some show-business photographs pinned to the walls. And though the room was cold, the bed itself was warm enough with its narrow confines again inhabited by two people, Kitty snuggling among the blankets while Richard Royle lay on his back alongside her, smoking and grinning.

"I've got a job - two jobs actually," he squeaked in mocking falsetto. "Dicky's got two jobs as well. But we go to church every

Sunday, don't we, Dicky dear?" He reverted to his normal voice. "However did you manage to keep your face straight? For sheer brass neck I must say - "

Kitty's laugh was more gentle. "I didn't say we went to church," she pointed out. "You did. I only said our jobs didn't stop us going, and that's true. So don't put the fib on to me."

"All right, you win." Royle chuckled. "No matter: it worked. Lordie me, the things you do for England!"

Kitty yawned and stretched herself. "I don't know about England," she said. "Actually it was for you. For you and me."

"Eh?"

"Oh yes. For you and me. You're no hero, you've said it yourself, and Blackpool's a good place to see the war out. Good billets, cushy paperpushing jobs, plenty of time off to run the shows. I mean, even though it's not an official duty they'll never post us as long as we can keep up the standard. You said we didn't need Terry, but we do - him and everyone like him that we can get hold of. They keep us fireproof."

Royle took a long pull on his cigarette and exhaled thoughtfully, the mask of flippancy temporarily peeled aside. "Of course you're right, Kit." He squeezed her hand. "Yes, you're right. If they posted me I'd die. I'd be useless at anything else."

"I know, love, I know." Her fingers smoothed his brow. "But you'll keep on doing the shows and I'll keep on helping you. And there's nothing to worry about because you're so good at it, you know you are."

"Thanks, Kit. I mean it." He held on to her hand tightly. "I daren't tell anyone this except you ... but sometimes I'm a bit, well ... you know ... tortured ... "

"I know."

After a silence, Kitty spoke again.

"And I did it for Terry as well."

"Oh? How's that then?"

"His Dad's hard on him. He's sincere and he means well. But he's holding Terry back, isn't he?"

Royle snorted scornfully. "Too damn right he is, the miserable old git. He's like a ship's anchor on a skiff."

"Well, Terry needs a chance. He's got to have his chance. I'd like to help him to get it."

Something in her voice made Royle frown and peer at her. "Crikey O'Reilly, Kit, what's it to you?"

"Oh, I don't know." Kitty's smile was hesitant, slightly uncomfortable even. "I can't help feeling sorry for him," she said defensively. "Just one of those things."

Royle reverted to his court jester role. "Ah, the wonder and the joy of maternal love!" he pronounced. "That fountain of selflessness and sacrifice poured forth from the hearts of half the human race, and that its better half - "

Giggling embarrassedly, Kitty removed the cigarette from his fingers and laid it on the ashtray on the bedside table.

"Hey, what the - ?" Royle began, but she smothered his protest with a pillow pressed to his face. He squealed in mock agony, wriggling and drumming his feet. The bedsprings creaked alarmingly.

"Shut up, you nitwit, do you want the landlady to hear?" she demanded, struggling to hold him still. "Now be told, will you? It's just one of those things, so leave it at that ... "

7
IS YOU IS OR IS YOU AIN'T MY BABY?

"Oh Terry, wasn't it sad?" sniffed Norah. She fumbled for a handkerchief and dabbed her eyes.

"Dead sloppy if you ask me."

"Oh, you! You would say that. It was lovely."

Terry grimaced. "Well, all that stuff at the end about having the moon but not the stars, or whatever it was, I mean to say, what a load of tripe - "

"Go on, it was beautiful. Don't be horrible!" Norah stifled another tear, half-giggling with embarrassment, and punched Terry's arm.

"Load of tripe, I said." He grinned, and she punched him again - then timidly held his arm as they continued shuffling slowly up the gangway from the warmth and comfort of the auditorium and into the foyer, whose portrait gallery of the stars, rich carpeting and marble floor eased the transition to the grim winter reality awaiting them outside.

The Princess was one of Blackpool's most luxurious cinemas, which was saying something considering that the Odeon, just along Dickson Road from North Station, was held, by "sand grown 'uns" at least, to be a close rival of its palatial namesake in Leicester Square, London. It was the Princess that had screened "Gone With The Wind" back in 1940. More recently it had shown "Mrs Miniver", that phoney seven-Oscar beacon of high-gloss heroics which bathed the Dunkirk days in a cosy sentimental glow and in so doing somehow provided a much-needed and far-from-phoney boost to wartime morale.

This evening's offering - "Now Voyager", to which Terry had accompanied Norah after a show of reluctance - was another Hollywood excursion into the never-never-lands of romantic love, where agonised displays of epic devotion and self-sacrifice kept audiences intoxicated and cinema tills clicking.

"Come on," urged Terry. "Better get a move on or we'll miss the tram."

They hurried through the swing doors, down the steps and across the road, where even the vast bulk of the Metropole Hotel failed to afford shelter from the biting wind or the raindrops gusting like machine-gun bullets.

Huddling into their coats, they put their heads down and fought their way to the North Pier tram-shelters, from which even in the blackout the murderous crashing of the waves against the sea wall of the Promenade could plainly be seen as well as heard.

"I could tell you enjoyed it, anyway," said Terry, as they joined the queue. "I thought I'd have to go for a bucket."

"A bucket?"

"Yes. To hold under your chin."

"Ooh, don't be horrible," said Norah again. "You liked it too, didn't you?"

"I told you, load of tripe."

"Oh, go on. You did, didn't you? I know you did."

"Wasn't so bad," he conceded, and added, in a rare burst of male honesty, "Only it doesn't do to admit it straight off about a picture as sloppy as that."

Norah smiled. "There! I knew you enjoyed it really." She was content.

The long lines snaked forward and slowly diminished as the trams arrived one after the other. Terry and Norah had almost reached the head of their queue when one of those long, exasperating intervals occurred which caused would-be passengers to wonder whether they had missed the last tram. A few people gave up, grumbling, and began walking home. Terry and Norah were about to do the same when another tram appeared. It was one of the green-painted, old-fashioned sort, open upstairs at front and rear, but nevertheless a tram. The trouble was it was already crowded.

"Two inside, four on top," snarled the beefy conductress as it swayed to a halt and the queue surged forward. "No shoving now, that's all I can take."

Terry and Norah were the last to board before the conductress's arm descended like a guillotine. The unlucky ones groaned, and the conductress uttered the customary hollow incantation as she rang three bells: "'Nother along in a minute."

The vacant seats downstairs were already filled. Upstairs another couple had taken the last inside places. Terry and Norah perforce squeezed themselves into the last two gaps in the bitterly cold open front.

"Br-r-r! What a wind!" Norah shivered. "Isn't it awful?"

"Better than walking," grunted Terry.

"I suppose so. It was worth it anyway. The film was good."

Terry dug her in the ribs. "Don't start that again or I'll thump you one."

They both smiled. This was progress, Norah felt.

In other respects, too, things had changed from before. Determined to free herself of guilt, Norah had tackled her parents and found to her surprise that they were prepared to tolerate if not totally approve of occasional evening outings with Terry. As to Terry's father, having let the wrangle over the Forces shows blow over it was easy for him to capitulate again about Norah. At least, Harold told himself, she was Salvation Army and decent. Norah's parents told themselves likewise about Terry.

The jolting of the tram gave Norah an excuse to snuggle up more closely than might otherwise have been proper. She looked about her. The other passengers on the hard wooden seats, like themselves, were jammed tightly together, bodies swaying in unison as the tram swished and clattered along. An airman and an ATS girl, careless of the lack of privacy, were dedicatedly pursuing their own solution to the problem of the cold by working their way inside each other's greatcoats. Norah's sense of propriety fought a losing battle against inchoate, darkly attractive sensations that would not be quelled. After some minutes of surreptitious observation she ventured a remark.

"Oooh, my hands aren't half cold, Terry. Are yours?"

"Mm. A bit."

"I ought to have brought a pair of gloves."

She took his silence for encouragement. Greatly daring, she slipped a hand into his.

"That's better."

The conductress came upstairs collecting fares. After the fumble with coins and tickets Norah linked hands with Terry again, more confidently now. The Forces couple resumed their explorations and Norah resumed observing them - in disgust, as she told herself.

The tram dropped them at the Royal Oak and they walked over the bridge past South Station. Norah's distaste for the behaviour of the couple on the tram seemed undiminished.

"They were so brazen, weren't they? I mean to say, it was so embarrassing for everybody else."

Terry shrugged. "Nobody has to watch."

"That's just the point. You can't help seeing whether you want to or not. That's what makes it embarrassing."

"What's it matter anyway?" Terry strode along purposefully

against the wind and driving rain, which hardly seemed to have abated despite their having left the Promenade well behind them. Norah clung to him and quickened her pace to keep up.

"A girl who'd behave like that on a tram can't think much of herself." She paused, lending emphasis to her next words. "Where everyone can see." She paused again. "After all, there are plenty of places in the blackout where people can't see, aren't there?"

"I expect so," returned Terry, humouring her. Why couldn't she give it a rest?

"I suppose you couldn't really blame a boy for taking advantage," she went on thoughtfully as they approached the entrance to a back street running between two rows of terraced houses. "I mean a place like that, for instance."

Terry grunted non-committally. Against such obtuseness drastic measures were needed, and Norah took them. She broke away, took a few steps into the back street and was gone. Terry halted in mid-stride and peered after her. Then her voice came from somewhere in the darkness.

"No one would see from the street, would they? Can you see me?"
"No."
"There you are then. That's what I mean."

Terry stood in the silence, waiting, increasingly conscious that the rain, trickling down his face and neck, had begun soaking into his coat collar and through to his jacket and shirt.

"Norah?" he called.

No reply. He took a few steps into the back street. At once there was a soft giggle as two small hands, cold and wet, closed over his eyes from behind.

"There, I told you," Norah whispered. "You couldn't see me, could you? No one can see up here in the blackout."

"Stop mucking about, Norah," Terry expostulated - but suspicion was dawning on him at last. He grasped her hands with his, pulling them away from his eyes. She resisted. A moment later they were engaged in the sort of playful physical scuffling of which Norah always seemed to disapprove when she witnessed others engaged in it. Yet strangely, the rebuff he still half-expected did not come.

Suddenly they were leaning against a wall, breathless, motionless and close together. The pale blur of Norah's face lifted to his.

"Go on, Terry. I'll let you."

He took her in a clumsy embrace. There were some minutes of rustlings, gaspings and shifting shadows amid the pouring rain and gusting wind.

"Your hand's cold, Terry." Norah broke away and put her own hand over it to restrain him.

"It's not."

"It is."

"It'll get warmer."

"No."

"It will."

Their scufflings resumed briefly, but Norah's next interruption was prompter and more determined.

"No, Terry, I mean it. It's wrong."

"Why?"

"You'll think I'm cheap."

"I won't. Why should I?" He fumbled at her again but was repulsed firmly and quickly.

"Because nice girls don't let boys do that, and nice boys don't try to do it."

"How do you know?"

But letting the argument develop meant he had lost. His final effort was crude, perfunctory and totally unsuccessful.

"No! Stop it!" She pushed him away decisively and began straightening her clothes. "It's what I've been taught. Now leave me alone, Terry."

"Oh all right then." He buttoned up again in silence, endeavouring vainly to prevent further inroads by the rain. They resumed walking slowly along the back street, parallel to their normal route home. After some moments Terry spoke again.

"And you believe everything you've been taught, I suppose?" The sulkiness in his voice reflected his frustration and puzzlement.

Norah's reply was cold.

"Most of it, yes. About that I do."

"Yeah," he sneered. Casting around for some weapon that would wound, he went on. "Just like believing in God and all that."

"Terry!" Her footsteps stopped. He stopped too, facing her.

"Well, do you believe it all?" he asked defiantly. "God, Jesus, heaven and hell, miracles - everything?"

"We're Salvationists, Terry. I'm in the choir. You're in the band. You like it, don't you, same as me?"

"Yes, but I didn't say like, I said believe." He had only wanted to shock her, but if she accepted the challenge he would fight it out. "Look, Norah, don't you ever ask questions about it all? Why did

God let my Mum get TB and die? All that pain she had! She hadn't done wrong; she wasn't a sinner. Why does He allow suffering like that all over the world? Why does he allow this war? Thousands and millions of people killing one another: why?" Suddenly he started to sing in a low, mocking voice, ignoring Norah's efforts to shush him.

There is a green hill far away
Without a city wall,
Where the dear Lord was crucified
Who died to save us all.

He took Norah's arms and gripped hard, frightening her. "Answer me this, Norah: if He did die to save us all, what did He save us from anyway? Not much, from what I can see, because the world looks pretty horrible to me with all the things that are going on in it - "

Norah flinched away from his grasp. "You mustn't talk like that," she protested. "It's blasphemy."

"Pah!" Terry let her go contemptuously. "You're just like my Dad. I'm only asking questions, but nobody wants to answer them. Listen, Norah, most families aren't religious like ours. Most of them don't go to church on Sundays: did you know that? Ask anybody at school. I tell you, at times I think there's a big world somewhere, much bigger than the one you and I live in, a real world with a more exciting life than we have, a sort of bigger life, and religion is just something invented by my Dad and a lot of others like him to stop us from seeing it. Why? Are they afraid we'll find out it's more fun than being Christians? Is that why most people don't go to church? Because Christians don't have as much fun as they do?"

The rain hammered at Norah's face, Terry's words at her spirit. This was not what she had bargained for. She peered at him, knowing that even in broad daylight she would find no clue to whatever inner forces drove him. What had just passed between them had been simple enough, clear enough to her burgeoning woman's understanding. She even understood Terry's anger at her sudden withdrawal of what she had begun by offering. But why did he have to start on about all these other complicated things, dragging her along uncharted paths where instinct told her not to follow? Why couldn't he just stay with her?

She could only say weakly, "Oh Terry, I don't know what you're talking about. It's fun being in the Salvation Army anyway. Isn't it?"

Terry sighed. What was the use? "Yes it is," he said impatiently, "but so is going to the pictures and - and dancing at the Tower and all that, and listening to what my Dad calls monkey music. And playing it too. I won't let my Dad stop me doing any of those things if I want to and I won't let the Sally Ann stop me. I won't let either of them stop me doing anything I want to. Neither should you."

He attempted another embrace, this time moved less by the desire to repeat the physical sensations of a few minutes ago than by a genuine and uncharacteristically generous affection which Norah failed to recognise and might have put her in peril if she had. At all events she dodged him adroitly, then picked unerringly on the one topic she ought to have avoided.

"Well, one thing I'd like to do is see this Forces show, but you won't take me."

Terry stiffened, glared and turned away.

"They don't have civvies there," he said sullenly. He pulled his raincoat collar ineffectually up yet again, then strode off once more, hands thrust deep in his pockets.

"You're a civvy," Norah called after his retreating back.

"That's different. I'm in the show."

His footsteps did not pause or waver as he disappeared. Norah scurried after him.

"I wouldn't mind standing at the back or something. You could ask."

"No."

"You won't even ask?" Her voice quavered.

"No," he snapped brutally. "You don't understand. I don't want anyone there, I've told you before. Not you, not my Dad, not anybody. I have to do it on my own, that's all."

"I think I do understand, Terry. I'm not good enough. That's it." Norah spoke quietly, but when Terry continued walking without making any reply, she grabbed his arm and forced him to stop. "That's it, isn't it? Oh yes, you don't mind snogging with me in the blackout, trying to - to make me do *that*, but I'm not good enough to meet your new friends. Well, I'm glad I found out in time. I suppose you think I'm no different from that ATS girl on the tram, really, just an easy" - she hesitated over the words she'd heard but never used, wondered if she dared say them, then spat them out - "piece of crumpet."

Her vehemence took Terry by surprise. He floundered.

"Norah, listen - "

"No, you listen. I wish I'd never let you kiss me - "

This was too much.

"You didn't let me," Terry retorted. "You made me."

"Oh, how dare you, Terry Cullerton!" Her indignation exploded, rendered no less intense by the uneasy recollection that there was truth in the rebuke. She drew herself up ceremoniously. "Well, I'm sure I don't want you thinking any worse of me than you do already. What you'd better do is look around among your new friends for some girl that's really common. I'm sure it won't be too difficult. She might let you do the things you want to do in the blackout, because I certainly won't. Goodnight, Terry."

This time it was Norah who strode purposefully away into the darkness while Terry gaped.

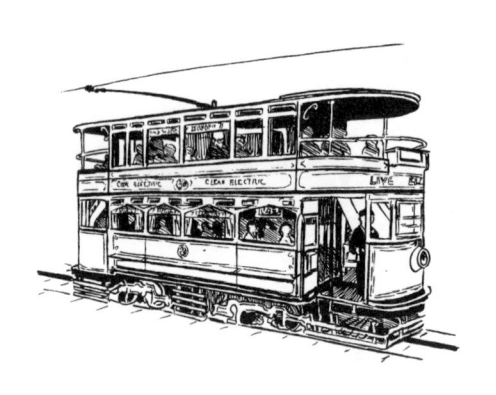

8
SILVER WINGS IN THE MOONLIGHT

Terry pushed the button and waited. The Coronation Theatre was on an upper floor of the department store building, so he might as well take the lift as climb the stairs, encumbered as he was not only by his usual cornet case but also by a bulky brown paper parcel under his arm. Wait till she - well, they - saw what he'd brought for the show tonight!

Pleasurable anticipation mingled with the heady tension, the tingling of the nerve-ends, that he was beginning to recognise as the prelude to show-time. This was the drug that bound stage folk to the world of dressing-up and let's pretend. True, he had had many a foretaste of this intoxication at the Citadel. But in the Salvation Army music and religion were inextricably interwoven. Until recently Terry had not doubted, as his father still did not doubt, that the music they played and sang was a prayer flung to the heavens in reverence and devotion, or that the sense of uplift that followed was God's reward to His faithful flock.

Now, with the rats of adolescent dissent gnawing at the foundations of faith, Terry was learning that music - the music he knew how to make - need not, did not, depend on the Citadel or the religion practised there for the intensity of emotional response it could generate. The realisation frightened him a little. It also excited him beyond measure.

A swing door opened, and Terry turned as a familiar voice broke in on his reverie.

"Wotcher, sport. In good time tonight, then? That's the stuff to give the troops."

It was for Richard Royle's companion rather than for Royle himself, of course, that Terry's face lit up with pleasure and undisguised devotion. And indeed the sight of Kitty Norton, smart and correct in her corporal's uniform yet carrying effortlessly with her the glamorous aura of the theatre, was enough to turn older and more experienced heads than Terry's.

"Hello, Mr - er - I mean Dicky," returned Terry, then shyly, "Hello, Kitty."

Her smile made his head swim. "Hello, love. Ready to knock them cold, are you? You and Auntie Kitty, eh?"

"I hope so," was all he could manage.

The lift arrived and they entered. Royle closed the gates and pushed the handle that sent the contraption wheezing and clanking upwards. Kitty nodded at Terry's parcel.

"Uniform in there, is it, Terry?"

He hesitated and essayed a mysterious look.

"Er - well - sort of."

"Sort of?" queried Royle. "Come on, sport, either it is or it isn't. I've got it! The mystery's solved! You've brought the tunic but not the trousers. In and out of six bedroom doors in your underpants and sock-suspenders like Robertson Hare. You'll get us done by the Lord Chamberlain."

"I can't explain exactly." Terry sought words to match Royle's waggishness but had to abandon the attempt. "It's really meant to be a surprise."

The lift reached their floor and they got out. Terry pushed open the swing door to the theatre and held it for the others.

"I don't know what you're talking about," said Royle as he passed through, and poked Terry in the ribs. "Come on, my lad, you're dying to tell us."

"Well, I - "

Royle made a playful snatch at the parcel as they walked down the side aisle of the auditorium.

"Now, young Cullerton," he pontificated schoolmasterishly, "don't you know that stage people have no secrets from one another? How can they have, when they spend half their lives jammed together in insanitary matchboxes called dressing rooms, and in this dump not even that? But out of the cesspits of squalor the sturdy flower of team spirit grows! 'Tis one of the glories of our calling ... "

Again he snatched at the parcel as they paused at the pass door, and Terry capitulated.

"All right," he said, and opened a corner of the parcel for Royle to peer inside.

"Well, well," said Royle, lifting an eyebrow. "Well, well, well."

"What is all this?" asked Kitty in mock-exasperation. "Come on, Terry, if this lunatic's entitled to look, why not me?"

Terry let her open the corner of the parcel further. She examined the contents.

"Oh, how lovely! And this is yours?"

"Yes."

"And you did it for the show?"

"Yes." He blushed furiously.

"Well, just fancy that! You are nice! You're a real pro, Terry."

Kitty's words, and another dazzling smile, were sufficient reward for Terry, though Richard Royle struck an attitude and had the last word as usual.

"Greater love hath no man than this, that he dress himself in sandpaper for his friends."

Which was not an unfair description of the first touch of the unbelievably coarse material from which were manufactured the millions of uniforms thrown over quartermasters' counters at dismayed recruits during the war. The Air Training Corps uniform contained in Terry's parcel was made from the same material and in fact was identical to the ordinary RAF uniform save for its silver-coloured buttons in place of brass.

Little did that matter to Terry, however, when he stood alone on stage to electrify the audience with the storming jazz virtuosity of Louis Armstrong's "Struttin' With Some Barbecue", still less when Kitty joined him to sing "I Had the Craziest Dream" while he backed her with a flowing lyricism reminiscent of Harry James.

But best of all for Terry was the finale, when the cast entered from the back in ones and twos, forming lines angled towards the audience from opposite wings, performing a simple dance step and singing in unison until the entire company was assembled on stage.

When Terry's turn came, Kitty walked on simultaneously from the other wing and they marched to the front together. He bowed; she curtseyed; the applause broke over them and he suddenly realised deliriously that the audience regarded them as partners - and so did she. The fact that he now wore an Air Force blue uniform to match hers seemed to set the seal on it.

The simple, emotion-charged words of "We'll Meet Again" rang out, and Terry found a special meaning in them as Kitty caught his eye, grinned broadly and winked. Richard Royle's entrance at the end of the first chorus completed the assembly and the company moved forward to form a single line at front of stage. Kitty squeezed Terry's hand as they went into the second chorus and the audience joined them in singing hearty defiance of the miseries of war.

Then it was attention with the house lights up for "God Save the King", and after that the rush and bustle of changing, clearing up and "goodnights" hurriedly exchanged before the lonely plunge into the blackout with a cold bed at the end of it. Still, Terry was one of the lucky ones, sharing a taxi home with Richard Royle and Kitty and one or two others.

It postponed the evil moment, though: it did not mitigate it. What made it worse, when the dim red tail light of the taxi had been swallowed up in the darkness, was that the fast-fading after-the-show exhilaration was complicated by an emotion which Terry could no longer ignore or suppress.

The only remaining passengers were Richard Royle and Kitty Norton. It was always so. Where did they go to? They always arrived together too. Where did they come from? Above all, what did they do?

It was a quiet, clear night. The moon peeped out from behind a cotton-wool cloud, drawing a ghostly pale blue-and-white beauty from the shabby rows of terraced houses, the unlighted gas-lamps lining the otherwise empty pavements, the railway bridge, the silhouette of the gasworks and the stark latticework of the Tower. But Terry had lived here all his life and naturally enough had eyes for none of these things, certainly not tonight. All he was conscious of, as he inserted the key in the lock and opened the front door of his home, was a sickening, near-physical pain that he had never felt before.

He was jealous.

Terry stood to attention before the desk in the CO's office of his ATC unit. The "office" was actually a corner of what Terry otherwise knew as the staffroom of the grammar school which he attended during the daytime, and the "desk" was a trestle table. The room was both familiar yet alien territory, for though Terry had stood at the portal on some errand or other many times, he had never previously set foot inside. Half-listening to the CO chuntering away at him, he made the most of the opportunity to glance around.

Not that there was much to see apart from the disorder customary in school staffrooms everywhere - shabby armchairs, random piles of battered textbooks and exercise books, boxes of chalks and packets of paper, a duplicating machine with huge half-squeezed tubes of a black tar-like substance that got all over the hands and clothes of the unwary, a teamaking corner with unwashed mugs and repellent messes of stubbed-out dog-ends swimming in brown splashes. Reminders of war were provided, as in all other public or official premises, by worn and chipped paintwork, heavy blackout curtains, and exhortatory, nannyish notices on the walls - "Dig for Victory",

"Careless Talk Costs Lives", "Coughs and Sneezes Spread Diseases", "Be Like Dad, Keep Mum", "Is Your Journey Really Necessary?"

Another reminder of war, actually, was Old Plate-Pate, a brutally apt nickname as schoolmasters' nicknames often are, and based on the unfortunate coincidence of the surname of Paton with the permanent wearing of a large and highly-polished silver plate secured by a band of black elastic to the back of its owner's head. The plate's only possible purpose, obviously, was to prevent the brains from falling out, but there was some dispute as to whether in that case it was superfluous since everyone knew that Old Plate-Pate, like all other members of the teaching staff, did not have any.

Then the ATC unit had been formed and Old Plate-Pate, to everyone's astonishment, had suddenly assumed an *alter ego* as an acting flight lieutenant to command it in his spare time. The 1914-18 pilot's wings and medal ribbons on his uniform tunic had caused much half-ashamed rethinking among the pupils about the origin of the silver plate and the callousness of the nickname. They could have saved themselves the bother, since Flight Lieutenant Paton himself was well aware of the nickname and rather fond of it. After all, his own schoolboyish sense of humour, along with much courage and determination, had been a valuable aid to survival during the Western Front air battles of the earlier war, until he got his Blighty in the form of a machine-gun bullet in the back of his head from one of von Richthofen's circus.

A little puzzled as to why Old Plate-Pate had thought it necessary to call him in specially, Terry half-listened to the recital of his progress.

" ... so all in all you've done well in navigation, which of course isn't really surprising considering you're in the "A" class for School Certificate maths." There was a pause. "But there's another reason I wanted to see you privately."

"Sir?"

Old Plate-Pate relaxed and leaned back in his chair. "Stand easy for a moment, Cullerton. Let me ask you a question. How do you like being in the band?"

Terry was taken by surprise. "Oh, er - "

"I know you're a very advanced musician yourself - I've sometimes suspected it interfered too much with your ordinary school work but that's by the by. Don't you find the ATC band very elementary, though?"

"Yes, sir. I suppose I do. The music's terribly simple." Terry tried to soften it, as though he had to excuse himself. "But it's good fun. There's more to it than just the music, isn't there? It's sort of - I mean it's like putting on a sort of show, really, with the uniforms and the marching, having to have all your badges and buckles shining and everything ... "

Old Plate-Pate pursed his lips in a slight smile. "Hm. Well, I can tell you've got the right idea." He tapped his pencil on the desk. "All right then, I'll come straight to the point. Young Stephenson's leaving. He's volunteered for aircrew and been accepted. He'll be off in two or three weeks. That'll mean we want a new bandmaster. You've not been with the ATC long, Cullerton, but obviously you're far and away the best musician we've got. There'll be three stripes for you straight off: you'll be a cadet sergeant ... "

Eagerness began to boil in Terry's stomach.

At last.

"I knew no good would come of it," growled Harold Cullerton. "I knew you'd leave the Salvation Army in the end."

At the other side of the scrubbed deal kitchen table, Terry shifted uncomfortably. He'd done what he could to prepare for this conversation - set the paper and sticks and coal in the old black kitchen range and got a good blaze going in time for his Dad coming home from work, boiled a kettle of water on the hob and made a pot of strong tea, warmed the slippers at the hearth. But that was all expected of him anyway, so it hadn't made a scrap of difference to the reaction when he'd dropped his bomb.

"Not the Army, Dad, only the band," he said as disarmingly as he could.

"Aye, and what for? A tinpot Boy Scout outfit blowing bugles that hardly knows one end from t'other."

"It's not Boy Scouts, Dad, you know that: it's the ATC, the Air Training Corps."

"Aye, and you joined it without asking me."

So here it was, the same old story. Nothing you ever did was right, and even if it was right, deciding it for yourself made it wrong anyway.

"You'd have said no," replied Terry, the sullen note of defiance creeping into his voice.

"That I would," snapped Harold. "This war's no different from every other war. It's against religion, against God. Hitler may be wicked, I don't deny it, but making war isn't the answer. What your

Air Training Corps is doing is teaching you and other young lads to kill, and that's wrong. Murder is still murder even in uniform."

Terry rose from the table and went over to the window. This constant, predictable dogmatism had once made his father seem so strong, so sure, so - so right, a man to be feared a little, perhaps, but anyway to be respected and depended on. Now ... he seemed just narrow-minded, intolerant, incapable of seeing any other point of view than his own. Staring out at the tiny backyard, with its flagstones and wooden outhouse and brick end-wall with nothing beyond save the back of another terraced house identical to theirs, Terry felt imprisoned. He muttered, "I wish I could be so sure."

His father bridled. "To take human life's a sin. It's never justified, no matter what the reason. You know that. I've taught you that. It's what we believe."

Terry faced round again. "Dad, I don't know what I believe any more. Honestly." He added: "I've tried to tell you."

But Harold was not listening. "So this is what it's come to, is it? After all I've done to bring you up properly, give you an education, keep you at t'grammar school - "

"It was me that got the scholarship," protested Terry.

"Don't you answer back: just listen! Do you think that scholarship keeps you? You could have been out working since you were fourteen, paying your way, but I've slaved and sacrificed so you shouldn't have to, and I've never begrudged it. But not for this ... " He shook his head. "Don't you see, Terry? I had such plans for you. With your education you could be an officer in the Salvation Army, make it your career, mebbe go right to t'top ... "

Realisation struck Terry. His Dad was pleading with him. Behind the bluster and the hectoring he was beaten again. All Terry had to do was stick it out.

Why hadn't he understood it before? He'd won: he was free! The evenings at the Tower, the talent competition, the Forces shows, going out with Norah, joining the ATC - it was a pattern of continuous victory. In the end his Dad hadn't stopped him doing any of these things. It was because he couldn't stop him. Neither could he stop Terry leaving the Salvation Army band, or doing anything else he set his mind to.

He was stronger than his father. It was a revelation. Better put the knife in and make sure.

"I don't want that, Dad," he said flatly. "You want it, perhaps, but I don't, and it's my life we're talking about."

He forced himself to stare unblinkingly at his father. It was Harold who spoke first.

"I see. What do you want then?"

This was surrender. Terry set forth his terms with quiet determination. "I want," he said, "to be a professional entertainer, a musician. Not playing in the Sally Ann, not in the ATC either, not in a symphony orchestra or anything like that. In a dance band. A - dance - band. I want to play dance music, swing, jazz and all that. I'm going to have my own band one day, so I've got to know how to manage one. And that's why I'm going to be bandmaster of the ATC. It's a chance to learn how to manage a band."

"But Terry, Terry, you'll do all that when you're bandmaster of t'Salvation Army band, and that's real music - " Harold began, but Terry cut him off.

"I know all about that. Yes, the ATC is a tinpot bugle band. But the point is, I'll be running it, telling them what to do. That's what matters. I'm not waiting for old Joe Braithwaite to drop down dead so I can have the Sally Ann band. I'll be away in the Forces by then, or the Germans may have won the war and there won't be a Salvation Army at all. I want to do it now. And I'm going to."

Harold clutched at the only straw left to him. "I'll stop your pocket-money."

"You wouldn't do that." Terry was incredulous, scornful.

"You live under my roof. If you choose to live in a way I don't agree with, why should I pay for your pleasures?"

Terry set the seal on his triumph. "I shall have to do without, then," he returned coolly. "I get five shillings a time expenses from the Forces show. I'll make do with that."

The huge ten-engined bomber plane gleamed in the moonlight over Blackpool Promenade. Terry's gloved hand manipulated the control column delicately, coaxing the giant machine into a wide sweeping turn around the Tower. Even in the light of the full moon it wasn't going to be easy. Pity they couldn't turn on the Illuminations for a couple of minutes: that would have helped. Swiftly he pulled back the glass canopy, whipped off his goggles and peered downwards through narrowed eyes, calculating the chances. Hm, a trifle tight - he'd have to be careful of the tram-shelters - and rather short for the landing-run he needed, but if the worst came to the worst he'd whip into a left turn on to the North Pier for the last bit.

He closed the canopy, set his jaw, flicked switches and levers with delicate fingers. The revs fell away and the monster aeroplane swooped towards the Starr Gate end of the Prom in response to his masterly touch on control column and rudder. The wheels touched down with the incredible gentleness that only a supreme pilot could achieve; trams and buses flashed by; amazed holidaymakers and RAF drill squads stared; then Terry guided the aircraft to a halt, perfectly positioned at the North Pier facing the war memorial and Hotel Metropole.

He donned his gold-braided uniform cap and white gauntlets, opened the canopy and climbed down, returning the barrage of salutes with casual waves of his swagger-stick. A cornet and mace were handed to him by a flunkey, and at his bawled words of command a gorgeously-caparisoned RAF band struck up the official March of the Royal Air Force. With Terry strutting in the lead with mace and cornet, they marched the length of the Promenade, cheered endlessly by the crowds of spectators lining the route.

After a while he was able to make out the words. "You're a real pro, Terry!" they were shouting over and over. He responded with a modest grin and a flourish of the mace. Then the white blobs grew and miraculously merged and became recognisable as a single smiling face that filled all his consciousness. "You're a real pro, Terry," whispered Kitty fervently over and over again until the tinny ringing of his Dad's alarm clock came through the thin bedroom wall, dispelling the dream.

But not the vision.

9
I DON'T WANT TO SET THE WORLD ON FIRE

"I'll murder the little bleeder, messing me about like this," muttered Richard Royle viciously. "Just who does he think he is?"

Kitty, busy putting the finishing touches to her makeup, turned away from the cracked mirror and placed a restraining hand on his arm.

"Cool down, Dicky, he'll be here. He must have been held up somewhere."

"Held up?" Royle exploded. "Held up? The little blighter, when I've finished belting him all round the stage, he'll need holding up, I promise you that. Just wait till I get my hands on him ... " His words trailed away into a grunt of annoyance as he looked at his watch. Then he raised his voice to address the company at large. "Five minutes, everybody! Curtain up in five minutes!"

He turned to the pianist and drummer standing chatting nearby. "Are my purveyors of philharmonic pleasures prepared to rattle the rafters?" A casual nod and half-smile answered him. "OK, places then. On my signal, right?" They made off and he spoke again. "You OK, funny man?"

Stanley Moffat, in red-nose makeup and a battered morning suit, did not pause in the complex evolutions which he was practising with cane and broken-lidded topper. "But naturally, dear boy." His tone was slightly hurt.

"Yes, of course," agreed Royle. "I don't have to worry about you." He consulted his clipboard, then muttered again. "Damn his eyes, it's the second time he's done this to me." In a threatening tone he addressed no one in particular. "There's not going to be a third, I promise you that."

Kitty stood up and planted a placatory kiss on his cheek, then bent to the mirror again momentarily to repair the damage while Royle dabbed irritably at his face with a handkerchief and tapped his clipboard. "We'd better think about some changes."

"Hang on, Dicky," she urged. "He can still turn up."

"I don't care if he does turn up," Royle retorted. "After this he's out."

"Dicky, listen, I've got an idea," pleaded Kitty. "I'm in uniform for the recruiting office sketch, then after that I've nothing at all until well into the second half, so as soon as I come off I'll scoot over to his house in a taxi, see what's up, and bring him back with me unless he's dying or something."

"Don't be daft. Then I'll have two of you missing."

"No you won't. There's bags of time. With or without him I'll get back easily, I promise."

"Dammit, Kitty, why do you want to fuss?" Royle's tone changed as he weakened. He glanced at his watch again. "He's just a kid. I'll cut him out, rearrange the order a bit and no one'll be any the wiser."

"A minute ago you were raving as though the end of the world had come." Kitty smiled, then she shrugged. "Well, OK, I admit it, I've got a soft spot for him. His mother died a few years ago, you know. Consumption it was - TB. Came on sudden, then there was all the pain and wasting away for months, the whole business. Terrible for a young boy to see."

"Who told you?"

"He did of course. He still misses her. His Dad doesn't seem to be much help: means well but he's a bit strict - you've seen it - and they get across one another."

"When did he tell you all this?"

"He chats with me when you're busy."

Royle laughed, glancing at his watch yet again. "So you've been giving séances, eh? Bless my soul, you really do want to mother him, don't you?" He searched her eyes and laughed again. "Now that's a turnup for the book: Corporal Kitty Norton, psychologist, clairvoyant and frustrated custodian of the maternal instinct. Horoscopes cast, palms and entrails read, crystal balls examined - which could be quite painful - but just watch out while you're holding the client's consultation or you might get a nasty surprise. He may not be as childish as you think."

"Shut up, Dicky. Don't be crude." She punched his arm and he slapped her bottom, his good humour restored.

"OK, Kit, have it your way. Charge the taxi to exes. I'll shift Mavis the mouth-organ maniac into his first-half slot and juggle the second half about a bit." He wagged a finger. "But don't waste time. Get yourself back whatever happens - "

"Don't worry. And on the subject of time, by the way - "

"Ouch!" Royle started, glanced at his watch again and called out, "Places everybody! Two minutes! Intro coming up! Last call! Places!"

He watched until the final scurry settled down and silence descended, then made for the break of the curtain, called for lights and signalled the musicians.

The blacked-out vestibule of the poky terraced house made a useful light trap. Harold Cullerton closed the inner door behind him before opening the outer one to peer at the shadowy uniformed figure silhouetted on the step and the faint lights of the waiting taxi at the kerb beyond. The melodious feminine voice took him by surprise.

"It's me, Mr Cullerton, Kitty Norton. You remember?"

"Good gracious me, whatever in the world ... ?" He recovered himself quickly. "You'd better come in, Miss."

He stood aside for her to pass, closed the outer door and followed her into the hall. They faced each other awkwardly for a few moments. The melancholy strains of Bunny Berigan's "I Can't Get Started" wailed scratchily from a wind-up gramophone upstairs.

"It's young Terry," explained Harold apologetically.

"It's about Terry I've come, Mr Cullerton," said Kitty. "We've the show on tonight. I know you're not keen on it, but Terry's supposed to - "

"It's not me that's stopping him, Miss - "

"Kitty. I told you."

"Yes: Kitty. He were right as ninepence this morning - quiet, like, but he always is these days. Never tells me anything. But then he weren't home when I got in from work this afternoon and when he did come in it were straight up to his bedroom without a word, locks the door and starts playing them jazz records. Wouldn't come out when I called him. Just listen to t'din! I made us teas, then I called him again. Even reminded him he were supposed be going to t'theatre - "

"Yes, I've got the taxi waiting to take him there with me - "

"But he won't come. He won't even answer. To tell t'truth, I don't rightly know what to do with him. He's always been a good lad, but these last few months - "

Kitty interrupted. "Yes. Look, Mr Cullerton, I don't have much time. I've got to get back to the theatre myself. Do you mind - I mean could I just go up and try?"

Harold stood aside. "I don't see what harm it'll do. In my own mind I've blamed it all on him starting with these theatricals. No offence, but it seems to me - "

"Yes, I do understand, Mr Cullerton." Kitty flashed him a winning smile from halfway up the stairs. "But it's not just that, you know. He's growing up, learning to have a mind of his own."

"Oh aye, he's doing that all right, but - oh well, see what you can do." Harold switched the upstairs landing light on, returned to the kitchen and after a moment's thought closed the door behind him.

The trumpet solo bringing the record to a close made it unnecessary to wonder which was Terry's bedroom. Kitty knocked on the door. No answer. She knocked again, more loudly.

"Terry?" She called. Then, more forcefully, cutting through the blare of the music, "Terry!"

Again there was no response and as the trumpet solo climaxed and ended she almost shouted into the sudden silence. "Terry, it's me, Kitty. I want to talk to you." She waited, knocked again and coaxed. "Come on, Terry. Please, love."

There was a slight shifting sound from inside and a small tense voice at last replied from behind the door. "It's no use. Please go away."

"No, love," said Kitty. "I won't go away until you've opened this door and let me talk to you."

She waited. "Come on," she insisted. "Let me talk to you."

The door opened a crack. "There isn't anything to say. Leave me alone."

"Just let me in, Terry. You're late for the show."

"I'm not coming."

"Why not?" She pushed the door gently, testing the resistance. "Have I done something to upset you?"

"No."

"Well what is it then?"

"Nothing."

Kitty gave the door a shove and bustled her way inside. The tiny room was like an oven, hot and airless, the ancient gas-stove recklessly turned full on. The gramophone was open on the stand chair, a litter of records scattered on the bed. Terry, jacketless but wearing open-neck shirt and grey flannels, backed away defensively and stared out of the window, hands in pockets, pretending nonchalance.

"Right," said Kitty, her tone businesslike. "Then if nothing's the matter, just get your cornet, put on your ATC uniform and come with me. I've a taxi waiting outside."

Terry shook his head vehemently, his back to her. "I - I can't come. I just can't."

Kitty looked at her watch, then sharpened her tone. "I'm sorry, Terry. I've no time to waste. Get your things and come, or tell me what's the matter. One or the other. And quick." She turned to the door.

"I can't." The misery in his voice melted her and she gathered herself for another try. She went up to him, took him by the shoulders and spun him round to face her.

"Now listen, Terry," she said firmly, gripping his arms, digging her fingers into him. "You want to be a musician, an entertainer?"

He nodded dumbly, and she went on.

"I called you a real pro the other week, remember? Well, I was wrong, you're not one yet, not a real one, and I'll tell you why. You've heard the saying about "the show must go on", haven't you? Everybody has. Well, the most important thing you have to learn if you want to be a real pro is that it's true. If you're in the business you have to live by it. The show must go on. You've got to be *there*. You've got to *be* there and do whatever it is that you do, because people have paid good money to see you do it. No excuses, no feeling not quite like it or not very well. You go out there and you do it and then you sort out your private troubles afterwards. Now: there's something wrong - OK, tell me and I'll try to help, but" - she smiled sympathetically to soften her words - "it mustn't take more than five minutes. Is it your Dad?" He shook his head. "Is it me or Dicky?" Again he shook his head. "What then?"

"I can't tell you. Not now."

"All right, tell me later then. And I'll listen, I promise I will. But in the meantime" - she tapped a finger against her wristwatch - "if you want to be friends with me you come and do the show." She lowered her voice and pleaded softly. "Please, Terry. Do it for me."

For an instant they stood in frozen silence. Then Terry threw himself into Kitty's arms. She led him to the bed, pushed the records out of the way and sat down with him, stroking his head.

"Oh Kitty," he choked, and began weeping.

"It's all right, baby," she crooned, cradling him. "It's all right. Just tell me about it."

He fought back the tears and gazed at her anxiously. "You won't tell anyone else?"

"Of course I won't, love."

"Not even - not even Dicky?"

She regarded him earnestly.

"Especially not Dicky," she replied, then consulted her watch again. "But it does have to be quick, love. I'm sorry."

"All right." Terry gripped her hand tightly, marshalling his thoughts. "Well, it was at rehearsal on Wednesday. I was talking to Mr Moffat - Stanley. He's always been friendly. He keeps telling me how important it is to be versatile: not just to rely on the main thing you do."

Kitty nodded. "He's right about that. Singers have to learn to dance and tell jokes. Comics have to sing and dance."

"Yes. He says we're all entertainers, whatever it is that we do. So a musician has to do more than play an instrument."

"Go on."

"Well, he said he'd teach me some dance steps. You know he's in the fire service? The NFS?"

Kitty half-smiled. "Yes indeed. It must have been Hobson's choice for our Stan. He wouldn't survive a week in a barrack block."

"Well, he said he'd be off duty at the fire station about four today and would I come round and meet him there ... "

The squalid little story was commonplace enough. It started in the fire station with a brief tour of the gleaming red fire-engines and ended in Stanley Moffat's flat with a dance lesson that quickly turned into a clumsy and ill-judged attempt on Terry's virtue.

" ... It was horrible," concluded Terry, his voice trembling with shame and embarrassment. "I - I didn't know what to do at first. I wasn't really sure what he - well, what he was after. But when I did realise, I felt sick ... I couldn't get him off me ... and then he went wild, holding me down and saying horrible things ... I was frightened, he was that strong ... and suddenly he started crying ... I couldn't believe it but he was crying, sort of begging me ... I ... well, I just got out somehow and ran home as fast as I could ... and he followed me to the door and said I mustn't tell anyone ... "

"All right, love, I understand," said Kitty, shaking her head sympathetically. She patted his hand. "Dicky should have warned you. Or I could have. But I'd never have thought Stan would ... Everyone knows he's as queer as a nine-bob note. Well, it's hard luck, Terry, but no bones broken, and it's an experience. You'll have learnt something from it, I expect." She glanced at her watch and jumped to her feet, straightening her uniform, her manner brisk. "Just look at the time: we'll have to shift ourselves. The taxi's waiting."

Terry remained on the bed and gazed up at her with a woebegone expression. "But Kitty, how can I?"

She frowned. "How can you what?"

"How can I ever come to the theatre again now?"

"Why not?"

"But isn't he there?"

"Stanley? Of course he's there," replied Kitty cheerfully. "Where else would he be? The show must go on, remember?"

"But what will he say?"

Kitty chuckled. "Nothing, if he's got any sense."

"What will I say?"

"The same. Forget about Stan. You just get out there and blow your horn."

Terry did not move. "I can't."

Kitty looked down at the tearstained, bewildered face, the crumpled, defeated figure. Too many new experiences and emotions heaped on top of one another. Her heart leapt with sympathy. She steeled herself.

"Now Terry, I'm telling you for the last time," she warned him harshly. "You must, do you hear? You've got to." She put all the emphasis she could into her words. "Because if you don't you're a coward and a bloody amateur and I never want to see you again." She made a show of consulting her watch once more. "I'm going now. You can either come with me or else stay here and watch me walk out for good. Suit yourself which."

She went over to the door and put her hand to the knob. Then she paused, turned and deployed the ultimate weapon.

"I'll give you a kiss if you come," she promised.

There was a tense moment, then Terry rose to his feet and flung himself into her embrace.

She meant her kiss to be maternal, or thought she did. But whatever she meant it to be, it was certainly much warmer than was wise.

10
THIS IS THE STORY OF A STARRY NIGHT

The grim wartime patriotism held the Forces audience of the Coronation Theatre at rigid attention until the last note of "God Save the King" died away. In this they did not differ from civilian audiences. No more than the merest handful at the back slipped out before or during the Anthem, even though the two or three minutes' start it gave could make all the difference in the queues for the last trams and buses.

However, all restraints were loosed once the curtains closed and "Who's Taking You Home Tonight?" began squeaking and scratching its way through the Tannoy system: the vigorous if good-natured scrum which then developed at the exits sufficed to empty the theatre long before the record finished playing.

It was not very different backstage. Scenery was dismantled, props were packed away and belongings collected together at lightning speed amidst the excited post-mortem chatter. On this evening, however, conversation and horseplay were more subdued than usual by virtue of the presence of a Royal Air Force group captain. In the splendour of number one uniform, with scrambled-egg cap and brown kid gloves in hand, he had appeared backstage directly before the Anthem and was now deep in conversation with Richard Royle.

As Kitty and Terry began shrugging on their coats the group captain departed and Richard Royle came over to them.

"Well, kiddies," he announced, "you'll have to find your own way home tonight. I'm summoned to the presence."

"Oh?" Kitty lifted an eyebrow. "What's that mean?"

"It means, o moon of my delight, that I'm mingling with the mighty, that's what. Fame and fortune are within my grasp! After the years of penury, the struggle and the heartbreak, my genius unrecognised and unrewarded - "

Kitty made a face and resumed the battle with her greatcoat. "When he gets to the point, Terry," she said with a show of exaggerated patience, "you could just send me a postcard - "

Royle raised a hand. "Peace, peace, my dearest love, I surrender!" he proclaimed. "The point is this. Groupie's been in the front row with his brown job oppo, a rather beautiful colonel no less, plus His and Her Respective Washups the Mayor and Mayoress. Between them this sinister crew have dreamed up a dastardly plot for putting on a Forces show at the Winter Gardens or Hippodrome or somewhere: they think it'll be good for morale, though exactly whose I'm not sure - "

"Oh, Dicky!" Kitty smiled with pleasure. "It'd certainly be good for my morale. Just think: a proper theatre with dressing rooms and everything!"

"Hole in one, my flower. Only snag is, they naturally haven't the least idea how to do it. Officers and gentlemen propose, sergeants dispose! That is to say, a-dither to arrange matters over a nightcap this very minute, Colonel Beautiful invites Their Collective Nibses to his lair at the Headlands down South Shore. But stay! The Headlands Hotel is an officers' mess. Shall it be polluted by the unclean presence of the non-commissioned, however handsome, talented and vital to the proceedings? Total discombobulation, resolved only by mayoral quick thinking and a change of venue! Thus I now take the high road to Their Washups' des res with all mod cons, while you take the low to your proletarian hovel, enduring the loneliness" - Terry missed the exchange of glances with Kitty - "as best you can. Taxi's booked as usual, so just fill it up how you like. Take care of Terry here for a start." He dropped his waggish tone and addressed Terry kindly. "You did well this evening, sport, once you got here. Kitty told me I had to forgive you, though she wouldn't say why. Her wish being my command, I hereby absolve you of sin, only you're not to mess me about any more, right?"

Terry felt a surge of gratitude, and his reply was sincere. "No I won't, Dicky. Honestly."

"Attaboy. Now: just you protect Kitty from the dangers of the night, think up something to knock them for six with in the next show, and I'll see you at band call."

Terry was on tenterhooks lest any of the other passengers in the taxi should have a destination further distant than his own. His heart sank when Mavis, the WAAF girl who had played the mouth-organ, said her billet was "on the front" beyond the Pleasure Beach, not far short of the Headlands in fact. But he need not have worried: after dropping off two airmen near the Manchester, Kitty directed the taxi-driver to carry straight on down the Prom to deliver the other girl home.

Goodnights were exchanged ; the door slammed; Terry and Kitty were alone in the back seat.

"Where to now?" enquired the taxi driver.

Terry would not have objected if it had been next stop Aberdeen. But prosaically, Kitty answered, "Burtenshaw Terrace please," and Terry felt unreasonably disappointed, knowing the magic just beginning would be over in minutes.

The driver U-turned, sped back along the near-deserted, blacked-out Promenade and and swung up Waterloo Road towards the Royal Oak and South Station. The taxi was unheated, but Terry was conscious of Kitty's warmth through her greatcoat. He said nothing because the million things whirling around his head were unsayable. It was Kitty who broke the tension.

"It went fine tonight, didn't it, Terry? I told you."

"Yes."

"You played beautifully. Same as always."

He searched for the words he wanted. "I - I play with you best," he said clumsily, then corrected himself. "I mean when you're singing."

Kitty rewarded him with a smile and a squeeze of the hand. "Thank you, Terry. You know I'm getting really spoilt these days having you to do the backing for me. That's why I had to come to your house and fetch you, you know. I needed you." She paused, aware that his hand was still in hers. "What about Stanley? He didn't bother you, did he?"

"No. He didn't speak to me at all."

"There you are, you see. You've come through a big test."

He lowered his voice, not wanting the driver to overhear. "It was you that made me."

"Rubbish. You did it yourself."

He shook his head vehemently. "I did it for you. I couldn't have done it for anybody else," he whispered, and willy-nilly Kitty was warmed by his guilelessness and devotion.

"I do believe you mean it," she said. "Just fancy! That's one of the biggest compliments anyone's ever paid me." She calculated, then abandoned calculation, told herself what-the-hell-it-doesn't-mean-anything but knew that it did, and went on: "You've earned a kiss. There!"

She planted a kiss on Terry's cheek. The light in his eyes melted her and without conscious volition she leaned towards him, put both hands in his and allowed him a kiss on the lips that lasted far too long. Familiar sensations began assailing her at unexpected voltage.

Panicking, she fought them back and pushed Terry firmly away, resolved now to evade the disastrous complications that suddenly seemed to loom.

"Well well!" she murmured a little breathlessly. "I can't say that was any pain at all." She tried to be matter-of-fact. "But it had better be enough for one evening."

Her emotions churning, she let the silence endure until the taxi turned into Burtenshaw Terrace, while Terry leaned against her, holding her hand tightly. Hell's bells, talk about cradle-snatching! What must the taxi driver be thinking? The vehicle pulled into the kerb and came to a halt.

"There you are: Burtenshaw Terrace," said the driver as he reached a hand over and opened the rear door.

Terry essayed another kiss. Kitty caught it deftly on her cheek and used a squeeze of the hand to propel him out of the car. But as his feet touched the pavement he hesitated, climbed back in and closed the door.

"Terry, what are you doing?" began Kitty, knowing the answer.

"I - I'm not getting out here," he said quickly. A desperate eagerness made him bold. "I'll see you home first." He tried to imitate Richard Royle's facetious style. "After all, Dicky said I had to protect you from the dangers of the night."

Crumbs, that's torn it, thought Kitty, and contemplated the back of the driver's neck, half expecting to see his ears waggle. She schooled herself to speak lightly.

"You don't want to do that. You'll have to walk all the way home again afterwards."

"I don't mind," replied Terry. A note of pleading entered his voice. "I - I just want to talk to you a bit longer."

She tried to hedge again, but she was being swept away and she knew it. "Well, I'm not sure - "

"Look, Miss," the driver interrupted sourly, "It makes no difference to me what you decide, but make it quick. I've got other passengers booked that do know what they want to do."

Kitty noted the choice of words, resented the sneer, knew exactly what he was thinking and asked herself why she should care anyway, it was none of his bloody business.

"Drive on," she gritted, then flung herself into the corner of the seat in unaccustomed ill-humour and brushed Terry away when he attempted to snuggle up to her.

The rest of the ride took place in silence, with Terry puzzled and hurt, unable to understand Kitty's sudden coldness. He shouldn't have done it, he knew. He'd gone too far. But he'd thought she'd wanted him to kiss her; she'd encouraged him. Yet she couldn't really have meant to, could she? Why should she when she belonged to Dicky?

The jealousy came to torture him again. In what way did she belong to Dicky? They weren't married, so were they engaged, were they "walking out", was she his girlfriend, what did it all mean? Dicky seemed so offhand towards her, sometimes quite rude in fact, always making jokes at her expense, though she didn't seem to mind it and gave back as good as she got; and then this evening he just casually packed her off in a taxi while he went somewhere else. Did she let Dicky kiss her, "snog" with her? He supposed she must. At this his imagination seized up, refusing to picture such a scene.

The trouble now, though, was that none of this mattered any more because he'd spoilt it all: through wanting too much he'd lost what he already had, and he counted the times she'd kissed him and knew that she would never kiss him again.

The taxi slammed into gear and moved off. Miserably, Terry watched it disappear into the night. Neither he nor Kitty had spoken on the way from Burtenshaw Terrace, and Kitty's words, when she did break the silence in a carefully neutral tone, did nothing to help him.

"That's it then, Terry. You've done it now: he's gone. This is my billet."

It was a semi-detached house, considerably larger than Terry's own, far from the beach, not a real boarding-house but the sort of place that hung a "vacancies" card in the window at peak-season periods to catch holidaymakers stranded without pre-booked accommodation, packing both them and the owner's family together in conditions which in a later age would have warranted immediate closure under the fire and health regulations. Now in wartime the landlady was doing well with Kitty in one room and two junior WAAF clerks in another, giving her a steady income all the year round and plenty of help with the washing-up. And if Kitty's boyfriend sometimes seemed to stay very late at night indeed, it was very discreetly done and never spoken about; after all he must be a gentleman, him being that Richard Royle from the BBC, and there was much reflected glory to be had from telling neighbours how polite and friendly he always was, not at all la-di-da like you'd expect; and somehow that seemed to make it all right.

Kitty stopped at the gate to the short garden path, hand on the latch. "You'll be walking home from here. Won't your Dad worry about you being late?"

"It doesn't matter," Terry said dejectedly, waiting for the formal dismissal. It came.

"Well, thanks for bringing me home, Terry," she said breezily, and opened the gate. She turned. "You didn't really do much talking after all, did you?"

"No," was all he could manage.

"I thought that's what you wanted to bring me home for."

Was she teasing him? She couldn't be so cruel. Could she?

"I couldn't talk. I - I - you seemed cross with me."

Her low laugh did not seem unkind. Neither were her words. "Cross? Good heavens, no. Not with you, love."

Had he misunderstood her? He found words.

"Kitty, I just wanted to be with you."

"I know that, Terry. And now you are with me," she replied. She really was teasing after all. His heart sank.

"Yes," he returned glumly, and could say no more.

Kitty leaned forward, kissed his cheek and walked quickly up the path to the porchway, leaving the gate open. Confused, Terry bent to shut it.

"Terry, I told you I'm not cross with you." Her voice from the porchway was soft and inviting.

He looked up and made out her shape deep in the shadows. He walked up the path towards her as if on eggs.

"For a minute you had me thinking you didn't want to kiss me goodnight," she whispered coquettishly, and drew him close. Some moments later she broke away and chuckled. "No need to take it all at once, love: I'm not going to run away. Just a sec." She fumbled with buttons and took his hand. "There."

After a rather longer interval it was Terry, inevitably, who spoke next. "I love you, Kitty," he choked, and Kitty sighed.

"Oh no you don't, ducky," she pronounced decisively. "I'm getting on for twice your age, you know." She paused, then whispered in his ear. "But just for tonight, I think I'm going to pretend that you do."

She groped for her key, put her finger to her lips, opened the front door and beckoned.

11
I DON'T WANT TO WALK WITHOUT YOU, BABY

The letter arrived two days later. Fortunately Terry saw it on the mat inside the vestibule when he went down for the morning paper while his father was in the bathroom shaving. Not that the contents gave him any cause to reflect on the kindness of Fate - rather the reverse, for the letter could not fail to hurt him deeply despite the time, trouble and tears which Kitty had spent composing it:

Dear Terry,

This will be a short letter, because I have to say goodbye to you and it's no use prolonging the agony.

I told you I'm a lot older than you are. You don't think that matters, but it does. You and I ought never to have done what we did, and it was my fault we did it. I'm sorry about that - not for myself, but for you.

I thought I wanted to stay in Blackpool for the rest of the war, and I probably could have, but now I've got to go away for your sake. Think of the trouble between you and me and Dicky if I didn't, not to mention your Dad!

My officer's a good sort, and I'm friendly with her. I asked her to get me posted away quickly. She thought I was mad but she did it. I shall not come back, and I shall not see you again. Don't ask the RAF where they've sent me, because they won't tell you without my permission.

You're going to be a fine musician and you'll go a long way. Not only that, you're a dear boy, and I'm more fond of you than is good for either of us. I shall always remember you. But you must forget about me, for a long time anyway. Later, when you've got over the pain I've caused you, I hope you'll be able to forgive

Your

Kitty

That day, for the first time in his life, Terry played truant from school, and next day, because it was so out of character and he pleaded desperately with his form master, his offence was quietly overlooked and no word reached his father.

Even so he adamantly refused to tell his form master what his trouble was or how he had spent the day. For two hours he had composed and torn up useless tearstained letters. Then he had picked up his cornet case, walked down Waterloo Road to the Promenade and taken the tram to Starr Gate. During the remaining hours until it was time to go home again in the afternoon he walked the sandhills in loneliness and pain, pausing every now and then to sit among the marram grass, blowing his heart out with agonised renderings of every Tin Pan Alley love-song he knew.

It was impossible to hide his distress from his father, of course, though he tried. Nevertheless he stonewalled every enquiry, and found it less difficult than he expected. It never occurred to him that this might be because Harold, albeit a man of narrow vision, had certainly had enough experience of life to put two and two together with some assurance that they were not five, and for once was endeavouring to exercise tact. It was a time, in fact, when to confide in his father might have evoked a more sympathetic response than in the past. On the other hand it is doubtful whether such a reconciliation at the cost of having lost Kitty would have been an acceptable exchange in Terry's eyes. In any case the issue never arose.

Norah was easily dealt with. She and Terry had neither met nor spoken since their last quarrel. He continued to avoid her, and this time she made no attempt to contact him.

Terry's attendance at Salvation Army meetings, already much curtailed by his new interests, fell to zero. His father's pleas and protests, fierce at first and accompanied by vague hints of further reprisals, had already become perfunctory and now ceased altogether. It was as though Harold realised the game was irretrievably lost.

What to do about Richard Royle and the Forces show was a very different matter. The instinctive, easy solution was to evade the problem by not turning up for the next band call and never going near the Coronation Theatre again. That would put an end to the whole business.

But would it? Would Richard Royle leave it at that, or would he pursue Terry to his home as Kitty had done? What might he know or guess about the reason for Kitty's sudden departure? What might he say to Terry's father? There could be trouble from Richard Royle. If so, better to face it at the Coronation Theatre than at home.

There was another factor at work too, and that was Terry's rapidly-developing professional instinct, quickened by Kitty's words of only a couple of weeks ago. What was it she had said? "You've got to be *there*. You've got to *be* there and do whatever it is that you do .." The show must go on, in fact. If he could defy his heartbreak, be a real pro as Kitty had taught him, wouldn't it be a sort of link to hold on to so that he wouldn't have lost her completely after all?

It was tortuous thinking and poor consolation, but it was something. Since he had nothing else, it was everything.

Butterfly wings fluttered in Terry's stomach as he pushed through the swing doors of the Coronation Theatre. Richard Royle was already on stage, deep in conversation with Stanley Moffat and one or two other early arrivals - including a dark-haired, very young-looking WAAF with a petulant expression constantly threatening to break through the simper that she evidently reserved for Richard Royle. Naturally Terry disliked her on sight. Had she looked like Rita Hayworth he would still have disliked her, simply because she was not Kitty.

A silence fell over the group as Terry entered. Richard Royle muttered a few words to the WAAF girl, who said something in return, giggled, put a proprietorial hand on Royle's arm and watched Terry appraisingly as he approached down the centre aisle. His footfalls on the proscenium steps echoed like cannon shots. He did not know what to say when he reached the group, so he came to a halt and said nothing.

Richard Royle nodded coolly, his customary bantering manner little in evidence.

"Evening, young Terry," he said.

"Hullo - Dicky." It had always been difficult to use the name naturally, and even more so now.

"Got some numbers for the show then?" queried Royle without preamble, and went on before Terry could answer, "Because I'd better just say this: Kitty's been posted and we won't be seeing her again." He regarded Terry keenly and added in a carefully neutral tone, "In case you didn't know." Leaving Terry no time to ponder what that might mean, he continued with his old facetiousness, "Ring out the old, ring in the new. It is now my privilege to introduce you to our new canary-bird, whom I have rescued from durance vile in the quartermaster's stores, where the safeguarding and dispensing of regulation Air Force blackout knickers has hitherto been her principal contribution to the downfall of Hitler, though not, I trust, of the knickers. In short - no, not in shorts, in knickers, should I say? - this is ACW1 Violet Roberts, and since you're going to have to work with her the two of you had better try to get along, though not too well, I trust."

Once more Terry wondered apprehensively about the significance of the last few words, but Royle's face was expressionless. The reaction of the girl herself to Royle's vulgarities was an oh-isn't-he-awful giggle and another proprietorial clutch at his sleeve. Royle went on: "Violet, my pet, this is our Terry. He's even younger than you are, as you see, but beware, he has more talent with his horn than you might expect."

If there was further ambiguity in Royle's last remark it went unnoticed by Violet, who regarded Terry with open disdain before pointedly addressing her first unpromising words not to him but to Royle: "Hm, I hope so. What tunes can he play?" Terry detected a trace of lisp in her sibilants, and took some slight satisfaction in that.

"Better ask him, my poppet. My experience is that if he's heard it, he can play it."

Violet stared at Terry. "Oh, I see, quite the infant prodigy, are we?" she exclaimed accusingly. "Go on, then: what can you play?"

A quick stab of anger came to Terry's aid. "The cornet," he replied abruptly.

"You don't need to be clever with me," snapped Violet.

"I do," retorted Terry, and prepared for storms when she gasped "Well, really," and flashed her eyes at Richard Royle in indignant appeal.

But the latter merely remarked mildly, "I can see you're going to be great friends," admonished them to let him know in ten minutes what they had been able to work out, and went off to exchange greetings with other arrivals.

Despite the bad start Terry and Violet soon agreed on their first number: they settled for "I Cried For You" in the Helen Forrest-Harry James manner, which suited Violet's sentimental delivery; but at the first mention of "You Ought to See Sally on Sunday", which Kitty would have gleefully joined Terry in clouting into the next street, Violet raised objections. Number one: the lyric was written for a male not a female singer. Number two: the song was centuries old, dating back ten years, and that meant that, number three: the pre-swing style of the piece would not suit her voice, which was altogether too refined and highly-trained to be wasted on crude belters of that sort.

Terry remained adamant. Called on by Violet to arbitrate, Richard Royle surprised them both by curtly instructing Violet to fit herself in with Terry's requirements as best she could. He then turned to Terry.

"The Nat Gonella solo, right?"

"Yes, I think I could - "

"Good." He addressed Violet. "He'll blister them with it, so you couldn't have a better lead-in. But then you'll have to give the vocal lots of stick or you'll fall on your face." He turned back to Terry. "The number's in. Do what you like with the solo. If Vi's not strong enough to carry the vocal, get Bobby to sing duet with her from the piano: we'll fix an extra mike. You get it organised, chum, OK?"

From that moment, of course, Terry knew that Violet's hatred for him was unappeasable. But he knew also that, although obviously Kitty's successor in more ways than one, she was powerless to harm him.

Nothing could be the same as it had been before, though. Richard Royle made this clear as the cast were dispersing at the end of band call, when he called Terry aside and led him to a corner out of earshot of others. His demeanour held no trace of raillery.

"Now just a word to the wise, chum. I took your side against Violet over the "Sally on Sunday" number - "

"Oh yes," said Terry. "I'm very grateful - "

"Whatever makes you think your gratitude could interest me?" Royle cut in icily. "Don't talk, listen. Just understand that I backed you up because business is business, and as far as that goes nothing has changed: I need you and you need me. But it doesn't go any further. And if you ever try to make it go further, in any way at all, I'll knock your block off. From now on you find your own bloody way home, understand?"

Terry did understand. He understood that the reason for Kitty's departure was no secret from Richard Royle. He also understood that Royle, like Kitty, knew what it meant to be a real pro and this evening had given him a demonstration of it. And as Terry thus added another brick to the growing structure of his own professionalism, he further understood that a hard and ruthless streak was going to be one of its components.

Somehow life went on, as it always surprises the brokenhearted victims of calf-love by doing. The searing anguish of the first few days subsided to a dull nagging ache as the weeks went by.

Terry's growing preoccupation with his music did much to cauterise his hurt. His inventiveness, perfectionism and energy soon elevated him virtually to star status on the Forces show. His range broadened too as Richard Royle used him more and more to support other turns, not only with his cornet but with walk-ons and speaking parts in sketches. The time even came when he was experienced enough and tough enough to face Stanley Moffat without a qualm in one of the latter's knockabout acts, coldly keeping his distance yet performing efficiently everything that was asked of him.

Terry worked hard with the ATC bugle band as well. It did not take long for his natural managerial instinct to reveal itself. Within a few weeks he had disciplined his charges to standards of turnout, drill and instrumental performance which, within the musical limitations of the bugle, would not have shamed a regular Forces band.

Still Terry's obsession was not slaked. In whatever spare time he had left from his stage and ATC activities along with his ordinary school work he began to explore more of the entertainment world. His father's protests, invested with all the killjoy puritanism, as Terry now regarded it, that previously had set the bounds of Terry's life, were no longer a problem: Terry simply brushed them aside as he had so newly discovered he could do with impunity. In the end his father stopped making them.

A more serious inhibiting factor was the need for cash, since Harold Cullerton remained obdurate in refusing to restore Terry's pocket-money. Terry took on a paper round before school every day, saving part of the proceeds for the trumpet he was more determined than ever to have and spending the rest on regular visits to shows and entertainments - variety at Feldman's Theatre near Central Station, "On With The Show" at the North Pier, plays at the Grand, revues and musicals at the Opera House.

He not only enjoyed, he absorbed and stored for future reference. There was always something for an acute observer to learn: timing from the comics - whether Blackpool's own like Frank Randle and Albert Modley or visitors like Winston Churchill's improbable son-in-law Vic Oliver - dramatic devices from Coward and Rattigan, spectacle and sentiment from Ivor Novello, rhythm from George Formby's double-syncopated ukelele beat, self-projection from Ann Shelton, Vera Lynn and other band-singers now emerging into the stratosphere of personal stardom from their former concealment behind the ignominious record-label description "With vocal refrain".

Closest to Terry's most direct interests and purposes, however, were the nationally-famous dance orchestras which gave concerts in Blackpool from time to time. It was at a Joe Loss performance in the Winter Gardens that Terry suddenly realised that these "dance orchestras", when touring anyway, were not dance orchestras at all but show bands, and that the difference was crucial. Playing music for dancing meant being imprisoned by dance tempi, but playing for an audience gave free rein to the musicians' virtuosity. Without that freedom, how could Harry Roy ever perform "Tiger Rag" or Harry James "The Flight of the Bumblebee"? This decided him: when his time came, a show band was what he would have.

And at an Oscar Rabin concert a few weeks later he resolved that come what may, his band, his show band, would be built around a single individual, himself, Terry Cullerton. No one else would filch the applause, the glory, the glamour that would rightfully be his.

For although Terry, watching and listening carefully, found little to choose between the Joe Loss and Oscar Rabin orchestras on grounds of musicianship, the two leaders were poles apart in presentation. Joe Loss, dapper in white tie and tails, smiling, bouncing with vitality, had dominated the performance from first to last, announcing the numbers, flourishing his baton like a fencer's foil, tapping his feet, capering around the stage, leaving no room for doubt as to who was in charge - and reaping all the plaudits. Oscar Rabin, on the other hand, turned out to be an unassuming figure who sat behind a huge bass saxophone somewhere in the reed section and left all communication with the audience to his front man Harry Davis, a tall, genial, handsome fellow with black brilliantined hair who looked well in tails and had a smooth line of patter but after all was not Oscar Rabin.

To have an orchestra and let someone else present it in public? Never, Terry thought as he emerged from the Winter Gardens exit and headed down Church Street for the Promenade: if I were a two-foot tall Martian with three legs and a face like a gargoyle's I'd do it by my own personality or I wouldn't do it at all. Going home on the tram the incantation hammered through his brain, and he was still muttering it to himself when he put the light out and climbed into bed:

"I have to do it on my own."

12
TAKING A CHANCE ON LOVE

It was after rehearsal on an ATC evening that Terry encountered Norah again. At about nine o'clock he and the other cadets emerged from the Scout hut in the school grounds which also served as the band room. Terry walked over to the bike-sheds to collect his machine, put on his clips, switched on the dimmed-out lamp and rode across the playground.

"Hello Terry." The shadowy figure in the darkness just outside the gate was in Salvation Army uniform. Terry braked and put his foot to the ground.

"Norah!" His surprise was genuine. "What are you doing here?"

"I came to find you."

"Oh," was all he could say. It was Norah who had to break the silence.

She stumbled on: "I haven't seen you for ages. Now that you don't come to band practices - "

He tried to cover his unease with Richard Royle-inspired waggery. "I've just been to band practice," he said, waving an arm towards the ATC hut.

"You know I mean the Salvation Army," said Norah.

"Is that where you've been now?"

"Yes." Another silence. He did not help her, could not. "And you seem to go to school a different way from me these days."

There was nothing to say.

"Could I walk with you?" Norah asked diffidently.

"I suppose so." He had been trying to think of some way of disengaging himself, but it was too late now. He dismounted and began wheeling his bicycle along beside her.

"Terry, don't you want to see me any more?" Norah blurted out at last.

He hedged. "I thought you didn't want to see me." And it was true that Norah had not attempted to seek him out. Somewhat to his surprise - perhaps dismay even - her reply confirmed that she had chosen not to.

"I was frightened of what you did - tried to do - that night," she said, and went on plaintively, "It's - it's hard for a girl sometimes, you know." Her words made him feel uncomfortable even though he was not totally certain what they meant. He evaded replying by feigning exaggerated care in avoiding a lamppost with his bicycle. "I'd still like to be friends, Terry," Norah resumed, then hesitated. "I don't know about you though." She sank her pride a little lower. "Perhaps you don't want to be friends with me."

They stopped and waited for a dimmed-out bus to go by before crossing a main road. They reached the opposite pavement, started to speak simultaneously, then both broke off.

"Sorry," said Norah. "Go on, Terry."

"No, you go on."

"Well, I suppose it's not my place to say it, but - it's that girl, isn't it? That singer. She's really the reason you went off me, isn't she?"

"Who told you about her?" asked Terry petulantly.

"Your Dad."

"My Dad ought to mind his own flaming business."

"He's only thinking about your good."

Terry grunted and resumed wheeling his bicycle at a faster pace, leaving Norah to catch up as best she could. After a while she spoke again, seeking words to mollify him.

"I suppose she's very glamorous." No answer. "It must be wonderful being in the show with her and everything." Still he said nothing. Resentment snapped the bonds of self-control, and she burst out, "Terry, your Dad said she's a lot older than you are. Too old."

Terry stopped walking and rounded on her fiercely. "She's not! You keep your nose out of it."

He moved on again so quickly that this time she feared he would mount his bicycle and leave her altogether. She ran after him, plucking at his sleeve.

"I'm sorry, Terry. Please stay with me. I'm sorry."

He slowed down. They were on a side road again now. With no traffic at all the silence seemed deafening. After a strained interval Terry spoke.

"Anyway, she's gone away now. Weeks ago."

"You mean for good?"

"Yes. Didn't my Dad tell you that?"

"He did say he thought she'd been posted."

"Yes, well she has, and I don't know where. She's gone for good all right." He added bitterly, "So you and Dad don't have to talk behind my back any more."

"I'm sorry, Terry. Truly I am. I'm sorry you're unhappy."

"It's my funeral," he returned ungraciously.

"I'd make it up to you if I could," ventured Norah, ignoring the snub. She hesitated. "I was thinking: perhaps you'd like to go dancing again? To the Tower perhaps?" She waited. "I haven't been there since that last time with you." Again no response. "I did like it, Terry." She lowered her voice and determined her fate for the rest of her life. "And afterwards too."

"My Dad stopped my pocket-money," grunted Terry, hedging to the last.

"I've got enough," offered Norah eagerly. "We could go tomorrow if you like ... "

The homegoing queues at the tram and bus stops on the Promenade outside the Tower were immensely long as usual but orderly and good-humoured, even high-spirited - also as usual, for everyone was accustomed to long waits for public transport. A whiff of spring was in the air, and since the "balmy Blackpool breezes" were not in evidence, it was not particularly cold.

A tram trundled ponderously to a halt and the crowd surged forward, bearing Terry and Norah with them. The folding doors opened and the conductor stationed himself defensively on the step.

"Gently now," he warned stridently. "Don't all rush or nobody's getting on."

He allowed two couples through, then Terry and Norah attempted to board. He raised a strict hand. "One only."

"We're together," protested Terry.

"Can't help that. One only!"

"Oh please!" Norah pleaded, but the conductor, one finger poised magisterially on the bell, was not to be moved.

"I don't make the regulations. One more standing! Who's it to be? I haven't got all night."

"You go," said Terry, but Norah had already turned away, and he followed her.

"All right, one more standing and be quick about it!" bawled the conductor, and rang three bells as a lone soldier swung himself aboard.

"That's that then: there won't be another," said Norah ruefully as the tram was swallowed up in the gloom. Most others in the queue seemed to share this opinion and were slowly dispersing. "Should we try for the bus?"

"We wouldn't have a hope. There's a queue a mile long now," said Terry.

"We'll have to walk then."

"Yes," said Terry, then after a pause: "If we've got to walk anyway we could go up to Talbot Square first. Let's go to Yates's."

"Yates's?" repeated Norah incredulously. "Yates's Wine Lodge? Why? What for?"

"A quick one. Before we go home."

"Oh Terry!" Norah was dismayed.

"Why not?"

"Terry, it's a pub. We're both under age."

Terry put on a swagger. "So what? They'll never ask."

"You haven't really started drinking, have you?"

Torn between prosaic truth and the show of bravado to which he seemed to have committed himself, Terry did not reply directly. "Nothing wrong with the odd half now and then," he said. "Helps you to wind down."

In point of fact he scarcely knew what an "odd half" was: he was quoting more or less verbatim from an accordeon-player on the show, a rookie airman whom he had accompanied to Yates's after rehearsal a week or two before. His companion, little older or more sophisticated than Terry himself, came from Bradford and was evidently preparing himself for the adult role of the blunt Yorkshireman who knows his ale. He had drunk - less effortlessly than he let appear - a pint of what he had called "wallop" to the accompaniment of lip-smacking exclamations of "By the 'eck, but that's t'stooff to put a bit o' lead in yer pencil," while Terry, after anxious enquiry and negotiation, had cautiously accepted a half-pint of shandy so weak as to be virtually indistinguishable from lemonade.

Norah having yielded to Terry's persuasion, they walked to Talbot Square in silence, passed the Town Hall and crossed over to Yates's. Norah's footsteps were palpably dragging, and a few yards from the entrance halted altogether.

"What's the matter?" asked Terry impatiently.

"Oh, I don't know." Norah quavered, fearing Terry's reaction if she expressed her misgivings again. A few stragglers emerging from the arcade gave her inspiration. "Terry, isn't the Tivoli entrance in here?"

"What about it?"

"Well, let's just walk through and see what's on."

"Why? It'll be closed. Second house must have finished."

"We can just look at what's on. If it's a good picture we might want to see it later in the week."

"How'll we do that?" Terry objected. "You said you couldn't go out again this week."

"It'll only take a second," Norah pleaded weakly. The subterfuge was pathetic. Terry sighed exasperatedly, but Norah clutched his arm. "Please, Terry."

He decided to humour her. They walked through the short arcade and saw that the Tivoli billboard advertised a routine Western. Turning left into the darkness at the arcade's other end, they bumped into a stout figure in Salvation Army uniform who turned out to be Vera Braithwaite, wife of the Salvation Army bandmaster and a gossipy old soul more inclined to ask questions than listen to answers.

"Well I never! What are you two doing here? We've not seen much of you at t'Citadel lately, young Terry: where've you been? Were you coming up to t'Red Shield? We could just do with someone like you giving a hand now and then. A bit late to do anything tonight, though: I'm just off home myself. P'raps you'll be coming up another time, then ... ?"

As she chuntered on Terry remembered. Never having visited the Red Shield Club, a Forces canteen operated by the Salvation Army, he had overlooked the fact that it was housed above the ground-floor bar of Yates's Wine Lodge, a location consistent with the sturdy Salvationist view that a good way of getting God's word to sinners was to take it to places where sinners were to be found. Lucky nobody had been around the bar selling the "War Cry" the other night when he'd been there with his accordeon-playing friend: then there'd have been trouble!

He had second thoughts. Trouble? What trouble? They're only the Sally Ann, not the police! I'm out of the band. For that matter I'm as good as out of the Sally Ann altogether. And I don't care what old Ma Braithwaite says to my Dad: I'm not afraid of him. Still, there was Norah to think of after all. She was palpably nervous. They had to get out of this.

"Sorry, Mrs Braithwaite," he interrupted. "We have to try and get our tram. We may have missed it already." He knew she lived over towards Whitegate Drive so would hardly suggest accompanying them.

"Oh yes. Aye. Well, goodnight then." Vera let them go but was slow to move herself. There was no alternative but to make off in the direction from which they had come.

More determined than ever on an "odd half", if only to save face, Terry steered Norah back to Bank Hey Street, whence despite the double doors of the light trap a muffled roar of conversation and song betrayed to the now infrequent passers-by the location of the Grey Goose, a pub of some notoriety and universally nicknamed the "Randy Gander".

Terry secretly shared Norah's trepidation as they entered, for there was one fact he had not mentioned to her. According to current legend among his fellow sixth-formers, the Grey Goose was the resort of "hoo-ers" in search of trade. Terry had not to his knowledge ever seen a "hoo-er", nor would he have recognised the word "whore" as the correct spelling. What did "hoo-ers" look like? He had no idea. What did they do? How many of them would there be? Did they really, as his school friends insisted, wear gold bracelets round their ankles to signal their availability? If not, how did they find customers? Did they come up and ask you? If they asked him, what would he do? Or did they wait for you to ask them? Suppose someone asked Norah by mistake ... ?

Inside the vast spit-and-sawdust bar a kind of ordered pandemonium prevailed. Every chair at the round marble-topped tables was occupied, every square inch of the oak settles likewise. At many points, indeed, the press of bodies was double-layered where girls perched precariously on their boyfriends' laps. Such gaps as existed between the tightly-packed tables were jammed with standing customers. A near-impenetrable scrum six or seven deep lined the brass rail at the polished bar-counter. Waitresses gave as good as they got in badinage while carving swift pathways through the tumult, overladen trays held high, never pausing, never spilling a drop. The reek of beer was overpowering, the din deafening. Over all hung a swirling blue fog of tobacco smoke.

Virtually all the male customers and probably half the females were in uniform, Air Force blue predominating. No one here seemed to care a toss about last trams and buses, though they would certainly have to be off the streets and in their billets somehow before lights out. Rival groups of patrons were singing coarse versions of "The Quartermaster's Stores", "I've Got Sixpence" and "She'll Be Coming Round the Mountain". A circle of Americans, in well-cut uniforms that made them look like officers, gave forth in barber-shop style with "Wait Till the Sun Shines, Nellie". When the song ended they dispensed Luckies and Camels to all and sundry, peeled pound notes from fat bankrolls and ordered gin-and-limes for faithless girls who knew the British boys could only afford beer.

In a corner near the door sat two raddled-looking women in late middle age, one fat, one skinny, but both with stringy peroxided hair, garish pancake makeup and a superfluity of Woolworth's bangles and beads. They seemed to be taking a motherly interest in the plight of a pair of helplessly drunk Canadian sergeants to whom they were offering beds for the night. With a shock Terry suddenly understood that it was not altruism that actuated their concern.

Was this the reality, then, behind the jaunty would-be-man-of-the-world sniggerings of his schoolfellows? Was this what you did when you "bought a bit of tail"? Could these two repulsive, pathetic old hags be "hoo-ers"? He glanced swiftly around, identified others like them, realised it was so.

Now he scrutinised the scene with new and critical eyes. This must be the "good time", much extolled by his schoolmates but rarely described in specific terms, which you were supposed to have in pubs. If so, it was not for him. Not here or in any other pub.

Nor, for that matter, in any other place of mass entertainment, not even the Tower, Winter Gardens or Palace, he thought, realising with a flash of insight why he was indifferent to dancing though he loved the music. His distaste had nothing to do with "hoo-ers": it came from inside himself, from his inability to forget himself, lose himself in the crowd, let himself go as others let themselves go.

For he was an entertainer. His role was not to receive pleasure but to generate it. He could give himself to the crowd without stint, but he would not, could not, be one of them.

"Terry?" Norah called him plaintively back to the present.

"Sorry, Norah, I was thinking," he muttered. To pretend enthusiasm was difficult. "What'll you have?"

She plucked his sleeve. "I don't like this, Terry," she said in a low voice. "I don't want anything. I'm sorry."

Terry felt a surge of relief but still gathered himself to put on a show of scorn at her faintheartedness. A sudden stentorian cry of "Last orders, please!" from behind the bar spared him the necessity. He clicked his teeth in feigned annoyance. "It's too late: we'll never get served now anyway," he said. "All right, we won't bother."

Norah clung gratefully to Terry as they made their way to the Promenade for the walk home. That they were by no means alone was attested by the snatches of laughter and conversation emanating from shadowy figures in the murk, by the glow of cigarette-ends and the occasional flash of a dimmed-out hand torch. One high-spirited group a dozen or so strong was making slow but strenuous homeward progress by performing the Palais Glide to the tune of "Poor Little Angeline". Another danced and sang the Hokey-Cokey by the railings overlooking the beach. An empty tram bound for the depot hooted a warning to a party of hopefuls standing at a stop. Their catcalls and jeers as it raced past at full speed were perfunctory, such annoyances being the familiar small change of wartime inconvenience.

By the lifeboat house at Central Pier, some couples sat on the steps leading to the beach, talking, smoking, "snogging". Others threaded their way purposefully downwards.

"Tide's out," remarked Terry with affected nonchalance.

Norah glanced at him sharply but said nothing.

He went on. "We could walk along the sands."

"Terry, no!"

He halted and faced her."Why not?" he challenged.

"I don't think we should, that's all."

"Plenty of other people doing it."

"That's not all they're doing."

"Oh? What else are they doing then?"

"You know very well," Norah retorted. She pulled at his arm, trying to make him walk on, but he held back.

"Well, you said you liked going dancing with me."

"Yes, I do."

"And afterwards too. You did say that, didn't you?"

Norah looked away and was silent.

"Go on," he persisted. "Be honest."

Her whispered "Yes" was barely audible.

"Well then?" He paused. "Oh come on, Norah, just five minutes."

"No, Terry, I shouldn't." Her voice was apprehensive, but "shouldn't" is not the same as "won't" and Terry knew it.

"Come on," he wheedled, and took her hand.

Norah's footsteps dragged as they reached the steps. "Just five minutes then. But you're not to try to - you know."

The pace of the couples strolling on the beach was slow, their conversation hushed. In the black shadows under the pier there was barely any conversation at all. Dim pairs of swaying figures leaned against the great iron pillars. Other couples half-sat against the lower sea-wall or lay on the sand, defying the dampness, clearly at the more advanced stages of "snogging".

After a few moments of indecision, Terry took off his raincoat and spread it on a vacant patch. "There you are," he said.

"Oh Terry!" Norah's voice was small and frightened.

"Come on. It's all right." They both knew the reassurance was meaningless. Terry pulled her swiftly down beside him. With the confidence learnt in a night from Kitty, he began unbuttoning Norah's coat. She was trembling.

"Oh Terry!" she pleaded after a time. "You won't ever tell anyone I let you do this, will you? Promise me."

13
OUR LOVE AFFAIR

Terry had selected the shop with care. It was on a quiet thoroughfare in the Caunce Street district, not far from where a stray German aircraft had dropped Blackpool's only bombs of the war during the Liverpool blitz of May 1941. The only other shops nearby were a tobaccanist and newsagent next door and a small general store on the opposite corner. Pedestrians and wheeled vehicles were few and far between, and above all the street was sufficiently distant both from Terry's home and from his school for there to be little risk of his being recognised. He had, of course, taken the precaution of discarding his school blazer and tie in favour of an open-necked shirt and nondescript sports jacket.

The sign above the shop front bore the legend "J. Wright & Co. - Surgical Appliances". The window display was meagre but somewhat startling, not to say macabre. The two central items consisted of a rupture truss of intricate design and an artificial leg complete with hinged foot. Accompanying advertising placards cited a wealth of "unsolicited testimonials", each outdoing the other in expressions of gratitude for the comfort which these devices afforded their wearers. The remaining offerings for the enlightenment of window-shoppers were more modest: a faded copy of "Health & Efficiency" magazine featuring a cover-picture of a nude young lady decorously posed in a sylvan setting; another, almost identical, of "The Naturist"; a few boxes of anal suppositories; a discreet notice saying "Rubber Goods" - along with a small-print admonition to the effect that customers under 18 would not be served. A sheet of roughly varnished plywood behind the display blocked any view of the interior through the window. A permanently-open front door facilitated rapid ingress and egress. Another plywood screen just inside the doorway ensured the discreet transaction of business.

Terry's intention of entering the shop, had anyone been interested in observing his movements, would have been obvious from the furtiveness with which he lurked outside it and the number of false starts he made. Several times the street filled magically with pedestrians and cyclists just as he was about to take the plunge.

Slowly remustering his courage as the street emptied, he would be on the point of another foray when further potential witnesses to his shame appeared from nowhere, bringing him to a blushing standstill again.

He feigned interest in the newsagent's window-display next door, tried to appear lost in thought, walked past the shop purposefully then struck his forehead with his palm and reversed his footsteps as though having forgotten something, peered into the gutter searching for non-existent lost coins. Any plausibility these devices might have possessed had long been exhausted by the time opportunity and courage at last presented themselves simultaneously, and he dashed headlong through the doorway.

The interior of the shop was as dusty, threadbare and unlovely as the window display. A notice on the counter repeated the warning about customers' ages. Adjacent to it were stacks of "Health & Efficiency" and "The Naturist". Another notice, smudgily handwritten and badly spelt, invited connoisseurs of Parisian art to enquire of the proprietor. A run of unpainted deal shelving along the wall behind the counter was sparsely occupied by a miscellany of bottles, jars and boxes containing various brands of hair restorer, ointments for piles and acne, cures for corns and bunions, purgatives, enemas, ear syringes - and "rubber goods".

Presiding over this squalor was an oldish unshaven man in a greasy suit and filthy collarless shirt. He was seated on a broken kitchen chair behind the counter, warming himself at an inadequate gasfire. A wisp of smoke trickled unendingly up his blackhead-ridden nose from a drooping Woodbine. The News Chronicle in his hand was folded back at the racing page. He glanced up as Terry entered, appraised him cynically and sipped noisily from a chipped enamel mug of tea.

"Yes, young fella," he vociferated in a kind of emphatic wheeze that probably had more to do with the saucerful of expired gaspers on the counter than with actual conspiratorial intent. Nevertheless it did nothing to make Terry feel comfortable. "And 'ow can I be of service to you?"

Unable to meet the man's eyes, Terry took refuge in examining his shoes. "I - er - " he mumbled, and dried up.

"'Ealth & Efficiency', latest edition? 'Naturist'?" suggested his inquisitor, indicating the two heaps.

"No - er - "

"Art studies down 'ere." The old man fished about under the

counter and brought up a handful of grubby brown envelopes. "Good these. 'Andy for swops an' all - "

"No, those," said Terry desperately and pointed to the "rubber goods" on the shelves.

"Wot, all of 'em?" The shopman's mouth opened in a parody of a grin, displaying a set of brown and broken teeth. His salacious chuckle turned into a spasm of coughing. When it had subsided he wiped his mouth with the back of his hand. "Right then, what kind d'you like?" He reached one of the packets down. "There's these - "

"They'll do," said Terry quickly.

The man put the packet on the counter.

"'Alf a dollar," he said, and kept his finger on it.

"Two and sixpence?"

The man leered. ""Three in there. Anyway, you want the best you 'ave ter pay."

"Could I buy one?" asked Terry, his face burning but conscious of the constraints imposed by lack of pocket-money and the reckless spending of his scanty earnings on theatre tickets.

"Can't break a packet." The man put it back on the shelf. "Can't let customers think they've been interfered with, can I? Too much at stake for that." He leered again and brought down another packet. "There's these. Three for one an' nine."

"All right."

"Not as good, mind. Rougher, like, know what I mean?" The man paused, letting it sink in, his expression mocking Terry's embarrassment.

"They'll do," mumbled Terry, and made to take the packet, fearful that some other customer might enter the shop and see it. It did not occur to him that any such other customer might well be as nervous and shamefaced as himself.

The man flattened his hand over the packet. "One and ninepence then." He waited ostentatiously as Terry put down a shilling and a sixpence. "'Nother thrippence." Terry reached again into his pocket and found a penny and four halfpennies. The man counted them carefully before handing over the packet. "Over eighteen, are yer?"

"Er, yes," replied Terry. Well, he wasn't that far off. Surely he would not have to hand the package back now?

The man grinned sardonically. "An' little pigs 'as wings."

"Pardon?" asked Terry in confusion.

"Granted." Tiring of the game, the shopman thrust the money in his pocket, yawned mightily and picked up his News Chronicle again. Then he resumed his seat, slurped another mouthful of tea and called after the fleeing Terry, "Do call again. A satisfied customer is our best recommendation."

It was a warm, sunny Saturday afternoon some weeks later, and the ATC band in full uniform made a brave show in the quadrangle of the school. The school buildings themselves, built of bright red Accrington brick in the solidly self-confident Edwardian style, formed a dignified backdrop to the drill evolutions which the band performed under Terry's leadership while blowing the bugle-march "All For a Shilling a Day". A fair number of passers-by paused to watch, and their half-patronising smiles turned quickly to genuine appreciation as they observed the high standard of drill and music which Terry extracted from his charges.

Terry had shot up considerably in stature during the last few months, but he was still far from being the tallest or oldest-looking cadet. Nevertheless in his cadet sergeant's uniform with bandmaster's sash and mace he was certainly the smartest and most imposing figure, his uniform immaculate, his marching and handling of the mace imbued with all the swagger of a Guards sergeant-major.

Perhaps most of all, though, what made him an impressive figure was his sheer self-assurance - a quality as conspicuously present in his public performances as it still was absent in the ordinary transactions of daily life.

Terry gave a quick sidelong glance at the scattering of casual spectators ranged along the low quadrangle wall, their view unobstructed by the former iron railings that had long since been ripped out and melted down to make guns and tanks.

All right, if they wanted to watch, let them watch. Quickly he revised his intended line of march, solving instinctively an equation involving distances, bars of music and numbers of paces. He led the band to a halt a couple of yards short of the wall, brought the music to an end with a flourish and was about to execute an about-turn in order to address his charges when, to his surprise, a ragged burst of clapping broke out from the dozen or so spectators. Thinking fast, he froze his action before it had started, then waited as Kitty Norton and Richard Royle had taught him to do, milking the maximum applause while careful not to let it dwindle into total silence before his next movement.

It's not much, this bugle band, he thought, but it's something, and it's mine! I got that applause for them, and from people who aren't even a proper audience; they'd never have got it without me! I've made them into something they couldn't have been on their own! I can do it, I can do it: I can run a band!

The adrenalin surged. To do this was to be a god.

He about-turned crisply and faced the band sternly, checking position, posture, alertness and - above all - total immobility and silence. Satisfied, he addressed them in the formal no-nonsense manner to which he had accustomed them.

"A good rehearsal. Look like that tomorrow, march like that tomorrow, and above all play like that tomorrow, and we'll have a pretty good church parade. One small point: Blenkinsop, there's something wrong with the height of your drum. Stand fast when we dismiss and I'll help you to adjust it. Now everybody just remember tomorrow: people don't take the ATC seriously because they know we aren't real Air Force. So the band's job is to make them listen and look. If we do it properly they'll be impressed, and then they *will* take the ATC seriously. That's how important we are. Ten o'clock tomorrow morning then, buttons and bugles polished, uniforms pressed. Dismiss smartly now, wait for it!" He raised his voice to a bellow. "Ba-a-and!" He paused. "To the right, di-i-is - miss!"

The cadets right inclined, paused, broke formation and headed for the band hut. The youth Blenkinsop remained behind, looking slightly sheepish.

"Ah, Blenkinsop," said Terry, "let's get this fixed - "

He broke off. Norah was entering the quadrangle from the street. He frowned and addressed Blenkinsop again. "Just a minute. I'm sorry, Blenkinsop, I'll see you in the band hut later. Dismiss just now."

Blenkinsop made off and Terry waited silently. Norah seemed pale and tense.

"Hello, Terry," she said.

"Hello, Norah."

"Terry, I've got to talk to you." Her voice was strained.

"Yes? What about?"

"Can't we go over there?" She pointed away from the band hut to a more secluded corner of the quadrangle and began walking towards it while Terry followed. But before they reached it Norah looked around quickly to see there was no one within earshot, then blurted out, "Oh Terry, it's awful! I've got to tell you. I'm - I'm going to have a baby."

Terry stopped in mid-stride, stunned and disbelieving.

"You're not," he said stupidly.

She faced him, grasped his wrist and shook it. "I am, Terry, I am. I'm going to have a baby."

"You can't." Still his mind refused to take it in.

"What do you mean, I can't? Of course I can, Terry! I'm going to."

The enormity of it, the impossibility of it, most of all the appalling, rotten unfairness of it, began to hit him.

"How do you know?" he asked. "I mean are you sure?"

"Yes." She said it slowly. "I'm sure."

"Really sure?"

Such pigheaded gormlessness! Norah, near tears, threaded her voice down to a note of quiet certitude. "Terry, I wasn't sure at first: that's why I didn't say anything. But now I'm sure. Completely and absolutely. I'm going to have a baby."

Why did she have to keep saying it over and over? Surely it wasn't final, was it? There must be something that could be done? Anyway something already had been done. "But we've been - careful," objected Terry. "You know, those - things."

"Not the first time, Terry, not the first time!" she cried distractedly. "It must have been then. What are we going to do?"

Still he tried to hedge, as though procrastination could will it all away. Again he said, like an incantation: "But you can't - "

"Don't keep saying that, Terry! I can. I can. I'm" - she hesitated before the fearsome word, the fateful word she had never before uttered - "pregnant. What are we going to do?" A tear started at the corner of her eye.

Terry glanced round nervously. What if somebody should see them, hear them?

"I dunno," he muttered feebly. The cadets, having discarded their instruments and equipment, were re-emerging from the band hut and straggling in ones and twos to the gate. Only Blenkinsop hung back, looking towards Terry and Norah, wondering. Terry grasped at the straw. "Look, Norah, that cadet's waiting for me. I have to talk to him."

"Terry, you have to talk to *me*: this is serious! You've got to help me." She grasped both his wrists this time.

He tried to pull away. "We'll have to think about it. You might be mistaken - "

"I'm not mistaken," said Norah with quiet finality. "I know." She pleaded simply. "Help me, Terry."

He stood dumb, ox-like, motionless. Norah searched his face with

126

her eyes and read there the terrible truth. "You don't want to help me, do you?" she whispered.

"Perhaps you can do something about it. I've heard about that." His words were a mockery of hope. "There are ways you can stop it."

Norah recoiled. "No!" she exclaimed. "No, never! I'd never do that, even if I could."

He held his body rigid, tightening his muscles, trying to shrink inside himself. His mind thrashed wildly around its cage, seeking escape. Deadly words formed on his lips and like a stranger he heard them.

"You're sure it's me?"

It was as though he had struck her. "What?" she gasped. She swallowed, then challenged him with massive dignity. "Will you say that again, Terry?"

Suddenly aware of the weight of the mace he was still holding, Terry looked about him, wondering vaguely where he could put it down. He could not speak, but Norah persisted.

"Just say it again. If you dare."

"I didn't mean ... " Terry's voice tailed off and he licked his lips. Of course he hadn't meant it, hadn't intended to say it even; it had just come out. But how to explain?

"Yes, you did," retorted Norah. "Oh yes you did."

Her gaze withered him and he dropped his eyes. What difference did it make anyway whether he meant it or not? It was all a mess, a swindle, a trap.

She was weeping now, and through shuddering sobs she voiced her condemnation. "I hate you at times, Terry Cullerton. I really do. This time I think I'll never stop hating you." She turned on her heel to walk away, thought better of it and swung round again, brushing away the tears with a fierce gesture. "You know," she said quietly, "it's a pity I didn't realise sooner how much I hate you, because now you're going to be the father of my baby, and I wish it was someone else instead of you. Absolutely anyone."

Her eyes bored into his for an eternity. He flinched and looked away. Then Norah bit her lips and turned on her heel again. Her swift walk and erect carriage as she disappeared from his life expressed a pride, and a contempt, that Terry was unable to forget for the rest of his days.

He did try, though.

14
WISH ME LUCK AS YOU WAVE ME GOODBYE

When Harold Cullerton reported his son's disappearance, the police were sympathetic and quite encouraging.

"He's very likely joined up," said the desk sergeant, "and if he has, it won't take long to trace him."

"But he's under age," said Harold.

"He's over seventeen and a half," pointed out the sergeant. "They can volunteer at that age with their parents' consent."

"But I haven't given - "

"Quite so, sir, but between you and me the Forces don't always check the consents as carefully as they might. Your boy wouldn't be the first to forge his dad's signature. Now, you say he was a member of the Air Training Corps?"

"Yes."

"Very well, then, we'll start with the Raf. If he's there you'll be hearing from us quite quickly, I shouldn't wonder."

Three days later Harold took a day off work and made a tedious train-journey to Warrington. A draughty, rattling bus then carried him to RAF Padgate. This turned out to be a dreary wilderness of tin-roofed huts, drill squares and barbed-wire fences, where contemptuous barking NCOs received shambling streams of pasty-faced bewildered civilians, assured them that they were not, and could never become, worthy of wearing the King's uniform, then bustled them through the week of marching, medical examinations, form-filling and kit-issuing that began the process of making them exactly that.

A sergeant escorted Harold from the guardroom to a arab office in one of the huts, where a grizzled flight lieutenant wearing the "Mutt and Jeff" ribbons of the previous war received him. They exchanged formal greetings, then the flight lieutenant waved Harold to the shabby visitor's armchair and seated himself behind the desk.

"I've been informed about your coming, of course," said the officer. "Before I send for your son might I just ask what you've decided to do?"

Harold shook his head. "You can ask but I can't tell you. Before I say anything about that I want to talk to him. That's why I'm here."

"You're very wise, Mr Cullerton."

"In private."

"Of course. You can use this office."

"Has he been told I'm coming?"

The officer looked at the sergeant questioningly.

"No sir," replied the sergeant.

"Then don't tell him, please."

"Right, sir," said the sergeant.

"Very well, then, Mr Cullerton," said the officer. "Shall I send for him now?"

"I think that'd be best," said Harold. The officer nodded to the sergeant, who saluted and disappeared through the door.

Harold felt a need to explain. "I don't want him to have time to think up a lot of clever things to say. It'll only start a row." He paused. "Between you and me we haven't got along too well lately. I suppose that's why he ran away and joined up."

"I understand, Mr Cullerton," said the flight lieutenant. "You don't have to tell me any - well, private business. I will just ask, though, that when he comes in you let me speak first. He's still under Air Force discipline, you see."

"Oh aye, that's all right," said Harold, and the conversation dwindled to desultory small talk and then died.

Harold glanced round the room. Its claim to the title of "office" rested on little more than a desk, two or three chairs, an ancient typewriter, a telephone, a filing cabinet and a shelf of service manuals. A forlorn attempt had been made to brighten the walls with a framed photograph of the King and a couple of aircraft recognition posters. The latter seemed out of place: it was inconceivable that anything happening in these surroundings could be connected with the flying of aeroplanes or the training of young men to kill each other with all the bloody efficiency of modern science.

After a few minutes there was a loud double-knock on the door. The flight lieutenant glanced at Harold.

"Come in!" he called, and the door swung wide at once.

Terry stood framed in the opening, stiffly at attention in his ill-fitting light-blue "hairy". He caught sight of his father and started, then returned his eyes to his front while the disembodied voice of the sergeant bawled from the corridor: "Recruit Cullerton, T, reporting for interview as ordered, sah! Smartly now, lad - three paces forward - march! - salute!"

As Terry obeyed, the sergeant appeared briefly in the doorway, saluted, screeched "Sah!", and closed the door from the outside. The flight lieutenant regarded Terry sternly for some seconds before he spoke.

"Now, Cullerton, listen carefully," he said. "You must know why I've sent for you. You've joined the Air Force under false pretences, because you're under eighteen years of age and you didn't have your father's consent. You've caused a lot of trouble for your father, for the police, and for me. Do you understand what I'm saying?"

"Yes, sir," replied Terry, addressing the air some inches above the officer's head.

The flight lieutenant's manner relaxed as he resumed. "On the other hand you've been a satisfactory recruit in the few days you've been here. Now, your father's entitled to take you home if he wants to and that will be the end of the matter: you'll be discharged. Or if he gives his consent now, you can stay with us. Your father has had all this explained to him, and he wants to discuss the situation with you before he decides what to do. Is that clear?"

"Sir," responded Terry, still immobile.

"Right," said the officer, "then I'll leave you both in here to talk on your own. Take your time, Mr Cullerton: I've plenty of work to do elsewhere. But you might bear in mind that even if your son goes home with you now, he'll still be called up on his eighteenth birthday and then he may not get the choice of service that he wants. As things are, he's chosen aircrew and that's what he's been put down for. The sergeant's outside in the next room: tell him what you've decided and he'll send for me."

He got up from the desk and made for the door.

Terry licked his lips nervously. "Sir?" he said.

The flight lieutenant paused, his hand on the doorknob.

"Yes, Cullerton?"

"I thought the Air Force wasn't supposed to tell anyone where I was, sir? Not without my permission."

The officer frowned. "Hm. Who told you that?"

"Someone I knew in the Raf, sir," said Terry. "That's what gave me the idea. I didn't want anyone to find me."

"Hm. I'm afraid you were misinformed. That might apply to girlfriends, creditors, people like that. Your own father, when you're under age - that's a different matter." The flight lieutenant removed his hand from the doorknob, regarded Terry in kindly fashion and said, "Look, Cullerton, turn this way and stand easy." Terry complied and the officer continued. "Now I've no wish to pry into your personal affairs, but here's a tip. Your father's come a long way to see you. Talk to him. If he decides to take you home with him you'll have to talk to him. On the other hand if he lets you stay here - well, it's best to be on good terms with your Dad if you're going off to war: you'll both feel better that way."

"Sir!" was all Terry's response as he snapped to attention.

The flight lieutenant regarded him searchingly, opened his mouth as though about to say more, then evidently thought better of it.

"Right, carry on," he said.

Terry saluted as the officer departed and closed the door behind him. Then he remained at rigid attention, staring straight ahead of him. There was a long silence.

"Going to be like that, is it?" growled Harold. "Well, suit yourself. You're coming home wi' me."

Terry set his jaw. "I won't."

"You have to if I say so. You heard what yon officer said."

"I'll run away again."

"Don't talk daft. T'police'll find you."

"I don't care. I'll do it."

"And what about Norah?" Harold asked. "What about her condition?"

Terry deflated instantly. "Oh," he said. "You know."

"Of course I know, you daft ha'porth. How long did you think you could keep that a secret? After all I've done to bring you up decent ... well, I've promised her Mum and Dad she'll be made an honest girl of right quick - "

"No!" exclaimed Terry. His father knitted his brows incredulously. "What did you say?"

It came out in a rush. "I said no. I mean it. I won't marry her," said Terry fiercely. "You can't make me and I won't do it."

This was more than Harold had bargained for. To get a girl into trouble was bad enough, but then to refuse to do the decent thing - it was unthinkable. Yet along with outrage came swift realisation that this was another battle he could lose.

"And why not, pray?"

"I'm too young."

"Oh aye, you're too young, I'll grant you," agreed Harold sarcastically. "But you should have thought of that before you did what you did to that poor girl."

Terry's riposte was brutally to the point. "I didn't do it *to* her. I did it *with* her. She helped me."

Harold rose to his feet in fury. "I won't listen to that kind of filthy talk, Terry Cullerton - "

But Terry had beaten his father before and instinct told him his future depended on beating him again. "And I don't love her," he said determinedly.

"Then you'd no right putting her in t'family way," retorted his father. "Love! You don't know t'meaning o' t'word, so forget it. You've a responsibility now. You're coming home wi' me an' I shall see you carry it out. You'll bear t'shame as best you can. I'll pray to the Lord to forgive you, and 'appen 'E will in time - if you do what's right."

"I won't marry her," insisted Terry. "I don't want - "

"Don't you tell me what you want and don't want!" cried Harold. "You wanted young Norah's body and you took it. Now this mess is where your wanting's got you. It's not your wants we're on about now: it's your duty. Duty to Norah. Duty to your unborn child. Duty to the Lord."

Harold was on familiar ground again. It was a kind of comfort.

"I just made one mistake - " Terry began, but Harold interrupted him.

"A mistake, you call it?" he scoffed. "It was a sin. You fornicated. You knew it was fornication." To Terry he seemed to be savouring the ugliness of the word. "Fornication's a sin. If we sin we pay for it."

"Jesus Christ paid for our sins on the Cross," said Terry defiantly. "He's supposed to have taken them all on Himself, isn't He? But you're telling me I have to pay just the same."

"Don't you try to teach me theology, young man," snapped Harold. He went on confidently. This was a game he could play. "Oh aye, Christ atoned for our sins by His sufferings. But if we want His atonement we have to repent first, and repentance isn't easy. Paying for what you've done is the first step, and only the first - "

"What if I don't want atonement?" interrupted Terry.

"Don't try to shock me," Harold said wearily. "It won't wash. I'll see to it you atone whether you like it or not. You'll do right by Norah - "

"I told you I don't love Norah," persisted Terry. "I love somebody else."

Harold reddened with fury. "Will you stop all this claptrap about who you love and who you don't love? Don't you see it doesn't matter tuppence after what you've done? Somebody else indeed! Don't think I haven't a good idea who that is, filling your head with notions beyond your age."

It was Terry's turn to be angry. "You leave her out of this!" he gritted.

"It was you that brought her into it," Harold reminded him. "Any road you've no choice now - "

"I have, I have! I can choose whether I'll marry Norah or not. And I won't. You can't make me. I don't care what you do. I'll never marry her, never, never, never."

Harold glared silently at his son, then went over to the window and looked out. Barrack huts, marching men, a milling crowd around a NAAFI tea-wagon: no inspiration there. He turned his gaze back to Terry. His son's stare remained resolute, unblinking. He would have to make the best of a bad job, he realised at last. He seated himself behind the desk and gestured towards the visitor's chair.

"Sit down, Terry," he said.

Terry did not move. "I'd rather stand."

"Suit yourself," Harold grunted. He tapped his fingers on the desk, pondering. "All right then, Terry, I can't make you marry Norah," he said. "But you'll do right by her just t'same. We'll make a bargain." He looked up expectantly. There was no response. "You'll sign a paper, a proper legal paper, saying you're responsible for Norah's baby. Then when it's born you'll pay maintenance. If you do that you can stay here in t'Raf. If you don't I'll have you home in quick sticks and you'll face the world as best you can. And when Norah has you up in court I'll take her side, not yours."

Terry's thoughts raced. He'd won! Sign a paper? Of course he'd sign a paper if that was all he had to do, he'd sign anything, so what? If they forced you to sign things, made you agree to things by threatening you, you didn't have to keep your side of it, did you, why should you? He'd won! He was in control, he'd do what he wanted, not what other people wanted. He'd determine his own destiny. He'd show them!

He put on no more than a slight pretence of deliberating before saying, "All right, Dad, I'll do it."

Then he considered further. Was there anything more to say? Yes, there was! He'd stuck the knife in once before during this kind of conversation: it'd be just as well to do it again. Besides there was a bitterness in him that made him want to hurt - to hurt and hurt until the breach was total, irrevocable.

"But you'll have to listen to this," he went on slowly, articulating each word with care. "I've finished with religion. I've finished with the Salvation Army. I've finished with God. As far as I'm concerned it's all rubbish. And just remember this: every time I pay Norah the money it's not because I want to do it, it's because you've made me do it, that's the only reason. It's your atonement and I don't want it. He's your Jesus Christ and I don't want Him redeeming my sins. I want my life - my life - and I want it for myself, not for you, not for Norah and not for Jesus Christ. I want it for me. That's my religion from now on. That's what I believe in."

Harold seemed to shrink lower and lower behind the desk, as though physically stunned. When his son had finished he did not look up but fiddled with a couple of paper-clips on the desk. When he did speak it was not to deliver himself of the tirade which Terry had expected.

"You've made yourself clear, Terry," he said quietly, the gruffness gone from his voice. He rose to his feet and with slow steps went to the door. Then he turned. "You want your life for yourself, do you? What for? With an attitude like you've got, what can you do with your life that will ever be worth anything? Don't bother trying to tell me the answer. Try to tell yourself."

He opened the door and addressed the sergeant. Terry heard his choice of words distinctly.

"As far as I'm concerned you can keep him."

15
A LITTLE ON THE LONELY SIDE

From Terry's first day in the Air Force he had hoped that somehow his and Kitty's paths would cross. Indeed it was not just to run away from Norah that he had joined up: he had also been impelled irresistibly by an urge to do something, anything, to find Kitty. Even at Padgate he had looked for her. When he was posted to Scarborough for recruit training his heart leapt with irrational expectation that because Scarborough too was a seaside resort this somehow made it likely that Kitty would have been posted there from Blackpool. His initial enquiries at the orderly room having produced no result, he spent his first few hours of free time vainly scouring the streets in which the WAAF billets were located. A hatchet-faced WAAF sergeant finally warned him off.

If Kitty were indeed in Scarborough she would doubtless have gravitated towards whatever entertainments went on in the town. Terry therefore did the same. As far as Kitty was concerned he drew a blank, but he did come across three musically-inclined RAF recruits, of much enthusiasm, a little talent and no coordination, striving unsuccessfully to present themselves as a dance band in their spare time. Terry rehearsed them mercilessly for two weeks, then put them on, free of charge and with himself leading, at an impromptu NAAFI dance. When they performed at the sergeants' mess a week later they were paid, for the first time but not the last. Then a sudden posting deprived them of their drummer at a day's notice. Somehow Terry conjured up a replacement and knocked him quickly into shape. At their next gig no one knew the difference.

From then on Terry had found his part-time vocation. At unit after unit throughout his training he spent whatever he had of spare time on the assembling, teaching, disciplining and marketing of dance bands.

And he never stopped searching for Kitty.

All this left little time for feeling guilty about Norah. Terry's education, both at school and at home, had resembled that of all his contemporaries in its lack of straightforward initiation into what were coyly referred to as "the facts of life". Nevertheless he was aware of the concomitant social conventions. Norah would have left school and ceased attending Salvation Army meetings well before anything began to show. Everyone would know of her "condition" just the same, and to avoid the sniggers and tittle-tattle she would spend long lonely days trapped in the house, a prisoner of her disgrace. How she and her parents would face life after the baby came and she could no longer stay indoors was beyond imagining.

This was the point at which, when images of Norah intruded upon him, Terry blotted them from his mind. To acknowledge a duty to her would be to lose everything - his dreams of Kitty, his future career, his music. How could he practise the trumpet - he had now been able to afford one - amidst a forest of drying nappies, sharing a back room in somebody else's house with a soppy whining girl he did not love?

The baby wasn't all his fault, anyway. It was at least fifty per cent Norah's - perhaps more, if the truth were told. Oh yes, she'd acted scared and unwilling that first time, under the pier, but all girls did that, didn't they? And when it came to the point she could have said no but she hadn't, and all the other times after that she'd been eager enough: she hadn't even pretended to resist.

It wasn't as though he'd ever really been keen on her, she must have known that. It was Norah who'd made the running from the very first, Norah who'd sought him out at Sally Ann meetings, Norah who'd wanted to walk to and from school with him, go out with him in the evenings. Look at the way she'd pestered him over the Forces shows! Then as soon as she'd heard Kitty had gone away she'd come chasing after him again, egging him on even though she knew it was Kitty he wanted, not her. Yes, he could see it now. He wouldn't be surprised if she'd even intended him to get her into trouble all along, just so as to catch him.

Well, if that was her game, he was too fly for her - just as he was too fly for his Dad when he went home on his first leave. He arrived on a Saturday morning after a dreary all-night journey with three changes of train and long periods of waiting on windswept platforms. Practically the first thing his Dad did was to tell him to go round and see Norah. He refused, of course. What was the point? He wasn't going to marry her, that was already settled, so there'd only be a row with her parents and all for nothing.

"Aye, well, you're bound to 'ave a bit of a pantomime wi' them any road, an' if you don't like it you'll 'ave to lump it," his Dad had said rashly, forgetting that their relationship had changed. "I told them you'd be coming on leave, and if you're not round there like a dose o' salts, they'll be over here an' raise 'umpy - "

"Stop them," Terry said.

"Eh?" Harold's jaw dropped.

"I said stop them." Terry's voice was flat and determined. "Tell them they can't come here. Do it now. If you don't I'm not staying. I'll go straight back to Scarborough and spend the rest of my leave in my billet."

"You can't do that, lad."

"I can. I will if you let them come here." How easy it was really! All you had to do was tell people straight and they did what you wanted. Even his Dad. Why had he let him boss him about all these years? "Look, Dad, I signed that paper you wanted. I never said I'd do anything else, and I won't. I'm not going to see Norah, and I won't see her mother and father either. You tell them that."

"Be reasonable, Terry, How can I talk to them that way?"

Terry shrugged. "I don't know. But if you don't, I'm going, and you can't stop me."

That was the truth of it. He was independent and free as long as he kept his guard up, refused to submit to the emotional blackmail which was his father's only real weapon. Even the paper he'd signed was just a paper. When Norah had her baby he'd have to start tipping up, true enough. What did they call it?- an allotment or something. Still, he'd afford it easily as a sergeant, especially with flying pay on top. And after the Air Force... well, he'd have to see when the time came just how long they could make him keep it up.

Harold had done as he was told, disappearing without a word and returning three quarters of an hour later looking badly shaken, but all he'd said was, "They're not coming." Then he'd spent the rest of Saturday morning in his easy chair behind his newspaper. Such talk as he and Terry exchanged during the rest of Saturday and Sunday was stilted, coolly polite and punctuated by tense silences. They both carefully avoided raising the one subject that was in the forefront of both their minds.

By Monday morning Terry was longing for the moment when his father would set off for work. But once on his own he felt at a loose end - almost imprisoned like Norah, in fact, for he was reluctant to venture out in case of a chance encounter with her or her parents.

When at last he did stealthily emerge it was with no clear idea of where he would go. He had cut himself off from old Salvation Army friendships, and too many new things had happened in his life for him to feel any affinity with his former schoolmates. As far as the

Forces shows were concerned, Richard Royle had made clear that he was unwelcome save on a strictly professional basis, and his leave was not long enough for the latter to be feasible.

That left the "amusements", a feature of Blackpool life previously forbidden to Terry as a Salvationist and which most local people in any case took a perverse pride in ignoring save as a source of employment. Yet now in the late spring the "amusements" were beginning to open, Terry had nothing else to do, religious qualms no longer restrained him, and his RAF pay, though meagre, represented more money than he had ever had in his pocket before.

Terry turned his footsteps towards the Pleasure Beach, but few people were about and there could be no laughter without others to share it. On the Big Dipper he was the sole passenger. The only car to bump against his at the Dodgem arena was driven by an attendant who took pity on him. The Hall of Mirrors was tawdry and boring without panic-stricken trippers colliding among the plate glass partitions. The glass-encased mechanical dummy writhing and screeching endless peals of recorded laughter outside the Fun House seemed to promise not fun but empty idiocy to the few dispirited pleasure-seekers trying to decide between it and the nearby alternatives of the Whip, the Water Chute and the Reel.

Terry fed a few pennies into the slot machines in one of the covered arcades. He bought a waffle. He wondered vaguely what was inside the Noah's Ark but decided against finding out. Even the barkers at the various stalls were lethargically disinclined to waste their breath on him or the two or three other passers-by. Terry decided that enough was enough.

He emerged on to the Promenade at the Casino end of the Pleasure Beach and drifted along towards Waterloo Road. He found a souvenir shop and examined the selection of comic postcards, in which skinny henpecked husbands, with bowler hats, red noses, soup-strainer moustaches, an eye for a winsome damsel and an insatiable thirst for beer, were doomed to eternal conflict with statues, nurses, toy balloons, vicars, public lavatories, policemen, small children and, above all, their own gorgon-like, domineering and huge-bottomed wives. After much cogitation and comparison he bought a card and looked for somewhere to write it. Few of the stalls, arcades and cafés in the area had yet bothered to open, but an ice cream parlour was in action and he was able to buy a sundae concocted largely of substitute ingredients. He addressed the postcard to the landlady of his billet in

Scarborough, mainly because he could think of no one else to send it to, found a post office, bought a stamp from the machine, dropped the card in the box, and saw from the post office clock that it still wanted a few minutes to midday.

He lingered as long as he could over a steak pudding, chips and peas in a café whose frontage, despite the war, still bore the legend POTS OF TEA FOR THE SANDS in huge black letters. It was now a quarter to one.

He left the café despairingly, crossed to the beach side of the Promenade and began walking. It would have been a relief to join one of the squads of RAF recruits drilling on the Promenade or doing PT down on the beach.

On he walked, past all three piers one after the other. At the Metropole he wondered if he'd done enough, decided he hadn't, then trudged on along the topmost of the three promenades to Gynn Square and up the rise to the cliffs beyond. Only when he reached Bispham did he pause at the Red Bank Road tram terminus - where the clock was well short of three.

Thirsty now, though hardly footsore - his RAF marching had already immunised him to that - he took the next tram back, but even with the time lost on connections, he was home again with a mug of tea in his hand by four. And it would still be a couple of hours before his father returned from work.

He made preparations as of old - laying the table, cutting the bread and butter and putting the kettle on, making sure the slippers were ready by the fireside chair where Harold would sit afterwards to read the newspaper and grumble about the war over a final cup of tea.

At last Harold arrived. They opened a tin of pilchards for tea, switched on the old Philco wireless set and listened to Bruce Belfrage reading the six o'clock news. Since the battles of Alamein and Stalingrad the previous autumn the tide of war seemed to have turned, and with North Africa wrapped up it was clear that an Anglo-American invasion of Italy could not be long delayed. Terry and Harold managed some innocuous conversation about these events while washing up, but both were aware of the looming problem of what to listen to next. Harold would want to stay with the Home Service for classical music or a talk, while Terry would prefer the Forces programme for ITMA, Hi Gang, a variety programme or dance music with Geraldo or Carroll Gibbons. In the present tense atmosphere such disagreement, once expressed, could trigger an explosion.

Terry averted the danger. As he put the tea-towel back on its hook he announced his intention of going out. Harold seemed relieved and made no enquiry or comment.

Terry could not have explained why he chose a dance hall rather than one of the couple of dozen cinemas which the town offered, or why he rejected the Winter Gardens, the Palace and half a dozen other possibilities in favour of the Tower, with its uncomfortable memories of Norah.

When he entered the ballroom the orchestra was playing "I'll Never Smile Again". The choice seemed appropriate, both to Terry's mood and to that of the few other patrons yet in evidence.

Always before Terry had had his own partner. Now, observing the pert manner and bold eyes of the two or three unattached girls in his vicinity, he found he could not bring himself to ask a stranger to dance with him.

For once too restless to keep loneliness at bay by studying the technique of the musicians, Terry sat through only one set before wandering out of the ballroom and through the "long bar" to the indoor zoo.

The vast high-ceilinged hall stank of sawdust and excreta. Apathetic lions and tigers paced away the tedious hours in bare and solitary cages. Bewildered birds screamed. Demented monkeys flung themselves around the few swings and ropes in their cramped prison, fighting confused, high-speed wars over heaps of rotting fruit and the crusts and toffees thrown to them by the public in defiance of the prohibitory notices.

Five minutes was enough. From the zoo Terry descended to the aquarium, a cavernous place of cool darkness punctuated by illuminated tanks housing a variety of exotic marine life. The benches strategically located in shadowed nooks were popular with patrons, though the biological studies conducted by the couples using them were unconnected with the denizens of the deep on display. Despite the sparseness of the Monday evening clientèle, business was booming here. This provoked disturbing thoughts of Kitty and Norah. Terry departed quickly.

The idea of a cup of tea among the potted plants of the deserted roof garden held no more appeal than did a shandy in the near-solitude of the bar. In the end Terry returned to the ballroom and managed to settle to watching the musicians until it was time to go home, but his heart was not in it. All in all the evening was as unsatisfactory as the morning and afternoon had been.

The days that followed were no better. Inside himself Terry knew why. He was a stranger in his own town, a stranger in his own home, a stranger to his own father. It was the price to be paid for defying the conventions by which their kind lived. He was an outcast.

To forget the guilt was impossible. To live with it was equally impossible. But purge it he would not.

There was only one thing to do and he did it. He returned to his unit three days early.

Next time Terry had leave he spent only two days at home before boredom, tension and the reawakening of guilt impelled him to cut it short. His father did not protest when he announced his intention of returning to his unit.

On his next leave after that he avoided the guilt completely. Instead of going home, he took a rail warrant to London and spent the whole week there, staying at a Forces hostel. That was the week when he learned to play jazz.

His first day in London was spent largely in riding the Tube trains haphazardly around the central area. Maps being unobtainable in wartime, he quickly found the Tube to be the one sure means of orientating himself among the multitude of exciting-sounding place-names familiar to him only from newspapers and books. By the end of the day he had discovered Buckingham Palace, the Houses of Parliament, Trafalgar Square, the Strand, Piccadilly Circus, Leicester Square.

On the second day he began navigating between these places on foot, absorbing the sights and sounds of a battered city, shabby in its wartime dress of peeling paint, sandbags and blast-taped windows, with unexplained barriers manned by steel-helmeted reserve constables and roped-off bombed sites that needed no explanation. The capital was at once a grim yet exciting place, where throngs of grey-faced, dogged civilians mingled with equally vast hordes of young and not-so-young men and women decked out in a greater variety and splendour of uniforms than even Blackpool could boast and seemingly from every country on earth. People queued patiently everywhere - for their rations, for buses and trains, for cigarettes and chocolate, for seats in restaurants, for service in shops, but most of all for cinemas and theatres. The queues for a popular show or film, indeed, could wind round an entire block even in the afternoon and, in the case of Vivian van Damm's Windmill Theatre with its celebrated nude chorus girls and the motto "We never closed", in the morning as well.

On the afternoon of the third day Terry managed to battle into a matinée performance of George Black's revue "Strike a New Note" and in the evening an Ivor Novello musical. The next afternoon, with some half-embarrassed trepidation not shared by the other patrons, he queued at the Whitehall Theatre to view the statuesque artistic poses of "The One and Only Phyllis Dixey" and her half-dozen - and half-frozen - nude acolytes. His own experience as a stage performer enabled him to appraise and appreciate the slickness with which these three shows, in their widely differing ways, combined music, speech, colour and movement to assault and excite the senses. These lessons in showmanship were as nothing, however, compared with what he learned at the Astoria Ballroom on Charing Cross Road on the evening of the fourth day.

He chose the Astoria partly because it was near to the Forces hostel where he was staying and partly because the Joe Loss Orchestra was billed as playing there. He wanted to study the bandleader's technique of self-presentation more closely.

The Astoria was far from the biggest of London's premier dance halls, and this was possibly one of its attractions, for it managed to combine the opulence obligatory in all such establishments with a sense of intimacy derived partly from the fact that wherever one stood or sat, the orchestra stand never seemed far away nor the sound unbalanced.

Terry found a seat on the balcony with a good view of both the dance-floor and the orchestra. The dinner-jacketed musicians were of course a well-drilled unit performing at the high standard demanded in the West End. Joe Loss was his usual energetic self. The patrons were noticeably smarter and more sophisticated than those to be seen in comparable establishments in Blackpool. Many were uniformed, of course, both men and women, but whereas at the Tower or Winter Gardens in Blackpool, sergeants and even corporals were comparatively few in number and commissioned officers never seen, NCOs here were ten a penny and subalterns rather small change. In fact nothing less than red tabs had a hope of causing heads to turn, as indeed they did for a gorgeously-attired though grey-haired major-general, of distinguished feature and bearing, whose energy and skill in propelling his blonde and highly streamlined ATS officer partner through the wilder antics of the jitterbug made it unlikely that he was merely a fond father taking his grownup daughter on a birthday treat.

Terry remained in his balcony seat until the interval. Once or twice, watching the crowds around the edge of the floor, he thought of asking one of the numerous unattached girls for a dance, but it was never a serious option. His teenage diffidence and lack of proficiency still hampered him. Moreover, to dance with someone else seemed an act of disloyalty to Kitty - with the inconsistency of youth he overlooked the far greater act of disloyalty, if disloyalty it was, that he had committed with Norah. But the most important obstacle was the now permanent sense of detachment that came from thinking of himself as belonging on the other side of the footlights, as being one of the fraternity who, by creating enjoyment for others, themselves experience a secret pleasure that goes deeper because it stems from the exercise of power.

At the interval he went downstairs and joined the queue at the soft drinks counter. Coming away with his orange squash he spotted a vacant seat at a nearby table, next to a dinner-jacketed young man with pebble glasses whom he recognised as the second trombonist of the relief orchestra playing back-to-back with the Loss band.

"Do you mind if I sit here?" he asked.

The other nodded. "Go ahead."

Terry scrutinised him covertly. This indeed was a real pro, and clearly little older than himself! Terry longed to speak to him and wondered desperately how to open a conversation. Suddenly the young man saved him the trouble.

"You a sand-grown un'?" he said.

Terry's jaw dropped in surprise. "Yes," he said, "how did you know?"

The other grinned. "You're accent's as thick as mine. I'm from Lytham myself. Name's Arthur, Arthur Ramsden."

The casual five-minute chat justified by such slender common ground developed deeper roots once Terry had shyly confided that he too played an instrument and, if not yet a fully-fledged professional himself, had done so in company with professionals. His eagerness to learn was obvious, as was his admiration for his new acquaintance, who although not much older than himself seemed a lifetime away in depth of experience and worldly wisdom. Arthur's weak eyesight had exempted him from call-up at a time when other young musicians were being swept away into the Forces, and this, along with his musical ability and happy-go-lucky nature, had enabled him to establish himself easily in the wartime West End. He knew everything and everybody, and was happy to share his knowledge with one whom, to Terry's flattered surprise, he regarded as a fellow-artiste. By the time the interval was over and Arthur returned to the stand, they were friends.

Terry went to the Astoria again next evening and after it closed found himself in a taxi with Arthur and two or three other musicians bent on having what they called "a wet and a blow" at a free-and-easy establishment known as the Hammer 'n' Nails - "calls itself a night club, but it's dead scruffy, bit of a knocking-shop really," declared Arthur cheerfully - which turned out to be a cramped and suffocatingly smoke-filled cellar somewhere behind Cambridge Circus, whose patrons could, and indeed more or less had to, buy rot-gut champagne at five pounds a bottle and the favours of a "hostess" by arrangement.

To lend gaiety to the proceedings music was provided by a pianist, bass-player and drummer, with a saxophonist doubling on clarinet. All but one of the dozen or so tables, grouped tightly together around a miniature dance-floor, were well filled. The empty one, adjacent to the band, was adorned with a "Reserved" notice. This, Arthur explained as they threaded their way towards it, was for the convenience of "sitters-in", dance-band musicians whose habit it was to drop in after hours to drink, gossip and let their hair down in impromptu and unpaid jazz jam-sessions.

This was a revelation to Terry. He had heard of this kind of music but never before witnessed it being made. At first he was content simply to listen, enjoying for the first time the sound of improvised jazz, observing and analysing the creative contradiction whereby self-expression and self-discipline fused to produce an exciting, vibrant music of soaring joy and low-down anguish. Later on, when dawn was breaking and chairs were being stacked on tables, he sat in for a few minutes on a final blues, filled in some background notes and at Arthur's insistence essayed a modest solo that elicited encouraging nods and smiles from the other participants.

For the remainder of his leave he slept during the mornings and spent the afternoons waiting for the Astoria to open. But the real day began and ended at the Hammer 'n' Nails.

By the time his leave ended, Terry could play jazz.

Also, in the course of some lighthearted switching of instruments during the jam-sessions, he had experimented with Arthur's trombone and found it both interesting and easy to adapt to.

It was to be more than ten years, however, before this would become a key factor in his life.

16
THERE'S A BOY COMING HOME ON LEAVE

The five RAF men forming the band for the sergeants' mess dance were clearly something of a scratch outfit. It was mainly Sergeant Terry Cullerton on trumpet and a bespectacled young corporal clerk thumping the battered piano who held the performance together.

The drummer, in his daytime incarnation, was a rotund and oldish flight sergeant cook. His beat had more than a touch of the nineteen-twenties about it. Just now he was doubling as vocalist with a rendering of "I'll Get By" that was somewhat marred by his tendency to slow down occasionally for what he conceived to be dramatic effect, with calamitous consequences for the dance tempo of which, as drummer, he was supposed to be both custodian and spark plug.

Not much could be hoped for from the sergeant navigator playing the bass, who knew how to keep time but not much else, while the saxophonist, also a sergeant pilot like Terry, was realistic enough to keep well in the background and allow Terry and the pianist to carry the main burden.

They went into the last chorus, with Terry and the pianist doing their best to prevent the drummer from dragging the tempo down too soon. In the end they had to give up as he bawled the last line in an ear-splitting crescendo. For a terrible moment Terry feared he was going to attempt a top-octave leap on the final note, but at the last micro-second he appeared to think better of it and fell back to the lower register. Even then his voice shook alarmingly, wobbled off balance and after two or three more beats died away for lack of breath like a sputtering two-stroke engine, leaving Terry and the pianist to improvise a camouflage job big enough to have hidden a couple of battleships.

Not that any of these things really mattered, any more than did the fact that even the considerable number of WAAF guests and wives of permanent staff NCOs did not fully offset the shortage of female partners for the large body of young aircrew sergeants making up the majority of those present. The mess was gay with bunting, the bar was open and well-patronised, and this was the evening of their passing-out, the great occasion that all these weeks and months of study and practice and "Good-God-that'll-never-do-go-round-and-try-it-again" had been leading up to. Tomorrow morning they would get their postings and disperse on leave.

After that they would report to their operational units, where many or even most would suffer death or terrible injuries, a few might find great glory and a very few perhaps disgrace, and the rest, thankfully, would simply survive.

This was not a time for morbid reflections, however: it was an occasion for celebration, for mutual goodwill and the anticipation of adventures to come.

Yet there were one or two whose misgivings would not be shut out, who had read between the lines of lectures, pondered the reality behind some instructor's reminiscence of battle, added together rumoured percentage losses and calculated how long it took to wipe out an entire intake of newly-qualified aircrews. These were the ones who paused now and then amidst the gaiety and banter and promises to write, gazed silently at nothing, and thought about the unthinkable. Would it happen to them? Would there be fear? Would there be pain? Would it be over quickly? Could there be some way of making it not happen?

Of course there could be: there was. Skill and teamwork would get you to and from the target on time, by the correct route and in the main bomber stream where comparative safety was to be found. Skill and teamwork would enable you to avoid flak, repel night-fighters, survive the hazards of wind and weather and mechanical malfunction. So said the instructors, veterans all, and their own survival was the proof.

That Terry was one of those for whom this did not suffice was something he kept strictly to himself.

It wasn't the flying. That was easy, and enjoyable too. His musician's fingers had as natural a feel for the controls of a four-engined Lancaster bomber as they had for a trumpet or a trombone. The disciplines required by technology and the division of crew functions were no problem either: he knew how to impose them. No: it was confrontation with the enemy - operations, battle, whose perils loomed more and more vividly as he had learnt more about them during his training.

On evenings such as this in the past it had not been too difficult to put aside such misgivings, since his trumpet and creative talent afforded a back exit from unwanted reality into a harmonious world of sound-pictures where everything came right in the last eight bars and they all, especially Terry Cullerton, lived happily ever after. Tonight, though, the customary exhilaration was missing and refused to be conjured up, try as Terry might to forget that only a brief leave now separated him from the cruel and imminent probability - not remote possibility, as it had once seemed - of mutilation or death.

The vocalist's excruciating closing notes did nothing to help. Feeling a sudden need for a few moments' respite, Terry exchanged a few quick words with the pianist and advanced to the microphone.

"Thank you, ladies and gentlemen, thank you," he intoned above the ragged clapping of the dancers. "Now, not all of you will want to stay on the floor for this one, but on the other hand some of the jive-merchants wouldn't want to be anywhere else. Old Smudger here is going to entertain you for the next five minutes." He waved an arm in the direction of the pianist, who smiled, nodded and launched into a quiet, fast vamp in the bass. "Well, Andy and I hope it will be five minutes, because that'll give us time for a swift half, which we desperately need. Smudger will manage very well without us" - he crescendoed his voice - "for his swinging version of 'Beat Me, Daddy, Eight to the Bar'. Take it away, Smudger!"

Drums and string bass came in with the piano as Terry and Andy, the saxophonist, descended from the stage and shouldered their way through the press of jitterbug enthusiasts invading the dance-floor. The barman gave priority to drawing their halves of shandy as they took a position in a quiet corner.

"Thirsty work," remarked Andy, nodding towards the jitterbugs performing their contortions. He lifted his glass. "But ours is thirstier. Cheers."

"Cheers," replied Terry perfunctorily. He still didn't like beer much and suspected he never would, but a shandy now and then did lubricate the mouth and throat when the atmosphere became smoky. For a few moments they listened to the piano, appreciating the inventiveness of the treble and the driving rhythm of the boogie bass.

"He's a good lad," said Andy.

"Aye."

"Solid bass."

"Mm."

Funny: Terry seemed a bit absent this evening. Andy tried again, changing the subject. "Well, this is it after tonight, eh, Terry boy?"

"Aye."

"Great, eh?"

"Mm." It seemed rather non-committal.

"Yeah. No more swotting; no more instructors pouncing on you, telling you what a ballsup you've made. The real thing after tomorrow."

"Leave first," Terry reminded him.

"Oh aye, smashing." Andy paused and took another pull on his drink. "You going home to Blackpool?"

"I suppose so."

"Suppose so? You don't sound too sure. Isn't your family there?"

"Mm. What there is of it," said Terry laconically.

Andy shot him a glance, then decided not to pursue the question. "I've got a girl waiting to see me in Glasgow. She's a cracker." He laughed. "Met her on my last leave. First thing she told me was 'I'm what they call a good-time girl: do you know what that is?' I said I wasn't sure, so she said she'd show me, and she did. The day I left she said she'd show me again next time I was on leave. What do you think about that?"

"Sounds all right," said Terry.

"More than all right, I'm telling you," said Andy with a wink. "Do you have a girl in Blackpool?"

Terry pondered the point. "I suppose I did have," he said at last.

"Mine's called Ishbel."

"Ishbel?"

"What's wrong with that?" demanded Andy. "It's a good old Scottish name. Ramsay Macdonald's daughter's called Ishbel: I bet you didn't know that."

"No, I didn't."

"Not that it's much of a recommendation. What's your girl's name?"

"Kit - " began Terry, and hesitated. "Well, Norah, I suppose."

"Is she a good-time girl like mine?"

The lighthearted question caught Terry unawares. He snorted sardonically. "You might say she was." He paused and reflected. "In a way."

"I bet she didn't tell you straight out like mine did."

"No. No, she certainly didn't."

The reminder of Norah triggered his memory. What had she said all those months ago? " ... after they've finished training and they go on operations - you know, bombing Germany - most of them get shot down in six weeks ... Well, he was reported missing a month later ... "

Norah. Damn Norah. If it hadn't been for her he wouldn't be here. Norah and his Dad. He'd only joined up to spite them, get away from them. Otherwise he'd have waited till he was called up at eighteen. With his Salvation Army background he could even have been a conscientious objector and perhaps escaped military service altogether. He conveniently closed his mind to his own responsibility - his joining the ATC to impress Kitty; his nonsensical notion that being in the Air Force himself might somehow help him to find her again; his ferocious determination to escape from Norah. The question whether he actually believed in the war or shared his father's pacifism was not one he had ever really considered. It was irrelevant to his personal concerns.

Andy was tugging at his arm. "Come on, Terry, stop dreaming. We've got to get back up there before Smudger runs out of steam." Andy peered into Terry's face. "Is something the matter, Terry?"

"Eh?" Terry started. "No, nothing. Why?"

"You're a bit quiet tonight."

"I'm all right." Terry willed himself back to the present. "Just thinking about something, that's all."

He drank up quickly, and they returned to the stand.

The barrack hut occupied by Terry and his crew was a spartan habitation at best. Now, after removal of the photographs, souvenirs and personal articles that had lent it some semblance of individuality, it was stark and positively forbidding in the light of the full moon. Though the ancient coke-stove in the centre of the hut was still glowing, a single window open the tiniest crack was the sole breach of the time-honoured barrack-room principle that death from asphyxiation is preferable to death from cold.

The voices of a group of late revellers penetrated the hut faintly from somewhere outside.

Coming in on a wing and a prayer
Coming in on a wing and a prayer

Terry stirred and grunted as the words invaded his sleep. It was suddenly a struggle to hold the bomber on course against the blast from the flak bursting all around them. Held solidly in a concentration of searchlight beams, it was a sitting duck for the dozens of night-fighters circling round in leisurely fashion, ready for the kill ...

Though we've one motor gone
We can still carry on
Coming in on a wing and a prayer

A bed-spring creaked. Its sound became magnified to a loud

metallic bang that made the aircraft lurch. The rustle of bedclothes crescendoed to a tremendous whoosh as an engine caught fire and the flames spread rapidly along the wing. Terry shut down the fuel supply to the dead engine, struggled to steady her.

What a show! What a fight!

Yes, we surely hit our target for tonight!

Terry writhed and kicked, his fingers gripping at the sheets. He wrenched the control column this way and that, kicked at the rudders, but none of the wild aerobatics that ensued could shake off the night-fighters. Cannons and machine-guns blazing, they zoomed and dived at their prey, magically avoiding the flak-bursts that never ceased to pepper the doomed bomber. In moments it was falling out of control, burning from end to end ...

And we sing as we fly through the air

Terry moaned in his sleep, and for answer came the screams of his crew as the flames reached them one by one ...

Look below, there's our field over there

Terry blinked once, but the nightmare refused to let him escape and his eyes closed again. Helplessly he watched the meadow growing as it spun faster and faster towards him ...

With a full crew aboard

And our trust in the Lord

Coming in on a wing and a prayer!

Terry's eyes blinked again, and from somewhere suspended in space he saw the wreckage of his aircraft and the scattering of scorched and mutilated bodies among and around it. He drifted unwillingly towards them, not wanting to see. One of the bodies had a charred New Testament protruding from a pocket of its flying jacket. He looked at the face, and it was his own.

He jerked to a sitting position, gulping with relief as the horror receded. He glanced uneasily around, but none of his crew was stirring. The thumping of his heart quietened. The luminous dial of his watch told him he had been asleep less than an hour. He lay back, composing himself, but it was a long time before he slept again.

The third-class compartment of the LMS railway carriage was of ancient vintage, with framed sepia-tinted photographs of desolate seaside resorts, leather-strap window pulls and luggage racks with torn netting that sagged perilously under the weight of bulging kitbags, suitcases and assorted impedimenta. The windows were steamed up, for naturally there was no heating. The only light was a faint glow from a single blue-painted lamp in the ceiling. Most of the passengers were servicemen, of course: all swayed rhythmically to the slow clickety-click of the train. The seats being fully occupied, a young naval rating was perforce standing at one end of the compartment and Terry's friend Andy at the other.

A sudden clattering and jolting told that the train was passing over points. Andy wiped the window with his sleeve and peered out. He leaned down and shook Terry's shoulder.

"Better be moving, Terry. It's Preston."

Terry came to life with a grunt and a yawn. "I must have dozed off. Preston, you said?"

"Yes."

Terry stretched himself and stood up clumsily as the train slowed to a crawl. "OK, Andy. Sit down quick while you've the chance."

"Aye. It'll be a long night to Glasgow," said Andy, sinking gratefully into the gap. "Might make it for lunchtime tomorrow, but I'm not betting on it. When'll you get home?"

Terry heaved his kitbag down from the rack. "An hour for a connection perhaps. Then half an hour or so to Blackpool South."

"Jammy beggar! Have a good leave then," said Andy. "And the best of luck after. You know."

"Yes, same to you." Terry yanked on the strap to lower the window and peered out at the surge of passengers eager to board the already-overcrowded train. As it clanked and hissed to a stop the station announcer's voice crackled over the Tannoy: "Preston, this is Preston station. The train now arriving at Platform 4 is the 9.15 for Glasgow, calling at Lancaster, Penrith, Carlisle ... ". He stepped down to the platform. Andy handed him his kitbag and was about to pull the door shut when a soldier swung up his own kitbag from the platform.

"Not much room here, chum," protested Andy mildly, but accepted the kitbag.

"Not much room anywhere," replied the soldier cheerfully, and climbed aboard. Seconds later an ATS corporal followed, triggering a stir of interest and an exchange of badinage while chivalrously - and miraculously - room was made, despite her protests, for her to sit.

Thus already shut out from the camaraderie of the other travellers, Terry felt relieved of the need for any dramatic leavetaking.

"Well, so long, Andy," he called casually, and was rewarded with a shout and a wave from somewhere among the press of bodies. Then the window was hauled up. He turned away, shouldered his kitbag and moved off down the platform.

The indicator showed a Blackpool train due in forty minutes. Terry also noted that there would be a train for Euston ten minutes later. He made for the Forces canteen, where case-hardened NAAFI girls dispensed Sweeney Todd meat pies, cardboard-textured cheese sandwiches and metallic-tasting cups of char. At the same time they returned measure for measure in backchat and sexual innuendo while never ceasing to maintain vigilance over the communal sugar-spoon lest someone should cut the string and make off with it.

Terry wanted to think - not an easy feat in this overcrowded place, with its constant comings and goings, its ever-shifting ramparts of baggage, its choking clouds of stale tobacco smoke and the almost continuous braying and crackling of the Tannoy in the background.

Unable to find a seat, he propped himself into a corner and defended it by placing his kitbag in front of his feet. He finished his tea and still had made no decision. He put the empty mug down among the breadcrumbs and dirty plates on a nearby table, trying furiously to concentrate.

At last the Blackpool train was announced. Still unable to decide what he intended, Terry made no move. Then, with less than two minutes to go before the train's departure, he picked up his kitbag, pushed his way out of the canteen and raced for the footbridge. Clattering down the steps to the platform he heard whistles shrilling and the last doors banging shut. The train began pulling away and a porter shouted a warning as Terry grabbed for a door-handle, ran with it for a couple of yards and finally had to let go.

Helplessly Terry watched as the rear of the Blackpool train receded into the distance. Then he turned about, climbed the steps to the footbridge again and made for the Euston train.

The decision had been made for him. More or less.

17
THE LAMBETH WALK

Terry sat on his kitbag in the corridor of the Euston train, swaying in unison with the rest of the sardine-packed throng and regretting bitterly the remnants of filial piety that had prompted him to declare Blackpool as his destination for this final leave before becoming operational.

"Becoming operational", he thought: that's a laugh. Becoming dead, that's what. The wraiths of immediate horror that had wrecked his last night's sleep had dispersed, yet the cold arithmetical truths remained and would not stop revolving around his brain: five per cent losses on normal Bomber Command operations, worse on particularly tough ones. Odds on being shot down, therefore, before completing the thirty ops that made up a "tour". Then if you survived, the same odds again on your next tour. He could not scoff and say he wouldn't let it happen to him, as his comrades did, as that airman had done whom Norah had told him about all those months ago.

Remembering Norah again shifted his thoughts to the other tack. Norah alone, after all, was still sufficient reason for keeping away from Blackpool: she always had been. Oh yes, she'd walked off all high and mighty that last time - he shuddered at the memory - and true enough she'd never tried to contact him since, but her Mum and Dad had, hadn't they? And you never knew, once she found out he was home on leave she'd be round like a rocket likely as not. Better not to take chances.

What a good job he'd come to his senses in time! As to what he would do now, that was simple. He'd do what he'd done on all his other leaves in recent months: play jazz in London.

After that though? His thoughts swung to the other pole again. Well, one thing he seemed to have decided: he wasn't going to go and get killed on ops over Germany. Better a live coward than a dead hero, he'd heard some say, and when it came to the crunch, weren't they right?

Yet even now, with the die cast and every click of the train-wheels reaffirming the momentousness of the step he had taken, he still could not fully admit what he was doing, still shied away from the direful implications.

It was easier to concentrate on the immediate practical problem of how to get off the train in London with a travel warrant and leave pass made out for Blackpool. While he could doubtless satisfy the ticket collector by paying the civilian fare, the Service police checking Forces passengers would not be put off so easily. They would ask questions ... and then?

In the end he was lucky. About halfway through the journey an inspector passed through the carriage scrutinising tickets and was indeed agreeably surprised at Terry's volunteering to pay the fare instead of attempting the tiresome toilet dodge beloved of servicemen. Accordingly he answered Terry's would-be innocent-sounding enquiries in friendly fashion and advised him, out of the side of his mouth, to alight at Watford Junction, where he could change to the Underground without having to pass through ticket barriers manned by Service police.

The unpredictable delays to which train travel was subject made it full morning before Terry, kitbag on shoulder, emerged from the Bakerloo Line into Piccadilly Circus, only one of many servicemen and women so burdened among the crowds. Packed buses queued to crawl their way round the Eros statue, boarded up for the duration. Over at "Rainbow Corner", on Shaftesbury Avenue, a sprinkling of Americans loitered around the entrance to the Red Cross Club. Terry made his way through Leicester Square, intending to avail himself of the wash-and-brush-up facilities of the Queensberry Club, the Forces recreational and entertainment centre housed in the London Casino.

At the entrance he stopped short at the sight of redcaps checking passes. Quickly he walked past, cut through to the Strand, merged with the hordes spewing from Charing Cross station. A few minutes later he paused at a tea-wagon parked outside the sandbagged Embankment entrance to the Underground.

The ferret-faced cockney behind the counter looked down at him incuriously. "Yus, mate?" he enquired, wiping a hand on his apron in an automatic gesture. His brilliantined hair and wispy smart-aleck moustache seemed incongruous affectations in the proprietor of such a modest establishment.

"Er - a cup of tea, please," said Terry.

"No cups, mugs," returned the man, taking one from the pile at the back and filling it from the urn. "Wiv or wiv'aht?"

"Pardon?"

"Wiv or wiv'aht? Milk an' sugar, mate?"

"Oh. With, please."

"Baowf?"

"Yes please. Could I have a sandwich as well?"

"Up ter you, mate. You're payin'." The man sloshed milk from a large jug into the steaming liquid, shovelled sugar in with a brown-stained spoon, gave a perfunctory stir and pushed the mug across the cinder-track of crumbs decorating the counter. "Bacon orf, Spam, cheese or dog fourpence, dog 'n' egg savoury tanner, take yer pick."

Terry opted for the sausage and egg savoury. Under government food restrictions the contents of the sausage would comprise more soya meal than meat. "Egg savoury" could only mean some kind of frizzled mess concocted from the dehydrated egg powder which, for civilians, industrial canteens and most restaurants, served in place of fresh eggs, the latter being reserved for Forces establishments. Still, the sandwich was hot, and a hefty dollop of HP from the huge bottle on the counter combined with the thin coating of now-melting margarine to reduce the grey wartime bread to a delicious warm sogginess.

Wolfing the sandwich down between gulps of stewed tea, Terry pondered his next move, which in the cold light of day suddenly seemed more difficult than he had foreseen.

Lacking a leave pass valid for London, would he be able to stay at a Forces hostel? What about a hotel or guest house? Did they have to check passes? He did not know, and finding out might be risky. What about Arthur Ramsden? They'd been good friends during his leaves, playing jazz together at the Hammer 'n' Nails Club. But how far did such friendship go? Last night on the train it had been easy to assume vaguely that Arthur would help him, but would he? Could he? He didn't even know where Arthur lived. Above all, could Arthur be trusted?

Then there were the police, both civilian and military. Wherever he went in uniform he would be vulnerable to their attentions, not to mention those of any commissioned officer who might take it into his head to check his identity.

Civilian clothes were the answer. But Terry had none in his kitbag. In any case he balked at the fateful step, even though he knew it had been implicit in all his thoughts, all his actions since Preston station.

Reluctant to move on until he had made a decision, yet fearful of making it, he lingered over the last of his tea. The wagon's proprietor eyed him covertly in between serving other customers. He spoke at last.

"Anyfink else, mate?"

An impatience born of his own irresolution made Terry suddenly blurt out, "Do you know anywhere I can buy a suit?"

An eye like a knife transfixed him. He quaked.

"A suit? You mean a civvy suit?"

"Yes."

"Got 'em in Burton's up the Strand. Fifty Shillin' Tailor further along. 'Course yer needs coupons in them places."

"I - I don't have any."

"No, well, you wouldn't 'ave, wouldjer?" He knew as well as Terry did that only civilians had a clothes ration. "Second-hand's the game for you then."

Encouraged, Terry plunged on. "Yes. I - I don't want a lot of fuss."

"No, I 'specs yer don't." The man paused, weighing him up. He began wiping the counter with a greasy rag and spoke again with exaggerated casualness. "Geezer I know dahn the Elephant don't arst no questions."

"Where did you say?"

"Elephant."

"What's that mean?"

"Cor stone the crows!" The proprietor paused in his wiping and shook his head disbelievingly. "Where you been the last five 'undred years?" Without waiting for an answer he continued. "It's a Tube station, mate. Elephant and Castle. Dahn Lambeth way."

"Can you tell me his name and address?"

"I might." Another pause in the counter-wiping. "Cost yer five bob though."

Terry stared in astonishment, and the other added slyly, "Well, it's valuable information, innit? Wot I mean is, e's the sort of geezer might look after yer kitbag for you as well if you wanted 'im to."

Another customer arrived, and the enforced suspension of negotiations gave Terry time to consider the impossibility of moving around London as a civilian without his very obvious RAF kitbag being noticed. By the time the other customer departed he had decided to pay up.

Twenty minutes or so later he was picking his way through a wilderness of shabby tenements, tight-packed terraced houses and streets disfigured by their wartime accretions of EWS tanks and concrete air-raid shelters. Ordeal by bomb and fire had shattered a house or two in almost every street, while here and there, appallingly, the mean panorama opened out into huge abandoned expanses where whole rows of dwellings had vanished, the resultant rubble having been tidied up and cordoned off but neither cleared nor rebuilt.

Amidst the wasteland Terry found at last the bustling oasis of market stalls, barrows and dingy shops to which he had been directed. Here a legitimate traffic went on in such meagre foodstuffs and trashy consumer goods as remained unrationed, along with antiques, second-hand furniture, clothing and household articles. There was also a thriving "under-the-counter" trade in which anything could be had by those in the know and with money - whisky, cigarettes, black market meat, bacon, butter, eggs or petrol, nylon stockings from America, parachute silk for making evening dresses or glamorous underwear, occasionally even bananas, tinned peaches and other such delicacies unseen in normal commerce since before the war.

Cautious enquiries led Terry quickly to a dingy shop with its frontage part-concealed by a pavement display of threadbare skirts and blouses, ragged, roughly-patched workmen's overalls and jackets, and a miscellany of worn-out shoes. Of suits there were none. If there was any hope, it must lie inside.

The shopman was busy behind the counter, his back to the door. "Yess, my boy?" he lisped softly, though it was difficult to know how he could tell the sex of his prospective customer since he had not yet turned round to face him.

The same sensation of embarrassment that had tortured Terry at his first purchase of "rubber goods" flooded back, overlaid this time with real fear - a fear of betrayal which by reinforcing his sense of wrongdoing impelled him yet further along a path from which there could be no return.

"I - I want a second-hand suit," he stammered.

The shopman turned round. He was past middle age, overweight, olive-complexioned, with bushy wings of grey hair and a broad bald patch on top. His cardigan was shapeless, his baggy trousers as shiny and worn as any of the nondescript offerings displayed for sale. "Ah," he said, and scrutinised Terry carefully with eyes like ebony beads. He wrinkled his nose and sniffed as though assailed by a smell of drains, then gestured towards a rack in the far corner.   "Nothing much your size just now, my boy, but you might find something over there." The hissed sibilants sounded somehow sinister. He turned his back again.

After a few seconds Terry, realising he was going to receive no further guidance, began rummaging through the rack. A few minutes later he had agreed to pay thirty shillings for a tattered salt-and-pepper sports jacket with cracked leather patches at elbows and cuffs, along with a pair of grey flannel trousers frayed at the turnups, faded, stained and well bagged at the knees. For another ten shillings the ensemble was completed with the only other items available in suitable sizes - a moth-eaten, garishly patterned grey-black-and-red Fair Isle pullover, a blue-and-white striped shirt with two worn, once-white semi-stiff collars, a greasy green tie and a pair of dark brown socks, well darned. In wartime there was, however, nothing about the wearing of shabby, ill-matched clothes to attract particular attention - rather the reverse.

As the cash he handed over disappeared, not into the cash till but down a capacious trouser pocket, Terry was uneasily aware that another problem was looming. However, the old man's next unexpected words, delivered in ingratiating, confidential tones, seemed to promise a solution before he even asked.

"Now, you'd like to get changed into your civvy gear right away, wouldn't you, my boy?"

"Er - well - yes, I suppose so."

"Yes." The other nodded. "Like to do it here, would you?"

"Here? Oh." He hadn't thought of that. Now that he did, it seemed an excellent idea. "Er - yes. Thank you."

"Not in the shop, though, of course." A crafty smile. "In the back room."

"Yes, please." Terry attempted a feeble nonchalance. "If it isn't too much trouble."

"Oh, no trouble. No trouble at all, my boy." A flabby finger pointed at Terry's kitbag. "An' p'raps you'd like me to look after that for a week or two, would you, my boy?"

That his difficulties should so magically and swiftly be dispersed! Terry was vastly relieved but adopted a careless pose of man-of-the-world confidentiality, as though the matter of the kitbag, being one of convenience rather than real importance, had simply not occurred to him previously. "It'd be a help, yes. I'd rather be out of uniform when I'm on leave. Away from all the rules and regulations."

"Ah, yess. The rules and regulations." His interlocutor nodded sagely, seeming to consider the rules and regulations for the first time. "Yess, of course." He wallowed over to the shop door and closed it. Hard lines incongruously creased his flaccid features and his voice sharpened as he turned to deliver the blow. "Well, my boy, that'll cost you another three quid."

Terry's burgeoning protest was cut off with a gesture. "Is that too much, my boy? Too much? You think it's too much for someone who's on the run?"

"I'm not on the run," expostulated Terry weakly.

"No? Oh well, if you're not on the run you don't need me any more, do you?" The man waddled back across the shop and from behind the counter stabbed a finger at Terry's purchases. "Off you go then, my boy: there's your clobber. Can't wrap it up for you; paper shortage, you know." He turned his back again.

"But three pounds is all I've got left," protested Terry, though it was not true, and the shopman knew it, and knew now that he would pay.

"Can't help that, my boy," he retorted brusquely. "Times is hard: there's a war on, you know. Besides, think of the risk I'm taking. Do you know the penalty for harbouring a deserter, giving him aid and comfort - ?"

"I'm not a deserter - " began Terry.

The old man straightened up and faced him again. "No? Not yet, perhaps, but you're aiming to be one: I'm not stupid." Suddenly he leaned across the counter, the cunning eyes flashing with something strangely akin to anger. "You think I should do you favours because I like you? Just lissen, my boy, lissen and learn. I'm a Jew, right? Lots of us round the East End. You got any idea what it means being a Jew these days? Relatives all over Europe - Russia, Poland, Germany as well: half of them probably dead and the rest in concentration camps. In one myself sure as a gun if Hitler ever comes here, and I got two lads in the army helping to see he doesn't. So in my book you're a washout, that's what you are, a turd, and I don't like turds." He paused. His tone moderated. "Still, there again, you see, a turd like you probably isn't much use to the Forces anyhow and I got a living to make till my lads come home." He paused as though forced to a distasteful decision. "So I'll do business with you, my boy, I'll do business." He shook his head to indicate regret at the necessity. "Not on the cheap, though, oh no. You want me to help you, you pay for it." During his discourse he had shambled to the door again. Now he grasped the handle. "So take it or leave it, my boy: make up your mind. Three quid to change your clothes and leave the kitbag or else get off my premises and take your belongings with you, double quick."

Was the reasoning false? Were the ethics twisted? Terry knew his own to be even more false and twisted. Ten minutes later, carrying his trumpet-case and a few personal items hurriedly retrieved from his kitbag while changing, he emerged from the back door into an alleyway giving egress to the street. In appearance at least he was a civilian again. The evasion and shilly-shallying were over.

The old man had been right. He had crossed the divide now. He was on the run.

18
RUN, RABBIT, RUN!

Terry had shed his military identity along with his uniform. Acquiring a civilian one would be a different matter. Without ration book, labour permit and identity card, he would have no legal access to essential food, a proper job or regular accommodation. Lacking any other recourse, many deserters simply headed for home in the hope of being sheltered and fed by family or friends. Not surprisingly, this was a sure route to the guardhouse. In any event it was not an option for Terry.

The only other alternative was the shady wartime underworld of "fiddling"- irregular, ill-paid jobs, black marketeering, petty skulduggery. Here danger would never be far away, but no questions would be asked, and Terry's musical talent would, he hoped, enable him to survive without becoming involved in more than a minimum of illegalities.

Still he needed immediate help - mainly somewhere to sleep - until he found his feet. The only possible source was his jazz-playing partner, Arthur Ramsden. But it would be late evening before there was any chance of finding Arthur at the Hammer 'n' Nails Club. Meanwhile he must kill time as best he could. The safest place for that was the cinema.

At Leicester Square a queue had formed round the block to see "We Dive At Dawn", a war film in which John Mills and Eric Portman, aided and abetted by the Admiralty, some excellent second unit photography at sea and a dozen character actors too old or unfit in real life to have been called up yet, reminded the nation that Britain too had submarines, which was true, and that their crews were superior to their German counterparts in skill and courage, which was less certain although no one doubted it at the time. The posters displayed outside the Odeon, the Empire and other first-run cinemas advertised other films of war heroics, none of which - especially "One Of Our Aircraft Is Missing" - appealed to Terry in his present situation. A little further afield, however, he found both "Stage Door Canteen" and "Orchestra Wives" on offer at second-run cinemas.

With much time in hand and still a fair amount of money in his pocket there was no need to choose: he went to see both. In "Stage Door Canteen" the parade of stage and screen stars moved too fast to make much impression, but Terry took a professional interest in the musical offerings - the relaxed jazz of Count Basie, the trilling saxophones of Guy Lombardo, the intricate South American rhythms of Xavier Cugat, the genial comedy of Kay Kyser, and the weary, hard-bitten cynicism of the young Peggy Lee's "Why Don't You Do Right?" counterpointed by Benny Goodman's pungent, stabbing orchestral commentary.

Watching "Orchestra Wives", Terry identified with George Montgomery as the star trumpet-player, accepted without question the impossibly innocent groupie portrayed by Ann Rutherford, and swallowed whole the film's depiction of the life of an orchestra "on the road" under the leadership of Glenn Miller. He did not suspect, for as yet he had no cause, how large a part the real-life Glenn Miller was soon to play in his own destiny.

Emerging into the blackout he bumped his way through hordes of torch-flashing pleasure-seekers towards Soho. The street-walkers infesting the West End had an almost telepathic ability, despite the blackout, to distinguish officers and Americans from the comparatively penniless British other ranks and civilians. Nevertheless there were a few exceptions, and Terry was sufficiently worldly-wise nowadays to ignore or make a firmly negative response to the hackneyed "Got a light, chum?" chanted from darkened shop-doorways.

Entering a milk bar he knew from earlier visits, he found that, moving with the times, its interior now attempted a perfunctory resemblance to an American soda fountain. A Coke machine, acquired no doubt through the good offices of some rogue quartermaster at an Eighth Air Force base, stood in a corner. Above the mirror on the back wall a pair of clasped hands had been painted, flanked by representations of the Stars and Stripes and Union Jack. The menu board offered not only the accustomed English wartime fare of sausages, rissoles and Spam or cheese sandwiches, but a selection of American items as well - hamburgers, frankfurters, French fries, cole slaw, eggs any style, waffles with maple syrup.

The good intentions thus displayed were scarcely matched by achievement, since the Coke machine was adorned with a tattered notice bearing the handwritten legend "Out of Stock", while all the American items on the menu were marked "Off" except hamburgers and French fries. These, when Terry ordered them, turned out to be virtually indistinguishable from the rissoles and chips familiar to everyone in Britain; and since the sole garnish available was HP sauce, the promised adventure in transatlantic eating was something of a let-down. Even so, the place echoed to the brash accents of the Middle West, California and the Bronx, so presumably this private-enterprise essay in promoting Anglo-American relations was both successful and profitable despite its shortcomings.

It was eleven o'clock when Terry emerged into the narrow Soho streets. Such passers-by as remained were mostly hurrying towards bus-stops or the sandbagged Tube entrances. A late-night newspaper-seller cleared his stand by dimmed torchlight. A stray taxi rattled past. A jeep-load of "snowballs", American military policemen with white helmets, gaiters, cross-belts and night-sticks, dealt roughly with a couple of drunken GIs while a peroxided harridan stood by shrieking obscenities.

The doorman at the Hammer 'n' Nails Club was new since Terry's last visit and made him wait while he fetched the manager to confirm his credentials. The manager, also new, eyed Terry's trumpet-case and seedy civilian rigout suspiciously, consulted his gold wrist-watch repeatedly and ostentatiously while Terry told his story, then adamantly denied acquaintance with Arthur Ramsden or any other "sitting-in" musicians. "We don't want no trouble here," he rasped when Terry tried to persist. "Throw him out, Bert."

"You 'eard 'im," said the doorman menacingly. Terry shrank away. But then the manager disappeared and the doorman's manner changed. He hailed Terry back.

"'Ere, 'arf a mo', you a real trumpet-player?" he asked conspiratorially.

"Yes," said Terry.

"I mean a good one, a proper one, a pro?"

"Yes." Well, it was nearly true, and this was no time for fine distinctions.

"Wanna job? Cash? No questions?"

"Yes."

"A quid gets you a hot tip. No muckin' abaht. Straight gear."

Terry's funds were now much depleted, but clearly this was no time for bargaining or procrastination. He handed over a pound note. The doorman glanced around furtively. "Sham-Bam Club, back o' Regent Street. Know it?"

"I've seen where it is."

"Manager's Tommy Ralston. Tell 'im I sent you. Now scram, quick."

The Sham-Bam was a cellar establishment virtually identical to the Hammer 'n' Nails save in the scruples, or lack of them, of its manager, who sensed Terry's dubious status at once, interviewed and auditioned him in five minutes, then offered him a wage which, though miserly, was strictly cash and nothing in the books, along with permission to sleep in a cubbyhole on the premises and instructions to get a dinner jacket and black tie by the following evening.

Possessing no clothing coupons, Terry again had recourse to a second-hand dealer, this time in Soho, partly because the Sham-Bam manager suggested it and anyhow it was nearer than Lambeth, but mainly because instinct told him that to go anywhere near his kitbag again would be suicidal.

Thus, by his prudence, and the preceding strokes of sheer luck, Terry had in little over twentyfour hours successfully consummated his disappearance. He settled quickly into a troglodyte routine consisting of jazz by night and sleep by day, punctuated only occasionally by brief and cautious forays into the world outside.

Meanwhile the war went on. The battles of Alamein and Stalingrad had turned the tide, and the ring was now tightening around Germany. The south of England teemed with men, armour and equipment assembling for the invasion of Europe which everyone knew must come. For troops on leave, London was the magnet. What they wanted, of course, was a good time while they could get it, for who knew what tomorrow might bring? Theatres were packed. Cinema queues lengthened. Pubs and dance halls bulged. Night-life boomed, for those who could afford it.

The Sham-Bam Club got its share of this prosperity, and more, thanks to its new trumpet-player, whose swiftly-flowering jazz genius galvanised the other resident musicians and brought both customers and sitters-in flocking.

This generated its own dangers. For one thing Arthur Ramsden turned up at the Sham-Bam one evening. Though puzzled that Terry had not contacted him, he was friendly to start with, but pointedly withheld comment on Terry's cagey account of an imaginary ailment occasioning his discharge from the Air Force. Arthur left again a few minutes later with only a perfunctory farewell wave. He never returned.

On another occasion several members of the official RAF Dance

Orchestra, the fabled Squadronaires, in London for a recording session, dropped into the Sham-Bam. To improvise jazz with them, to converse as a fellow-trumpeter with Arthur Mouncey on what the latter evidently regarded as level terms, to borrow Lew Davis's trombone and receive friendly tips on reproducing some of his jazz effects - such experiences could have been not only memorable but much more comfortable had Terry been able to stifle a nagging question: how might the Squadronaires men react if they knew the truth about him? For they themselves, first-rank musicians and most of them indeed from the Ambrose Orchestra, the top dance band of all, had made no small sacrifice by joining up voluntarily on the outbreak of war, placing their rare talents at the service of their country in return for the status, pay and discomforts of "erks", AC2s, the lowest form of RAF life.

At the same time it was frustrating for Terry to reflect that had he managed his life differently, he might himself perhaps have been a Squadronaire by now instead of a deserter skulking around back streets in the darkness.

Profitless to dwell on such might-have-beens, however. What was sure at any rate was that Terry was not one of those who flew and died in the RAF's hard-fought, and ultimately unsuccessful, six-month effort to end the war by destroying Berlin. He was still safe on the ground, too, when RAF Bomber Command, along with the United States Eighth Air Force, flew weeks of hazardous round-the-clock softening-up raids in preparation for D-Day.

Not that he allowed himself to think as starkly as that: the guilt would have sat too heavily. Instead, he avoided newspapers, the wireless, and conversations about the war or indeed anything much else with such acquaintances as he made, as though by isolation he willed reality out of existence.

Thus the mighty events of D-Day itself, when it came, passed him by almost unremarked. The German V-1 offensive, launched a few days later, was a different matter. No one living in London could ignore it. Like everyone else, Terry had to come to terms with the repeated air raid alarms, the menacing buzz of the approaching pilotless aircraft, the breathless wait for the moment of cut-out and, if by then the engine-noise was not receding, the dive to the floor.

Yet nothing could quell the rising optimism of those days, the sense that though there was more struggling and suffering to be done, the crusade was entering its final phase. The arrival in Britain of a flood of robust, breezy American entertainers already famous from their films - Bing Crosby, Fred Astaire, Dinah Shore and others - seemed symbolic of happier times just beyond the horizon. None of these created a greater stir than Captain, soon to be Major, Glenn Miller and his American Band of the Allied Expeditionary Force, whose sparkling, self-confident and above all *hopeful* music, holding a mirror to the mood of the times, hit the British entertainment world like a thunderbolt.

The echoes reached the Sham-Bam Club one evening when a Squadronaires musician arrived escorting a lanky, bespectacled American sergeant with an amiable smile, another sergeant, young and unmilitary-looking in dark glasses, and a short dark-haired corporal carrying a clarinet case. The first two took over drums and piano, while the latter added his clarinet to Terry's trumpet and the trombone of the Squadronaires musician. The hour of miraculous jazz that followed left Terry exhilarated, stunned and wishing desperately for more.

His wish was granted when the three Americans returned a few evenings later, accompanied this time, though they did not tell Terry so, by a grave-faced officer with rimless glasses who remained in the shadows at the back of the room, unrecognised and listening intently, particularly to Terry, while the three Americans joined the resident musicians in running the gamut of jazz styles, from "Basin Street Blues" and "Muskrat Ramble" to "Stealin' Apples" and a catchy number based on a simple repeated phrase, somewhat resembling a kind of upside-down version of "In The Mood". It was led by the Americans, who called it "My Guy's Come Back".

In a sense, the title was prophetic.

Ten minutes before curtain-up, the backstage uproar at the Stoll Theatre, Kingsway, was more chaotic than usual, partly because this was a one-off event without dress rehearsal, which made it more likely that things would go wrong, and partly because of the sheer numbers of performers involved, all highly gifted but none of them true "theatricals" in the sense that true theatrical people understood the term.

What was worse, the greatest star of them all had not turned up yet and no one was really certain that he was going to, not even the big built, middle-aged man with moustache and heavy jowls who had persuaded him to participate in the show and now pushed open the stage-door to gaze anxiously up and down Kingsway for the umpteenth time.

On a Sunday the traffic was sparse even by wartime standards: a couple of London Transport buses, an occasional private car or taxi, a bicycle or two, and nothing else - except, of course, for a vast and excited crowd, many in uniform, milling around the theatre entrance. The sixth annual British Jazz Jamboree, a musical marathon by Britain's top bands, was a sell-out like its predecessors. It would have been so even if the Melody Maker had not announced, only three days before the event, that Major Glenn Miller would take part along with the American Band of the Allied Expeditionary Forces.

The big built man sighed, turned and went in again. His head was on the block all right. His own fault too. He was the knowall, the fixer with contacts everywhere, the windbag who'd boasted he could get Miller. If it went wrong there was no one to share the blame with.

To make matters worse, there was this kid, supposedly an ace trumpeter. There he was now, sitting on a stool by the doorkeeper's glass cubicle the way he'd been told, cradling his instrument-case.

"You'd better be good, you short-arsed brat," he muttered *sotto voce*, and a cheerful voice replied unexpectedly from behind him.

"I'm always good. And I'm not short-arsed. I'm a tall guy with short legs."

The oft-repeated quip was sufficient trademark. "Hello, Billy," the other man said even before checking his stride and turning to face the speaker, his irritability undiminished. He jerked his head, indicating the kid. "I mean him. The kid Miller lumbered me with - "

"You, Ted? Lumbered?" The diminutive reed-player grinned. "I didn't know anyone could lumber you. God knows I've tried -"

"Yeah, well, you're Billy Amstell, you're not Glenn Miller. 'Get him, chum, or you don't get me': that's what he said. 'Course he smiled, but you know what they say about Miller - velvet glove, iron fist. Anyway I'd gone to him asking a favour, so what could I do? But I don't even know if the kid's any good or not. I never had time to find out."

"A couple of the Squads say they've jammed with him down that dump where he hangs out. According to them he's a genius." Billy grinned again. "Bit like me."

"Yeah?" The big man remained unappeased, unconvinced, unwilling to take up the banter. "Well, I tell you, my number one worry right now is whether Miller's going to turn up. If he doesn't, that kid doesn't get to blow a penny whistle. Bad enough with one fiasco: no sense risking two."

Billy shrugged. "Miller said he'd come, he'll come: why not?" He jerked a thumb and nudged the big man. "The kid probably feels like a cat with the squits: I'm young enough to remember what it's like even if you're not. Tell him to cheer up, he'll soon be dead like you." Billy grinned cheekily yet again, dodged the big man's upraised arm and moved off.

The big man grimaced, then shook off his disgruntlement. Billy was right: a bit of encouragement wouldn't cost anything. He put a friendly smile together and went over.

"All right, sonny?"

"Yes thank you, Mr Heath."

"Nervous?"

"No."

The little beggar! Well, maybe he wasn't at that. For a moment the quietly composed expression reminded the big man uncannily of someone else's. Whose? He frowned, wondering. Why, dammit, Miller himself, he thought wryly. Funny that. What a self-contained young devil! Utterly unflustered, bags of chutzpah, just like that other kid, the little Jewish laddie even younger, who'd be playing along with him later on if all went well. He shook his head, disgruntlement returning. The modern generation for you, too damn clever, too damn full of themselves!

He kept his thoughts to himself and smiled genially. "Attaboy," he said. "Once the show starts you can watch from the wings. Take stage left. Don't get in anyone's way, but don't budge from there until you're announced, then straight on stage." He paused. "I don't know when it will be, probably not for hours. All right?"

"I won't mind. I'll just watch until it's my turn."

Ted Heath nodded, moved off and was swallowed up in a crowd of chattering fellow-bandsmen whom all the efforts of the stage manager seemed unable to awaken to a sense of urgency despite the imminence of curtain-time. Capable of prodigies of endurance and discipline once the performance began, dance-band musicians away from the stand were an eccentric, bumptious lot, fully aware of their talent, immune to stage-fright, determined not to be pushed around by ignoramuses who didn't know a French horn from a Boulogne beach ice-cream cone.

Terry watched eagerly as yet more musicians arrived by the minute, some camel-hair coated and pork-pie hatted, others in carelessly-worn military uniforms; some empty-handed, others carrying instrument-cases ranging from slim clarinet size to double-bass. In these pre-television days faces were not easy to recognise, but

Terry knew that he was in the presence of the élite of his world.

This indeed was why he had come, defying the risk, aware of the disaster he courted by emerging from the obscurity which thus far had protected him. For this was where he belonged, it was what he was born for, it was his right, to be among the very best of his chosen vocation, unknown to them now but destined for glory before this evening was over. He had surrendered himself to his dream, because his dream was the only reality that mattered. Tonight he would have his moment: tomorrow could not take it from him.

The concert began, and the cream of British dance bands came and went, vying with one another to make this, as the banner headline of the next issue of the Melody Maker was to describe it, "The Best Jazz Jamboree Ever".

But no Glenn Miller. Ted Heath, coming off stage after his own stint on trombone with the Geraldo Orchestra, seemed to shrink two sizes. Brows beetling and shoulders hunched, accompanied now by an ever-growing throng of equally worried-looking hangers-on, he lumbered again and again to the stage door to peer uselessly along the near-empty street. He resigned himself to failure and the scorn of his peers.

Then it happened. A convoy of olive-painted trucks rounded the corner and roared up to the theatre. Flaps banged open, tarpaulins were flung back, and in seconds GIs were swarming into the theatre and over the stage like ants, setting up rostrums and equipment at lightning speed while the audience was giving its ovation, well-deserved and fortunately lengthy, to the last of the British bands.

Ted Heath grinned his relief, and the finest musicians in Britain, blasé recipients of fan idolatry in their own right, took turns to slap him on the back before rushing like fans themselves to the sides of the stage, awestruck and eager as children. There was a moment of stillness, the strains of "Moonlight Serenade" struck up and the roar of the audience lifted the rafters as the curtains opened on an orchestra unique in the annals of popular music.

They played for the best part of an hour, fifty musicians in disciplined array, directed unobtrusively by the reserved, dignified Miller. Every inch the officer and gentleman, he remained cool and unemotional throughout, his brisk, spare announcements contrasting strikingly with the brilliance of the music.

Like everyone else present, Terry was overwhelmed, inspired. Yet as number succeeded number - "Poinciana", "Caribbean Clipper", "Little Brown Jug", "String of Pearls", "Jukebox Saturday Night", "It

Must Be Jelly 'Cos Jam Don't Shake Like That" - and the clock ticked on, a small nagging doubt assailed him, puncturing his exhilaration. Nearly four hours the concert had lasted: well over schedule. Surely by now ... ?

The lights dimmed and "Moonlight Serenade" came up again to signal the end. Major Miller took the microphone, addressing conventional words of thanks and farewell to the audience.

Tears of disappointment pricked at Terry's eyelids. It was too cruel to bear. All his hopes! The risks he had taken! And for nothing. He had been cut, callously cut, or perhaps just forgotten. He turned away.

Someone took hold of his arm. "Where are you off to, sonny? Didn't I tell you to stay there till you were wanted?"

Terry looked up into the creased, heavy features.

"Yes, but it's over - " he began.

"Sh! Listen," said Ted Heath, and turned him forcibly to face the stage again.

" ... his name is Victor Feldman, and he's just ten years old, but from the way my boys" - Major Miller gestured towards the orchestra - "have been raving about him, he's a wizard on the skins. Well, I'd like to hear him, and I thought you might like it too." Glenn Miller paused, then went on. "Now while Sergeant McKinley lowers his drums so this pocket-sized Krupa can reach everything comfortably, I'd just like to tell you that I've made another discovery too. Of course, he's not exactly a boy wonder like Victor - actually he must be getting on for twice Victor's age, so he's practically an old man. But I've heard him play, and although you've never heard his name - as a matter of fact I only know him as Terry - you have my word that he's a terrific jazz trumpeter."

Terry looked up at Ted Heath, who pointed at Terry's trumpet case, raised a thumb and lifted a questioning eyebrow. Terry gulped and nodded, his stomach fluttering momentarily.

"Well, get it out," said Ted, and turned him round again, gripping him by the shoulders while Glenn Miller completed his introduction.

"Now just to show how real jazzmen work, what can happen when they let their hair down and improvise, we're making an experiment. I can tell you truthfully that Victor and Terry haven't rehearsed. In fact when they come on stage I'll have to introduce them to each other. All they know is the name of the number they're going to play. It's "Sweet Georgia Brown", ladies and gentlemen, and here they are to play it for you, any way they dream it up - Terry on trumpet, and Victor on drums."

Two powerful hands propelled Terry forward, though he needed no compulsion. As he walked towards Major Miller at centre stage, a jauntily grinning schoolboy in shorts, as confident and nerveless as Terry himself, advanced likewise from the opposite wing. Major Miller's handshake was firm and friendly, and when he smiled there was warmth and kindliness behind the rimless spectacles.

The voice was equally benign and encouraging. "Now don't you guys let me down after the build-up I've given you."

Then the tiny schoolboy figure planted himself among the drum kit. Glenn Miller retreated to watch from the string section, while Peanuts Hucko came forward to lend support with his clarinet along with Carmen Mastren on guitar and the exuberant Trigger Alpert on double bass.

Terry put up his trumpet, flexed his fingers and nodded. The boy drummer let rip a short, sharp, commanding break as pickup and then they were off. Aware that the delicate melodic texture of "Sweet Georgia Brown" adapted more easily to reeds or strings than to brass, Terry started cautiously, softening his effects with the mute and taking care to leave space for clarinet and guitar. But the Miller men held themselves in the background, kept their own solos quiet, efficient and restrained, throwing drums and trumpet into the limelight again and again. Only towards the end did they drive full-bloodedly along with Terry into what seemed to be the last couple of choruses - until Glenn Miller himself uncoiled from his seat, picked up his trombone and put it to his mouth to emit a long growling note that floated them all into a final breathless, ceiling-bursting reprise. It was a scintillating display of spontaneous creativity, telepathically coordinated, a supreme jazz moment that brought the audience to its feet cheering.

Terry and Victor grinned at one another, the orchestra joined in applauding them, and Major Miller took the microphone, shaking his head and repeating over and over the words that Terry was to treasure for the rest of his life.

"That's the greatest I've ever heard."

Terry's senses reeled. He'd done it! He was there, no longer knocking at the door but inside the citadel! He'd climbed Everest, and this was the pinnacle. The most illustrious figure in his world had paid him homage, and with an accolade like that there was nothing he couldn't do! For a few seconds he knew rapture, pure bliss, the fleeting reward that the creative artist pursues like the Holy

Grail - and which, even as he captures it, somehow eludes his fingers and dances away again, into the uncharted labyrinth of the future.

A few seconds were indeed all it lasted. Bowing to the audience across the footlights, some instinct made Terry glance into the wings.

Two figures stood there alongside the stage manager, impassive and a little apart from the crowd of cheering stage hands and musicians. They were both police sergeants, one civilian, one Air Force. Their faces were stony, their eyes fixed unwaveringly on Terry. They did not join in the applause.

There was nowhere to run to now.

19
IT HAD TO BE YOU

The rhythm section tapped out the beat and gentle saxophone ripples prepared the way, then Gary Milner signalled the whole orchestra to its feet - not that they needed any reminding - to blast out the celebrated finale of "American Patrol". The audience applause welled up, and Gary laid down his trombone and stiffened to attention, waiting his moment. Then he launched the abbreviated closing bars of "Moonlight Serenade" and turned to address the audience through the microphone while the curtains drew slowly across the stage.

"Thank you very much indeed, ladies and gentlemen. If you have enjoyed listening to the music as much as we've enjoyed playing it, then this has been a successful concert so far. But don't go away: we've got more good things for you in the second half. Meanwhile the boys and I will get ourselves ready for it over a couple of jars. No doubt you'd like to do the same: the bar's at the back of the hangar, in case anyone hadn't noticed. Thank you and see you again soon."

The musicians sorted their sheets as the stage lights dimmed. "OK boys," Gary called to them. "On places ready to go in twenty minutes, not a second longer." He nodded to Adam Gates, approaching from the steps at the back. "Right, Adam, where's this woman who's too high and mighty to come to press conferences?"

"I put her in your room," said Adam.

Gary nodded. "Right. I'll give her ten minutes at most. Save me a half of shandy."

Adam smiled and lifted an eyebrow. "Nothing more?"

"You know me."

"Just a sec," said Adam, as Gary made for the steps. "I'd better tell you this: there wasn't time before. She said she had to talk to you about Terry Cullis - Cunningham - no, Cullerton. She said you'd know - "

"What?" Gary halted in his stride and stared at Adam as though at a stranger.

"Cullerton. Terry Cullerton, that was it," said Adam. He regarded Gary curiously. "Why, is anything wrong?"

"No." Gary recovered himself. "Just - er - an old friend, that's all. I'll - I'll see you later."

He descended the backstage steps slowly and made his way to the dilapidated office which he had used as a dressing room. His mind was still whirling as he opened the door.

Inside, a butch-looking woman, in her late thirties he judged, was gazing through the dusty window at the aeroplane parked fifty yards or so away on the hardstanding, still visible in the gathering dusk and the threads of evening mist.

"Your - er - vehicle?" she queried in the tone of one accustomed to receiving immediate and truthful answers.

"Yes," he said shortly. He'd have to play this one very, very carefully, but how, how?

"Very nice."

"It avoids traffic jams."

"Hm," was all she said, and continued examining him through her library-frame spectacles.

She was playing on his nerves, doing it deliberately, damn her. Come on, come on, get on with it. "Now, I don't have a lot of time, Miss - er - ?"

"Cannon. Clare Cannon. And it's Miz if you don't mind."

One of those bitches, eh? He might have known. The anger rose, would not be contained. "I couldn't care less, *Miz* Cannon. Which newspaper are you from?"

"Not a newspaper. 'Open Eye' magazine. Perhaps you've heard of us?" She unzipped her shoulder-bag, extracted a card and handed it to him. He examined it perfunctorily.

"'Open Eye', eh? Gossip and muckraking, isn't it? What they call the gutter press, I believe?"

She smiled thinly. "'Investigative journalism' is the modern term. You got my message about Terry Cullerton, Mr Milner? Or Major Miller? Or Mr Cullerton? Which do you prefer?"

He held himself in, gave no outward sign of being disconcerted. "What about it? Gary Milner's a stage name. As near as I could make it to Glenn Miller, for obvious reasons."

"Please don't bluff, Mr Milner." She placed her shoulder-bag on the shabby table, rummaged in it and took out a sheaf of papers. "It's not a stage name: it's your real name - by deed poll. I expect you chose it because it was close enough to Terry Cullerton so you'd get used to it quickly. You took it long, long ago - actually quite a time before you dreamed of marketing yourself as Glenn Miller's lookalike. And you did it for a very good reason. You wanted to kill Terry Cullerton stone dead, and I know why. Shall we sit down?" Gary hesitated. "Shall we?" she repeated.

Gary faced her, his mind still racing. It wasn't fair, it just wasn't fair after all these years! For long seconds he willed himself to stare her out, but she was carrying the ball and she knew it. He sagged into a chair. She remained standing.

"All right then, what do you know?" he said, and added a feeble bluster. "Or think you know?"

Clare Cannon perched herself on the corner of the table. She looked down at Gary and did not hide her contempt.

"I'll tell you a story, shall I?" she began. "A man called Jack Yardley walked into the 'Open Eye' office one day." Gary started, and she nodded. "Yes, that's right. He's eighteen or nineteen years younger than you; he's never met you, but his mother's name was Norah Yardley and he hates your guts. Actually his Mum died a few months ago, though I don't expect you to care about that. Cancer it was, but our Jack tends to dramatise things and he says it was a broken heart from all those years ago. After the funeral when he went through her handbags and stuff he found a couple of old photographs and a diary from when his Mum was in her teens. Up to that time the only thing he'd known about his father was that he hadn't married Norah and hadn't done a damn thing to help her bring up her offspring - just disappeared after a few months and was never heard of again. In those days having an illegitimate child was a big disgrace for a girl, and if the father didn't cough up with maintenance money nobody did much for you, sometimes not even your own family. Well, Norah's family didn't throw her out in the snow, but she had a tough time just the same. She never married anyone else, of course: after all, who'd have wanted a fallen woman with a bastard brat? So she had to bring him up as best she could on her own. Well now, our Jack was so bitter about all this that he hired a private detective, gave him the photos and diary, and asked him to find his Dad. When he got the detective's report he toddled along to 'Open Eye' with it. It landed on my desk."

Gary had sat hunched and silent while Clare Cannon was speaking. Now she watched him take it all in. He looked up at last, defeated. "You know everything then?" It was part question, part confession.

"Everything that matters, I think. I know why Norah never got any maintenance from you after the first few weeks. And how and why you disappeared so thoroughly. Why you never even showed up for your own father's funeral. And why you changed your name."

Gary got up from the chair, walked slowly over to the window and peered out into the gathering mist. "Getting a bit foggy," he remarked. "Temperature must be falling."

Clare Cannon did not answer. He spoke again. "So now you're going to write an article about me."

"I've already written it, Mr Milner."

He turned round. "Exposing me?"

"Telling the truth."

"I'll sue you," he said.

"That's your privilege," she replied frostily. "But I don't think you will."

"God dammit!" he burst out. "You'll destroy me!"

Clare Cannon got up from the corner of the table, whipped off her butch spectacles and brandished them like a sword. She spoke with slow and deliberate emphasis.

"No I won't," she said scornfully. "You did that yourself forty years ago. If you want my opinion, you've spent all your time since then trying to convince yourself that you didn't. If you'd had any shame you could have just left things alone. But no, you had to set to work building a whole career out of other people's heroism, other people's sacrifices, other people's pride in their past, when your own past was nothing but a smelly little dog-mess of treachery and cowardice. And you did pretty well, didn't you, with your fake-Tudor gin palace in Surrey and your flat in Paris" - he shot a glance at her but said nothing - "and that - that toy out there." She waved a contemptuous arm towards the window. "Do you happen to keep an old portrait of yourself in your attic, Mr Cullerton-Milner-Miller? If so, I suggest you go and look at it sometime. You might get a surprise."

Still with her spectacles in one hand she thrust the sheaf of papers she held in her other under Gary's nose.

"Here," she said. "This is what we're going to print. Read it. If you want to make any comments, I'll write them in provided the length's reasonable. If you can show me that anything I've written is untrue, I'll delete it. Otherwise this is it."

Gary did not move. After a few seconds Clare Cannon put the papers on the table and made for the door. She opened it, and with her hand on the knob turned for a parting shot.

"I don't expect you to appreciate this, but actually I'm giving you more of a break than a lot of journalists would, more than you deserve." She paused, while Gary stared sightlessly at the floor, hands in pockets. "Oh, and I've also kept your lad Jack from beating you to a pulp, which he's for ever threatening to do. Keep the proofs, compliments of 'Open Eye'. I'll be in my office tomorrow until one o'clock."

Terry made no reply. The door closed quietly. Through it he heard her footsteps fade away. He fingered the business card she had given him, glanced at it again and dropped it absently into a pocket. He went over to the table, picked up the proofs and began to read.

A little later there was a knock on the door. Adam Gates entered. "Sorry to butt in, but - " he began. "Oh, she's gone, has she?"

"Yes." Gary was standing at the window, staring out, the bundle of proofs clutched in his hand. He did not turn round.

"Good riddance. You've just time for a swift one before curtain up."

Gary remained motionless. "I'm not going on," he said.

Adam's brow furrowed. "Pardon? What did you say?"

Gary turned round and repeated it with emphasis. "I'm not going on. I'm not doing the rest of the concert."

Adam stared disbelievingly. "What on earth are you talking about, Gary? Of course you're going on. Look, it's curtain up in five or six minutes - "

"Adam, I'm not going on stage again today. Perhaps not ever again."

"You're out of your mind," exclaimed Adam. He peered more closely at Terry. "Or are you ill? What's happened?"

"Here." Gary handed him the sheaf of proofs.

Adam looked at him questioningly, then began reading the top proof. "Oh my God!" he murmured after a moment. He reached absently for a chair, sat down as he went on reading, then muttered again, "Oh my God!"

It was Adam Gates, standing at front of curtain in the light of a single spot, who addressed the audience a few minutes later.

"Ladies and gentlemen," he said, "you'll be sorry to hear that Gary Milner will be unable to conduct the remainder of the concert." There was a rustle of disappointment, and he held up a hand. "Now we can manage the music anyway: Tommy Pearson, our very able leader of the brass section, will conduct. But there is another problem, which I want to put to you if you will bear with me for a few minutes. I've taken it upon myself to explain to you the reason why Gary isn't coming back on stage, firstly because it will be made public in a couple of days anyway but secondly because I believe that you, the men and women of the United States Eighth Air Force and Royal Air Force Bomber Command, along with your families and friends, have more right than most to give your opinion about it. I'm going to read out the opening paragraphs of an article which will appear in a nationally-distributed magazine the day after tomorrow. And sadly, I have Gary's permission to tell you that the allegations made are substantially true." He paused, then began reading from the sheaf of papers he was holding:

"'*Gary Milner - coward and fraud! Glenn Miller's bandleader lookalike exposed as World War II deserter. By Clare Cannon.*

"'*Only two days after his orchestra's triumphal appearance at an anniversary reunion of RAF Bomber Command and US Eighth Air Force war heroes, the shocking truth about Gary Milner, Britain's top bandleader, stands revealed by "Open Eye" investigators. We now expose the real war record of the man who, as well as cashing in for half a lifetime on the music and reputation of the famous and respected Major Glenn Miller, repeatedly laid claim publicly to an honourable record as a Royal Air Force pilot in World War II. This is what he really did during the war and after:*

"' *- he abandoned his pregnant gymslip sweetheart*

 - after the first few weeks he contributed not a penny to maintain his child

 - he cut all links with his father, who never heard from him again and died brokenhearted

 - he did indeed qualify as a pilot with the RAF as he claimed, but he ran away rather than fly on operations

 - he was caught, convicted of desertion and sent to prison, remaining safe and sound behind bars for the rest of the war while better men than he were fighting and dying for their country

 - on being released from prison he changed his name by deed poll to hide the truth about his past.

"'*For over ten years he lived abroad with his shame. When at last he skulked back to England, did he seek out the child he had fathered or the woman he had wronged? No! Did he at least have the decency to keep quiet about the war? Quite the reverse: he exploited it for his own gain, coolly identifying himself not only with the music but with the personality, the popularity, the heroism even, of one of the great figures of the Second World War generation, the legendary Major Glenn Miller. And he had the effrontery to back it all up by publicly claiming, over and over again, an honourable war record in his own right!*

"'For half a lifetime this impudent coward and cheat has enjoyed fame, admiration and a lavish lifestyle - including, ironically as some might think, his own private aircraft - based on this cynical abuse of the Miller saga, this peddling of cowardice for courage, of fraud for honesty. It is time for the real heroes of the war, those humble, brave, ordinary people who did not shirk or falter, to be told the truth ... '"

Adam broke from his reading and looked round the audience. They sat like statues. The silence was total.

"Now there's more in the same vein," he went on. But you've heard enough to realise the difference between what you did in the war and what Gary Milner did. What I want to ask you, ladies and gentlemen, is whether the pleasure which, over the years, Gary has given to people like yourselves outweighs the undoubted wrongs he has done, or whether those wrongs make him a moral outcast. This is a profound issue, ladies and gentlemen, with which you obviously did not expect to be confronted this evening. I'll sum it up in a simple question. Do you want Gary Milner to come back and finish the concert himself in spite of everything you've just heard?"

A commotion in the audience broke into his last few words as a stylishly-dressed elderly lady rose in her seat and made her way to the gangway. She paused there, erect and four-square, cupping her hands around her mouth like a megaphone.

"Sure we do!" she shouted in a strong American accent. The clarity and power of her voice belied her years. "Go get him back: we just want the music, not a court martial!!"

There were murmurs of surprise and heads turned towards her. She strode quickly down the gangway until she was level with the front row, where she turned round, opened her arms and appealed to the audience.

"The war's over, isn't it, folks? We've all changed since then, haven't we? Sure, there were some guys couldn't cut the mustard, we all know that - well, a lot of other lousy things happened in the war too, so forget 'em. But Gary Milner helps us to remember there were some good things in those days too, and that's got to be worth something, hasn't it?" She paused. "So bring - Gary - back!" She punched the air with both fists and repeated, "Bring - Gary - back! Bring - Gary - back!"

There was a stirring in the audience. One or two voices began to join in. Others followed, and the old lady turned round to face the stage, led the swelling chorus for a few more seconds and then made for the proscenium steps and mounted them. By the time she reached Adam Gates at the microphone the audience was roaring, some standing to applaud as well. Adam Gates smiled, took the old lady's outstretched hands and kissed her cheek. They embraced while the audience cheered, then Adam turned to the microphone, grinning broadly.

"Now that makes me feel like Humphrey Bogart, and this lady must be Ingrid Bergman," he said and paused for the puzzled laughter. "Well, you see, she always used to say that she'd kissed Bogie but she didn't know him. Now I just kissed this lady, but I don't know her either."

The old lady lifted the microphone expertly from its stand, put it to her mouth and through the renewed laughter said, "I'm just a friend of Gary Milner."

Adam retrieved the microphone, put his arm around her and replied, "Then you're a friend of mine." Over the further applause he continued, "Ladies and gentlemen, let's not forget, this is supposed to be a concert. The orchestra's ready back there to start the second half with a grand old flagwaver that's perhaps very appropriate in the circumstances. While they're playing it I'll go and find Gary and get him back on stage if it's the last thing I do." He opened the break of the curtain, popped his head through and gave a signal.

The orchestra struck up "When Johnny Comes Marching Home Again" and the curtains began to open. Adam shepherded the old lady towards the proscenium steps, but she halted and appealed to him urgently.

"Mr Gates, let me come with you!"

He started in surprise. "I beg your pardon?"

"Let me come with you." Her expression was intense, desperate even. "Please. To find him."

"Well, I - "

She clutched his arm. "Listen, Mr Gates. It's very, very important to me. Please. I've got to come with you."

He hesitated. "Come on," he said.

In the backstage area they hurried along the dusty corridor to Gary's dressing room. Adam knocked and they entered. The room was empty. They looked at each other.

"Is this where he was before?" the American lady asked.

Adam nodded. "I left him here ten minutes ago." He pointed. "He was sitting in that chair."

"Where else can we look?"

Adam consulted his watch. "Just now, nowhere," he said. "I'll have to make some sort of announcement at the end of this number. Goodness knows what I'll say. Wait here till I come back."

"OK."

Adam left the old lady alone. She looked round the dingy room restlessly. Where was he, for Chrissakes, where was he? There weren't so many goddam places he could hide after all. What was Adam Gates doing? If she had to just stand around in here she'd go out of her frigging skull. She paced up and down aimlessly once or twice, then glanced out through the window to where the darkness and mist were now rapidly closing in. She could just make out the shape of the aeroplane.

On the hardstanding outside the hangar, out of view from the window, Gary Milner, still in US major's uniform but now wearing the belted raincoat and service cap as well, paced up and down, carrying his holdall, his head sunk into his chest. The lyric of "When Johnny Comes Marching Home", sung by his close-harmony vocal group, came faintly from inside the hangar.

But the gruff voice to which he was listening was one that seemed to come from very far off yet at the same time from deep inside himself.

" ... it's your duty ... if we sin, we pay for it ... if we want atonement, we have to repent ... you've no choice now... you want your life for yourself, do you? ... What can you do with it that can ever be worth anything? ... I'll see to it you atone whether you like it or not ... atone ... atone ... atone ... "

He shook his head, squared his shoulders and strode towards his aeroplane shrouded in the mist a score or so yards away.

The old lady ran down the dimly-lit corridor, found an outside door and tried it. It opened.

Fifty yards away through the mist was the aeroplane. A dim figure in an American officer's uniform was climbing into the cabin. She raced towards the plane and yelled out, "Terry! Terry! Wait! Terry! Wait for me!"

Settling into the pilot's seat, Gary Milner heard the shouts and hesitated. A faint shaft of light came from the open door leading to the hangar. The sweet, emotional opening notes of "At Last" wafted from within. A scurrying female figure without coat or hat materialised at the cabin door. Gary opened it.

"Oh jeepers, thank God I caught you! Let me in, Terry. Please let me in!"

He frowned. "What the - ?"

"Don't go, Terry!" she pleaded breathlessly. "Oh please don't go."

He looked at her with a curious impassivity, as though already far away and unwilling to be drawn back. "No one's called me that in thirty years," he said. "Who are you?"

She tried to smile, but the tears were streaming down her face. She fought to get the words out.

"Don't you know me, Terry? Oh sweet Jesus, Terry! I - I guess I look a lot older now - a helluva lot older, God knows - but I'm still Kitty. Kitty Norton. Your Kitty."

Gary stared, stunned, beyond words.

"Let me in, Terry," she pleaded tremulously. "I can't talk to you from here."

"You - you'd better go round," he managed to get out. "Come in the other side."

He leaned over and opened the other cabin door. His mind spun. Kitty climbed in, closed the door and looked at him almost shyly.

"How the hell did you get here?" he asked wonderingly.

She bit her lip. "Oh gee, where do I begin?" She was calmer now. "Well, they posted me down south from Blackpool. I met an American. A bombardier on B17s he was. His base was near here. We got married. After the war we lived on the west coast, in Seattle. When you toured Canada with the band - must be ten, fifteen years ago, wasn't it? - we went across for the concert you did in Vancouver. We were in the front row. I got the jolt of my life when I saw Gary Milner was you - "

"You mean you recognised me? Actually recognised me? In all this - this disguise? Nobody else ever has - "

She smiled, and a faint trace of her old accent came through. "Oh Terry love, I'd have known you if you'd been painted blue all over."

"Then why didn't you ... ?" The words trailed away.

"I couldn't. Jeepers, Terry, I just couldn't. Well, Hank was with me - that's my husband's name - was - and I'd never told him about you. How could I have? It was nothing to do with him." She shrugged. "And can you imagine if I'd come out with it right that minute? Or even afterwards? What good could it have done? Besides, you might have had six wives for all I knew, and all of them jealous."

"One," he said briefly. "For a few years. It didn't work out."

"I'm sorry," said Kitty. She paused, gathering her thoughts again. "Well, Hank died a few months ago. But he'd wanted to make this trip. And I did too, though I'd never told him my other reason. So here I am."

Gary stared out through the windscreen, fiddled idly with one or two switches on the instrument panel in front of him. "No need to tell you my life-story," he said at last. "I guess you just heard Adam tell the world what a fraud I am."

"You're not a fraud, Terry. Not to me you're not." She clutched his arm. "And if you are, maybe it's my fault. If I hadn't run away from you ... I meant it for the best ... Dear God, how I hated myself ... Oh jeez, I don't know ... "

"You're not responsible for my life: I am. I've lied and cheated for forty years. I've got to atone for it."

"Don't, Terry, don't! Can't you see I don't care about all that stuff?" she cried fervently, gripping his arm again. "Those people in there, do you think they care either? God dammit, they're hollering for you fit to bust! They *love* you, Terry! Whatever you did it's a long time ago and they don't care. Anyway they understand: they were afraid too! Well jeepers, if they don't care, why should anybody else? No one gives a toot about the war any more. That article: so they print it, so what? It's no big deal, in one ear, out the other, you'll see. Come back in with me, Terry!"

"I can't." He shook his head dully. "It's over. I have to atone somehow."

"Atone, atone? Holy cow, what are you talking about? What can you do now? It's finished with, all finished with. Nobody cares, I told you."

"But *I* do," he said. "Don't you see, it's not finished for me just because you tell me I can still get away with it even though I got found out. That's not the point. *I don't want to get away with it.* Do you think I haven't known all these years that I'm a cheat and a coward and a fraud? Do you think there haven't been times when I've been sick of myself? Well, now I'm so sick of myself it won't go away and I don't care whether other people care or not. *I* care. " He paused and smiled ruefully. "I seem to have principles after all, you see. I used to think I didn't have, and I haven't lived by them, that's for sure. But I know what they are, and now they've come back to haunt me, full blast."

Kitty gestured impatiently. "Principles, principles - what are they?

Everyone's life's the same, one big mess-up after another and you just get through it the best way you can, that's all- "

He shook his head. "Not mess-ups. Sins. Wickedness. Wrongdoing. That's what I'm talking about." He paused, letting the words sink in. "I was brought up in a religious home, remember? Right is right and wrong is wrong. My Dad taught me the difference but I thought I knew better. Well, I didn't. I've sinned. For sin there has to be atonement. God wants it even if nobody else does." He turned suddenly in the cramped cabin, his eyes hard, his voice sardonic, defying ridicule. "Now isn't that just too bloody old-fashioned for words?"

She set her face obstinately. "Oh shoot, Terry, don't let's talk about it any more now." She plucked at his sleeve. "But if you're going away somewhere take me with you, please. Now, this minute. Anywhere you say." She smiled uncertainly, but he turned away without answering. Her tears came again and she struggled to get her next words out. "Terry, be honest with me. Have you ever thought about me in all these years?"

He swung round facing her again and gazed into her eyes expressionlessly.

"Every day," he replied at last.

"Then for Chrissakes take me with you!" she exclaimed. "I'm begging you!" She tried to smile. "You remember when I told you I was a lot older than you? Well, it's not such a lot now, not at our time of life, Terry, honest to God it isn't!" She hesitated. "And what's it matter? We're just a couple of old crocks and we don't have much time. Take me with you!"

Faintly from the hangar came the last few lines of "At Last":

You smiled, and then the spell was cast,
And here we are in heaven
For you are mine at last.

Kitty heard it and prayed.

Adam Gates found Gary's dressing-room empty and at that moment heard the aircraft engine burst into life. He saw the open door leading out to the hardstanding and ran out into the chill of late dusk. The sound of the taxiing aircraft receded. His eyes became accustomed to the darkness and he made out the figure of a woman, her back to him, motionless in the swirling mist. He hurried forward.

"Where's he gone?" he asked.

Kitty did not turn round.

"He said Paris." Her voice trembled.

"Where did you say?"

"Paris."

"Good grief, in this soup?"

Kitty nodded wordlessly. In the distance the engine sound crescendoed for the pre-takeoff check.

"He lived in France for a long time after the war, you know," said Adam, peering into the mist. "He always told me it was because he liked the jazz there. Now it seems...." He shrugged. "He still has a flat in Paris."

"Paris: that's where he said he was going," said Kitty. "He wants to atone."

"Atone? What? For that load of old cobblers, is that what he means? Atone? What a word! What does he think it matters - ?"

"I don't know. He doesn't know. But he wants to be by himself and think it out." She spoke slowly, spacing her words. "He says he's going to figure out how he can atone."

"And that's all he said?"

Kitty covered her face with her hands. "Oh God, there were other things, but they don't matter any more," she sobbed. "I wanted to go with him but he wouldn't let me. He said he had to do it on his own."

Adam Gates put an arm around her shoulders and began leading her slowly back to the hangar. But then the engine note from the aircraft changed as it began the takeoff run. They paused, turned and peered into the mist, seeing nothing. The sound faded quickly into the distance, then vanished altogether. Kitty spoke.

"He promised he'd phone me from Paris."

From inside the hangar the orchestra swelled up into the closing phrases of "At Last".

"I know he'll phone," said Kitty. "He promised."

"Yes," said Adam.

"It's just that first he has to - you know - do it on his own."

"I know." Adam paused. "He's always been like that."

Kitty shook her head. "Not always."

Adam weighed this and wondered. "You must know him well."

Did she? "We go back a long way," she temporised. Jeepers, she thought indignantly in the silence that followed, she knew everything about him, everything! What use to explain, though? When she spoke again it was only to add cryptically, "But we had too little time."

PROLOGUE AS EPILOGUE

On 15 December 1944, Major Glenn Miller took off with two companions in a Norseman aircraft from an airfield in southern England on a flight to Paris. Weather conditions were poor, with mist. The Norseman did not arrive at its destination. No trace of it, or of its occupants, has ever been found.

Too little time
Our love was strong but we had too little time
Farewell my heart

Too little time
Our love was wrong so we had too little time
And we must part

And as the years go by my love will burn
Until the magic day when you return

And we'll have

Too little time
For sad regrets about the days
Those golden days
Those fleeting yesterdays
When there was too, too little time

Keep in touch with the Miller Magic by joining...

THE GLENN MILLER SOCIETY
with
FRIENDS OF THE HERB MILLER ORCHESTRA

The Miller Magazine, free to members, gives latest news of CDs, cassettes, videos, personalities, books – everything connected with the immortal Miller style of music, including current concert engagements of the Herb Miller Orchestra directed by Glenn's nephew John Miller. For full membership details write to Doug Le Vicki, Miller Villa, 55 Wycombe Road, Princes Risborough, Bucks HP17 0EY.

* * * * *

EAST ANGLIAN AVIATION SOCIETY

welcomes visitors to the Tower Museum at Bassingbourn Barracks (north of Royston beside the B1198 road). The Museum commemorates the USAAF 91st Bomber Group (H), based there from November 1942 until June 1945, and the long association of Bassingbourn airfield with the Royal Air Force until its closure in 1969. It is a memorial to all who made the supreme sacrifice. To visit, or for membership details of the Society, contact Vincent A Hemmings, 53 Malthouse Way, Barrington, Cambridgeshire CB2 5RR, tel 0223-872947.

* * * * *

THE TED HEATH MUSIC APPRECIATION SOCIETY

was formed in 1988 and now has over 900 members throughout the world, all united by interest in the music of Ted Heath, both on record and at the live concerts still given by his musicians and vocalists. Regular record recital meetings are held in Central London and at branches throughout the UK. A quarterly newsletter keeps members in touch. For membership details write to Pete Jones, 2 Tempest Road, Egham, Surrey, TW20 8HX.

* * * * *

When in Blackpool visit the historic
MUSIC HALL TAVERN
(above Yates's Wine Lodge, Talbot Square)

where Miss Patricia presents Blackpool's finest Singalong, with good company, good ale, good food and superb artistes on the greatest open mike in Britain's greatest seaside resort!
Open every lunchtime and evening till late

Free admission   Tel 0253-28794

MEMORY LANE

A lively magazine for enthusiasts of dance music and jazz etc of those nostalgic years — the 1920s, 1930s, 1940s and 1950s — with accent on the great British dance bands of the period plus regular features on Al Bowlly. Published quarterly, each edition includes articles by top writers, picture pages, book and album reviews, readers' letters and discographical information. For sample copy and subscription details, send two first class stamps (or two International Reply Coupons) to MEMORY LANE, 226 Station Road, Leigh-on-Sea, Essex SS9 3BS.

* * * * *

What's your NOSTALGIA interest?

Jazz? The dance bands? Swing? Big band sound? From King Oliver to the Savoy Havana Band to the Ambrose Orchestra to Ted Heath, from Gene Austin to Denny Dennis to Dickie Valentine — if it happened *then* and you like it better than what's happening *now*, NOSTALGIA MAGAZINE is for you! Articles, photographs, readers' letters, discographies, record and book reviews. For subscription details and sample copy, send two first class stamps to C D Wilson, 39 Leicester Road, New Barnet, Hertfordshire EN5 5EW.

* * * * *

BETTY GRABLE'S HOLLYWOOD

Four issues per year dedicated to the films, songs, dances, career and life-story of the number one pin-up girl of the Second World War — and to the magic of Hollywood in the great days! If you believe "they don't make 'em like that anymore", send for subscription details to Tom McGee, 55 Elmore Avenue, Simshill, Glasgow G44 5BH, Scotland.

* * * * *

Stay IN TUNE with the golden years...

To discerning lovers of popular music, 1935-60 were the great days of harmony and melody. IN TUNE is the monthly magazine devoted to the bands, singers and songs of those years, with interviews, discographies, label listings and new releases with full track listings, record and book reviews, readers' letters, addresses of record dealers...you name it! For subscription details, write Colin Morgan, IN TUNE Magazine, 12 Caer Gofaint, Groes, Nr Denbigh, Clwyd LL16 5YT, Wales.

THE SYD LAWRENCE MUSIC SOCIETY

brings together admirers of the great Syd Lawrence Orchestra. To receive information about the Orchestra's engagements, audio and video recordings, local branches, personnel etc, read the monthly newsletters — free to members when you join the Society. For full details write to Ken Almond, 25 Carr Gate, Moreton, Wirral, L46 6EQ.

* * * * *

THE HARRY JAMES APPRECIATION SOCIETY

is a non-profitmaking organisation promoting interest in the music of Harry James, his vocalists and sidemen, together with other bands of similar persuasion. Regular recitals are held in Central London, and members receive the magazine "Music Maker International" three times a year. For membership details contact Eric Ward, 40 Oakfield Road, East Ham, London E6 1LW.

* * * * *

THE HARRY ROY APPRECIATION SOCIETY

was formed on 1 February 1972, the first anniversary of Harry's death, to enable admirers of his music to work for its appreciation and availability. Meetings are held in London three times a year, and a newsletter, "The Bugle Call Rag", is published. For more details write to Mrs Dorothy Cresswell, 68 Stoneleigh Avenue, Worcester Park, Surrey, KT4 8XY.

* * * * *

THE RAY ANTHONY MUSIC SOCIETY

In the Miller Mood...2 CDs of that title, the Dream Dancing LPs, plus many other recordings and concerts, testify to Ray Anthony's mastery of melody in the Miller style. Ray is still tops in America! For information about the Society contact Martin Java, 81 Whitchurch Lane, Edgware, Middlesex HA8 6QE (Tel 081-951-3351 evenings and weekends).

* * * * *

THE ARTIE SHAW MUSIC SOCIETY

was formed in 1986 to promote and organise recitals of the works of Artie Shaw, and to enable devotees of his music to meet, listen and exchange information and material. The Society holds regular meetngs ini Central London. For membership details contact the Secretary, Artie Shaw Music Society, 42 Fauconberg Road, Chiswick, London W4 3JU.

THE COUNT BASIE SOCIETY

was formed in 1980 to promote the music of William "Count" Basie, his bands, his sidemen and singers, to maintain the common bond between his followers, and to provide an opportunity for all lovers of his music to meet (three times a year in London). For details, write to Eileen Branch, 33 Barrington Road, Southgate, Crawley, West Sussex RH10 6DQ.

* * * * *

THE SINATRA MUSIC SOCIETY

was founded in 1955 and is the largest "easy listening" organisation in Britain. Its magazine, published six times a year, keeps you informed of the career of Frank Sinatra and of your favourite vocalists and big bands. Branches in London, Birmingham, Cardiff, Glasgow, Leeds, Manchester, Newcastle, Salisbury and Sussex meet monthly. For further details, contact The Sinatra Music Society, 49 Lincoln Avenue, London N14 7LL.

* * * * *

WELSHPOOL PRINTING COMPANY
(0938) 552260

We are pleased to be associated with Marchman Publications in the production of this book. We also print 4-colour magazines and journals, in fact anything from Business Cards to Annuals.

Please telephone for free quotations.